BOSTON BLUES SERIES

Pitcher Us

MOLLIE GOINS

To every woman that's apologized for rambling—let the MLB Pitcher encourage you to use your words.

Boston Blues Starting Roster
Bold - mentions in story

- Zane Mickels #01 | 2B
- Dante Newport #02 | CF
- **Adam Reyer #04 | C**
- **Mateo Keener #07 | SS**
- Keaton Locke #08 | LF
- **Tripp Pierce #11 | 3B**
- Wesley Nelson #18 | DP
- **Will Anderson #24 | P**
- **Beck Daines #36 | 1B**
- Grayson Nash #45 | RF

General Manager: Jim Olsson | Pitching Coach: Dex Larsen | Team photographer: Calliope "Callie" Reyer (Kuh-Lai—uh-pee) | Shannon Carlton: Team Secretary

For the full 26 man roster and teams in their division, please see molliegoins.com

Content Warnings

Pitcher Us is primarily a low stakes book, however, some topics may be considered sensitive to some readers. The following are mentioned through out the story:

- Complicated family dynamics with emotionally abusive parents.
- Past mentions of Alcohol abuse from a parental figure.
- Past mentions of sexual harassment in the workplace.

Thank you for reading Pitcher Us. Please see the Dick-tionary in the back of the book for chapters with explicit content.

Chapter 1
Will

"Welcome to the Blues," our new general manager, Jim Olsson, says as we walk in his office. He stands over his desk with his arms wide. "You boys had a long trip, please take a seat."

Do you know what whiplash feels like? Because I fucking do. I know the feeling all too well.

For years I've had one constant—my team. I played for the Seattle Mavericks for five years and won the damn World Series literally last week. But in the past forty-eight hours, I've had to pack up all my stuff, scramble to find someone to take over my lease, and fly all the way across the country because I was the first fucking trade to go through. Well, technically, I was the second.

My teammate, Adam, and I were made a package deal so now we're both starters for the Boston Blues. Me, the starting pitcher, and him, the catcher. I suppose I could have been traded with a worse teammate or by myself. Though, I'm not sure if alone would have been better or worse.

"Happy to be here," Adam says, and I know he means it.

While I've found this trade stressful and overwhelming, Adam seems unfazed. But that's probably because he didn't have to make this move alone.

Adam Reyer and his sister, Callie, have always been a "glass half full" kind of pair. She moved in with him earlier this spring and is now making the move as well. The six-hour plane ride from Seattle to Boston was the most time I'd spent with her. Key word being *spent*. While her beautiful fiery red hair and freckles galore make her sunshine and rainbows attitude more tolerable than Adam's, it also made her hard to miss—but if any player thought they were going to talk to her after a game, they were sorely mistaken.

Mr. Olsson takes a seat in his desk chair. "I know you guys are jet-lagged and still have shit to get sorted, but I like to be clear from day one on how I plan to run this team." He leans forward, putting his arms on the desk. "I won't tolerate bullshit or slacking off. I want to make this a top organization, period. Some general managers can be very hands off but that's not my style. I pushed for you both based on your experience and skill, but I'm not too attached, so sending your contracts back to assignment won't be an issue if you can't get on board."

Well, I can appreciate his bluntness. One major hesitation with this trade was the fact that this is Mr. Olsson's first year as General Manager. With the Blues having a pretty serious reputation in the league, and the last GM getting fired because of their losing streak last season, I know Olsson taking this position involved some serious hoops to jump through. He coached for years and was a hell of a player—I know a lot rests on his shoulders now as GM. The pressure is palpable.

"That won't be a problem," I clip. I don't mean to come

off rude, but this has been a long day, and Adam and I are good at what we do. We don't need to be lectured on the importance of dedication. You don't win the World Series by slacking off. "I also know that our contracts are up for renewal at the start of new year, and I want to add in a no-trade clause."

There are some major downsides to being traded to Boston, but one bright side is I'm now only an hour away from my mom and sisters. Ever since my deadbeat dad walked out on us, it's always been me and them. Being the "man of the family" is a little difficult when you're three thousand miles away, but signing with the Mavericks was a dream come true. This past season especially, with the original starting pitcher getting injured and me battling to claim his spot. I earned starting pitcher with the Mavericks, and then to get traded so quickly...yeah, the whiplash is real.

Mr. Olsson laughs, not sure if it's at my request or the boldness in asking. I don't really care. I'm not going to let it go without a fight.

Adam glances my way with pinched brows. I didn't mention any of this to him. He would have just told me to not even bother asking. Adam's been playing nearly four years longer than me and I know he'd never dream of asking for something so major in a meeting like this. But if these are the cards I'm being dealt, then I'm going to play my hand.

"I get this is your first trade, but a no-trade clause isn't exactly something you wager in the first meeting. I understand you are familiar with some people from the team, but you haven't even practiced with the Blues yet."

"I understand that. The Mavericks were my team for five years, the only team I've been with, but I've more than proved myself. This trade might not have been my choice, but this move puts me closer to my family, and I know an opportunity when I see one."

Olsson flashes a sly smirk as he leans forward on his desk. "Family man, I like it. I'll admit you've proved you're a damn good pitcher, but don't think I don't know you have a bit of a temper. I know you've been ejected a few times for some intentional hits. That won't fly here. And while we're being honest, I might have dug a little deeper into the both of you. It's part of why I'm not surprised that Adam got you all here in forty-eight hours. While you're now one of the top pitchers in the league, you're also anti-social. I don't give two fucks what you do with your personal time, but when it comes to the team, you will integrate yourself. I want this team to be great, I want my players to be great, and that requires you to make friends."

Well, shit. I can't defend myself regarding the hits. I never intentionally hit anyone from the Blues but there are a few players in this league that I might have let get the better of me. But as for the loner statement, I feel that's none of his concern.

I clench my jaw. So, just because I'm not Mr. Personality that means I'm not a team player? That's bullshit.

"I'll tell you what. I'll keep this conversation of family in mind. We'll renew your contract for one season and if you can keep yourself in check and give me your all—I'll agree to the strictest no-trade clause your lawyers can draw up."

"I can work with that." I hold out my hand to shake on our deal.

"Great. Now, like I said, I know this is the first trade for you both, so our team's secretary, Shannon, printed these for you. There's a list of some apartments that house several of our players, along with any information you will need to get in this facility." Sitting back again, Mr. Olsson taps his desk. "Now, you're free to go. We'll be in touch. I have a different fire to put out now as our team photographer decided to quit this morning with no notice."

I simply nod and then stand, ready to sleep off the past forty-eight hours, but Adam doesn't move. He now has his game-day face on. Is he going to try to add a no-trade deal too?

"Since we're all being bold for our first meeting, I think I have the perfect girl for the team photographer."

Chapter 2
Callie

I never enjoy playing the "let's contemplate my life" game. I'm enjoying it even less now as I stare up at the ceiling in my Hilton Inn hotel room. The popcorn ceiling was definitely a weird choice. How did someone even think this looked good? Also, don't they release asbestos?

"Ugh, focus, Callie! What are we doing with our life!" I shout to absolutely no one. Between the complete coastal change and only a seventy-two-hour window to make it happen, I'm jet-lagged and overstimulated.

My phone dings on the nightstand alerting me that it's finally back on. With all the texts I've been getting about Adam's abrupt trade and all the calls I've helped Adam make to get everything ready for the move, my phone was beyond dead by the time my butt hit my seat on the plane. My charger is packed in God knows what bag. That is if I even packed it at all. It very well could still be plugged in at Adam's old place.

The only reason my phone can even ding now, sans phone charger, is because I was able to snag a new one at one of the little convenience stores while manically rushing through the airport because my brother's teammate said he needed something too. I didn't pay much attention to what Will needed because I know my brother, he would have dragged me out of the store if I didn't get in and out. There might have been seventy-two hours to get here but Adam had got it in his head that we needed to be here in forty-eight.

You would think it would have been easy to not forget any of my things considering I randomly showed up at my brother's door seven months ago with only one duffle bag, a suitcase, and a shred of my sanity left. Who can't keep track of just the basic necessities? Me, that's who.

I also can't seem to get any of my sanity back either. I have no fucking clue what I want to do with my life. I'm twenty-five with a master's degree from Yale that I didn't even want and don't intend to ever use again.

If I had any other option, my butt would have stayed in Seattle. I hate that Boston is so close to home. But I didn't know what else to do. Right now, I'm living off my savings and mooching off my older brother, who, thank the Lord, loves me enough to not kick me out while I figure out who the hell I am when I'm not under my parent's thumb.

My phone dings a couple more times, and I internally groan. I've answered about a million questions about this trade. At this point, I want to call whoever in the MLB franchise made these trade rules and scream into the speaker.

My phone starts to ring this time, and my eyes nearly roll to the back of my head. Barely moving I blindly reach for my phone, not even looking at who's calling. "Hello," I groan.

"Oh, I'm sorry, Stevie. Auntie Cals is in a bad mood, we'll call her back later." My best friend's voice is condescending because she knows there's no way I'd pass up an opportunity to talk to my little munchkin.

Sitting up against the headboard, I push all my negative energy down. The only teammate of my brother's who I really talked to was Jett but that was mostly because of his girlfriend, Wyla. We became quick friends—my only friend, if we're being honest. And don't even get me started on their daughter. I worked hard to mold her sass to be just like mine. "You better let me talk to my mini me. I miss her already."

She chuckles. "Are you in the hotel? Wanna FaceTime us?"

"Obviously." Holding my phone out I click it over to FaceTime.

It takes a minute to connect but then Wyla's face shows on the screen. "Hi, I have someone who—"

In a flash a little hand blocks the camera, pulling the phone out of her mom's hands. "Hi, Auntie Cals! Why are you in bed? It's sunshine time."

A weak laugh bubbles out. "I'm so sleepy, Stevie Bug. I haven't slept very much in a few days, and I had a long plane ride."

Wyla scoots into the frame. "Remember how tired you were after our last plane ride?"

Stevie nibbles on her bottom lip as she thinks. "I guess so. I think I took a nap. Auntie Cals, did you take a nap? You should try that!"

This time my laugh feels a little lighter. "You know, I think you're right. Are you helping your mommy get everything packed?"

This trade has completely turned everything around on me, and Wyla's been in the same boat as they get ready to move back to her hometown since Jett decided to retire at the end of this season.

"Yes!" Stevie gives me a proud grin. "We've packed so many boxes that we ran out! We had to send Daddy to go get more."

"I'm sure you did." I give Stevie a soft smile. "You're leaving in two days, right?"

Wyla angles the phone in Stevie's hands so I can see her better before she says, "Yeah, I think this should be the last 'we need more boxes' trip I send Jett on. Lord willing. I'm so over packing, I think I've told him to just leave some stuff here a million times."

Sitting up a little straighter, I snort. "You're over packing? Try having to speed pack on Adam's crazy time clock."

"That man doesn't believe in fashionably late, that's for sure. Where are the guys now?"

"Meeting with their new general manager and hopefully getting a lead on some housing. They've put us in a hotel for now, but only for a week, so we gotta move fast."

Wyla shakes her head. "The guys can easily pay for some extra nights in a hotel, Cals. Y'all have been going ninety miles an hour. I think a few days of rest will do you good."

She's both right and wrong. Rest sounds nice, but... "Wyla, you know damn well I can't be stuck in the same hotel room as my type A brother for that long. We need walls! I have to hide my chaos somewhere or he will try to organize it."

Stevie rolls her eyes and huffs, "Language, Auntie Cals."

"I know, I know." Stevie is a stickler for cursing. Adam and I get reprimanded quite a bit.

Before anyone else can say anything Adam bursts into the hotel room. "Callie, get your ass up and get ready."

"Language, Adam!" Stevie yells through the speaker making Wyla laugh.

Adam stomps up and grabs my phone. "I thought I escaped the curse word police. Go yell at your dad."

I don't have to see the phone to know she just rolled her eyes at him. Stevie's four going on fourteen. "Daddy's not here, he's getting boxes."

As the words leave her mouth, she squeals, which tells me Jett just got back. Wyla's voice comes next. "Babe, come say hi to Adam and Callie."

I stand up and reach to take my phone back, but Adam jerks it to the side as his best friend comes into frame.

"I'm sorry, I don't know an Adam," Jett jokes.

"Yeah, yeah, listen. I don't have time for this reunion. Say bye to Callie and wish her luck because she has an interview at the complex starting in twenty minutes."

I'm sorry, what?

"What are you talking about right now? I don't have an interview!" My voice sounds all loud and squeaky.

Wyla's question comes next but in a less stressed tone. "Ooo, what job?"

Adam gives me a little nudge before reaching for my travel duffle bag and plopping it on the bed. "Team photographer. Now, say bye!" Adam tilts the phone to me for a second as they all yell "bye" and "good luck" before he clicks it off.

He tosses my phone on the bed before unzipping my bag. "Did you happen to pack anything other than sweatpants in this bag?"

I'm baffled by one, his fucking audacity, and two, the fact that he actually thinks I'm going to an interview right now.

"Have you lost your mind?!" My voice has gone up another octave.

He starts throwing clothes out of my bag before landing on the one pair of jeans I packed in my travel bag. "Here, these'll do."

"These..." I sputter as he tosses them to me. "Adam, I am not going to an interview to be your team's photographer. You're insane! You were supposed to ask about apartments, not a job!"

My brother huffs as he filters through my shirts next. "Cals, you know I love you, but you've been moping around for a year trying to figure out what you want to do."

Holding back an eye roll, I grumble, "I haven't moped."

To anyone else that statement would be true, but to Adam it's a bald-faced lie. There are not many people that I let see any other side than my happy-go-lucky attitude. Despite our differences, I'm pretty sure he's the only person I don't feel this pressure to fill the silences with.

"Here." Tossing me yet another article of clothing, Adam then goes and grabs my laptop. "You got five minutes to change. I've got an Uber waiting downstairs."

With the click of the hotel door, I'm left to argue with no one. Welp, I guess I'm going to an interview.

The entirety of the car ride over Adam fills me in on the details. The team's photographer backed out of their offer maybe an hour ago, and while it seems they have plenty of time to find someone before the season actually starts, my brother didn't hesitate to snag an interview for me as quickly as possible.

"You've got some pictures on your laptop, right?" Adam asks as he leads me down the hallways of the complex.

"Yes, but not a lot of sports pictures." I exhale, trying to let the nerves out and keep up with Adam's pace. "I mostly took pictures of the city back in Seattle. I doubt that's what they're looking for. This is just a silly hobby of mine, Adam."

Looking back with a half-annoyed look on his face, Adam huffs. "Don't do that. That's Dad talking, and I don't talk to him for a reason. Cals, they're looking for someone who loves photography and takes good pictures—that's you."

I do love photography. It's always been a passion of mine —one my father always aimed to snuff out. One that bit me in the ass before, but that's not a thought I want to have right now.

When I allow myself to think of what this job could mean, I get a little excited. My pictures could be used for a professional team. Used on their websites, socials, and possibly even for articles with ESPN. There's so much I could do—blogs, social media campaigns, revamping their brand. It's always been my creative outlet, but could I make it my career?

I used to take pictures of Adam playing all the time but after what happened at the beginning of this year, baseball players have been on my shit list. I honestly put photography on my shit list for a little bit too, but it's hard being mad at something you love.

Adam stops abruptly in front of an office, and I can feel my blood pressure shoot up. Hugging my laptop to my chest, my fingers fiddle with the edges. "Adam, I'm nervous."

Turning to face me, Adam places his bear-paw-sized hands on my shoulders. "Deep breath, Cals. You've got this. Nothing bad will happen if you don't get it, so relax. Forget every interview rule Dad taught you."

When I start to roll my eyes, he squeezes my shoulders. "This isn't Dad's company. Mr. Olsson's not going to grill you. At the core of any interview, it's just a conversation. And Callie Reyer knows how to fucking talk so just talk, okay?"

Breathing in through my nose and out my mouth, I nod. "You're right. Talking, I can do that. I know words...kind of."

My brother chuckles softly. "That you do. His secretary knows you're coming so, again, deep breath. You got this."

As Adam's hands leave my shoulders, I roll them back, standing a little straighter. "I got this," I whisper. "Wait, what's his name again?"

"Olsson. Jim Olsson." Adam laughs before clapping my back, which causes me to take an involuntary step forward. "Text me when you're done. I'm going to go explore my new office until then."

That makes me laugh a little bit. "Isn't this whole place your office?"

"Yeah, isn't that fucking cool?"

I shake my head as I take another deep breath.

I can do hard things...I've done harder.

Okay, I'm...kind of ready. Twisting the knob to the office door, I step in, and at first all I can see is the field. Windows from the ceiling to the floor make up the wall that overlooks the entire stadium. It's gorgeous and beyond massive. The stadium in Seattle was nice, but this one is incredible.

"Wow," I mumble.

"Pretty cool, right?" A female voice says off to the side.

Swallowing my startled yelp, I try to come off as poised as the girl my parents tried to force me to be. Adam might have told me to throw all those thoughts out the window, but old habits aren't that easy to kick.

Turning toward the voice, I find a woman, probably early thirties, who has to be the complete opposite of me—beautiful sleek black hair and porcelain skin. She looks so refined in her pencil skirt and silk blouse.

"It's quite the view. I imagine it makes the workday a little less dull." I smile as I hold out my hand. "I'm Callie Reyer. I'm here to interview for the photographer opening."

I get a quick glance from head to toe that I'm not really sure how to interpret. If my father saw me even thinking about an interview in jeans and a white button up, he'd have an aneurysm. My first instinct is to apologize, but this was not my plan. I didn't anticipate an interview for today—surely they can understand that.

Finally giving me a half smile, she says, "I'm Shannon, Mr. Olsson's secretary. He's been waiting for you. Follow me." She clicks her heels as she turns and I begin to feel I've lost before I've even started but letting her undermine my confidence won't help me.

I can do hard things...I've done harder.

Following behind Shannon, I repeat my mantra with deep breaths.

"Well, you must be Callie Reyer." A man stands from behind his desk as we walk in. His smile is wide, and a little weight falls off my shoulders when I realize Mr. Olsson is wearing jeans and a Blues t-shirt. "I told Adam not to force you out here today, but he was insistent that he had the right person for this job."

Ah, freaking Adam. Smiling through my internal curse to my brother, I laugh. "Yes, patience isn't exactly his virtue, but everyone needs a pusher in their life, don't ya think?"

"That they do." Stretching out his hand for a shake, he says, "Jim Olsson."

"Callie," I say as I return his hand but then shake my

head. "We established that already." A nervous laughter escapes me.

"I assumed. You were just confirming." Mr. Olsson sits back in his chair and motions for me to take a seat. "I imagine your brother filled you in on the current situation, so there's no need to get into those details. Adam said you were the perfect fit for the job, let's focus on that."

Perfect fit. Damn, Adam, pressure much?

I might not have a ton of sports pictures ready, but if I'm feeling bold, I've got some incredible shots that can back my brother up.

"Well, I could sit here and tell you all the reasons why I think I would be great at this job, but nothing quite shows that I'm capable as actual proof."

Chapter 3
Will

One benefit of this trade happening in the off season is now we have time—time to settle in and regroup before the season starts.

The negative—I got traded with fucking Adam 'no chill' Reyer. The pounding on my hotel door at seven in the morning was both unwelcomed and poorly received. I don't really mind early mornings, but would it kill the guy to just take a beat?

Adam and his sister dragged me out to walk to this apartment complex that Olsson's secretary mentioned. Apparently, he called around and this one happened to be four blocks down from our hotel. But by block two I was beyond annoyed.

Callie's teeth chatter as she wraps her arms around herself, clearly cold. Who cares if it is only four blocks away? I know how much we get paid, an Uber is practically pocket change.

"Is there a reason the meeting for these apartments

couldn't have been made at nine? Or any reason you felt I had to be included?"

"You're going to need somewhere to stay, and this was the only one of Shannon's listings that had places open. Excuse me for thinking you might not want to stay in a hotel all season," Adam huffs as we wait at the crosswalk.

Jamming my palm to my forehead, I try to ease the oncoming headache. "I could have—"

"Oh, that place looks good," Callie says low, under her breath. I'm sure she was only talking to herself as she fidgets with her oversized Yale sweatshirt and stares at the doors behind us.

Following her gaze, I see a small sign that says "Freshly Brewed" in the window. I don't even really like coffee but if I see her shiver one more time I might cuss Adam out for not getting a car.

Glancing at my watch, our meeting with the property agent isn't until eight and it's just past half past seven now. "If you're dragging me along, I'm going to at least grab a cup of coffee."

Blame it on my brotherly instincts, but I'm not letting Callie walk another block without at least a warm cup of coffee in her hand.

Not giving Adam any room for a protest, I turn heading straight for the shop with the purple door that Callie was locked in on. I knew I couldn't take her by the hand and drag her in with me, but I hoped the temptation of a warm drink was enough to make her follow.

Looking back, I can see she's hesitant but the moment I open the door and the smell of the caffeine is stronger, she caves.

"Cals, we—" Adam starts, but she ignores him.

"Thank you," she whispers as we enter the small shop.

Her smile is different from what I normally see from her. Instead of a wide grin accompanied with a loud personality, this one is subtle, softer... I've only seen this smile one other time and my only thought is *why does this one seem more genuine than the others?*

I try not to read too much into how much I like this smile more, and how I'm the reason it's there...maybe this wasn't my best idea. "I need some caffeine if I'm going to have to deal with your brother. It wasn't anything—"

"I meant thank you for holding the door." Callie's eyes narrow and the soft smile leaves.

Oof, okay, that wasn't my smoothest move. Just because I know I came in here for her doesn't mean she knows that. Pull it together, Anderson.

We walk up to the counter and the barista greets us with a voice way too chipper for the morning I'm having. "Hi, what can I get started for you guys?"

"Hi," Callie says, matching the girl at the register with that full smile I'm more familiar with. "I'll have a sixteen-ounce ginger tea, and I'm paying separately."

Callie pulls her bag up on the counter digging for her wallet. I should let her pay, there's no real reason I shouldn't let her pay for her own drink. Adam said she got the photographer job. She's a big girl, she's not one of my sisters, or my mom. She's not my girlfriend. She's my teammate's little sister—an acquaintance at best.

"No, she's not," I blurt out, despite every thought that just passed through my head. Maybe this is that brotherly instinct taking over again.

"Wi—" Callie starts, but I talk over her.

"I'll have a small coffee with a little bit of cream, please."

The girl behind the counter scrunches her face. "We don't have coffee. This is a tea shop."

Callie looks up at me with a confused look. "Did you not read the sign? It's called *Spilled Tea.*"

Oh, well this is great, double embarrassment. How am I supposed to respond to this? *"No, I didn't look because all I could see was you shivering."* Fucking hell.

"Didn't you hear me say I wanted coffee before walking in. Did it sound like I read the sign?" Shit, too snappy. Great, if this is any indication on how making friends with my teammates is going to go I might as well kiss that no-trade clause goodbye.

Callie quirks an eyebrow. "No, I didn't hear you. I was just standing there, freezing my ass off, thinking man, I really want a hot cup of tea. Then next thing I knew you were walking in."

Callie watches my blank stare, then just laughs and turns back to the barista. "He'll take a sixteen-ounce Chai latte."

Callie moves to pay again, but I toss some cash on the counter. "I said I would pay."

Rolling her eyes, she brushes some of her red hair away from her face. "You also said you were getting coffee. I wasn't going to make you pay for something you might not like, but you and I both know you have to walk out of here with some sort of drink unless we want to see Adam blow a gasket."

"Don't tempt me," I mumble. Sliding my change back, I put the rest in the tip jar as we step to the other end of the counter. "So, what did you order for me?"

"Chai latte." She shrugs. "Technically, it's not tea or coffee per se, but tea brewed with milk. I can't promise you'll like it, but it's got the caffeine you were searching for."

"Alright," is my only response. These past few days have

been the most I've spent around Callie all year. I was never one to hang out after games and if I ever did venture out with the guys, Callie was never there. I never heard of her going out with them in general, really. If it weren't for her sitting in the front bleachers with her beautiful red hair and loud cheers for Adam, I wouldn't have known she was his sister.

Again, the key takeaway there is I definitely noticed her, just wouldn't have known of the relation had she not made that obvious. All that being said, Callie's not a temptation—or at least, she *wasn't*. She's my teammate's little sister. She should never be a temptation. But ever since the trip over here, she's been a...distraction.

One I definitely shouldn't entertain, but when we sat down on that plane, Callie looked over at me with tired eyes and that soft smile on her face and asked how I was handling all of this.

This odd feeling came over me when I looked over at her and the words she said registered in my brain. As far as I can recall, no one had ever taken a second to ask how I was doing. My mom and sisters never asked, but I never would give them a reason to think that something was wrong. I'm the person who takes care of things in my family—and I like that role.

But with one sigh of stress out of me, she was there asking me what I needed, what she could do to help. Even if what I needed was as simple as her listening to me vent. Not that I was going to vent or tell her any of the thoughts running through my head, but something about how she looked at me when she asked told me she wasn't going to let it go without some sort of response. So, I grunted back a simple "I'm good" to appease her.

And she didn't stop with me. Callie asked Adam at least

five times what she could do to help once we landed. Hell, she treated everyone on that plane with such kindness and grace. Didn't matter that she probably only had a few hours of sleep in the past forty-eight hours, she never made one complaint.

After deplaning, all she wanted was to stop in and grab a new charger. But Mr. Schedule wouldn't allow for unplanned stops. So, she just smiled and asked him what she could do to help for the sixth time.

There wasn't a single thing I needed from that damn convenience store, but I wasted ten bucks on a crossword book, so Callie had an excuse to get her charger. And now here I am, about to get some drink that I probably won't even like because she was cold.

Maybe my subconscious is pulling me to care for her because she reminds me of my family. I've seen my mom and sisters go through some crazy things, and they hold that same overly optimistic attitude Callie does. Maybe that's what this whole distraction thing is about—me missing my family.

I've supported them from across the country for the past five years and leaving them weighed on me more than I led on, hence my loner tendencies. I guess I kind of wonder if Callie's rainbows and sunshine is a cover up for something weighing on her. I'm not sure why I care to know so badly, but I do.

Rocking on her feet she looks all around the shop. "This place is adorable. I'll have to add this to one of the perks of moving here."

"So, tea? Not coffee?"

Glancing my way, that soft smile tugs at her lips. "No, no coffee for me. I used to drink it all the time, but I realized the caffeine and sugar would make me feel really jittery and anxious, so I switched to tea."

"Couldn't you just order decaf?"

She shrugs nonchalantly. "I could, but turns out I like tea more. It has less sugar and there's tons of flavors with all sorts of different benefits to keep my hyper fixation from getting too carried away. Plus, it's just a safer order. I would forget to say decaf sometimes, so better just to get something that doesn't even have it."

Hyper fixation? For a drink? And how could you just forget to add "decaf" at the end of your order? Hell, make it the first word you say.

"That's fair," is what I decide to go with, because I have too many questions about her statement.

"Granted, some teas do have caffeine," she continues. "So I have to watch that too. But sometimes, depending on the amount of caffeine, it doesn't affect me too bad if I don't drink too much. I guess that's where the added sugar would come into play because...sorry, I'm rambling. See? Imagine me on caffeine."

I'm starting to understand why she stopped. How could there be this much energy in her already?

Her eyes study me. She's biting back talking more, I know it. Just as her mouth opens slightly, our order is called out and I quickly step up to grab our drinks.

Handing hers out she takes it with that soft smile again. "Thanks."

I simply nod back before heading toward the exit.

I don't really understand why, but I look down at the name of the store on the cup and make a mental note to remember it.

"Great," Adam says, clapping his hands together as we

make it outside. "Now that you two have your drinks, can we please get a move on?"

"Hold on." I hold out my finger telling him to wait another minute as I take a so-very-slow first sip of the drink Callie ordered me to really piss him off.

He huffs. "Seri—"

I hold my hand up for another sip. Shit's not bad. It tastes even better when I notice Callie trying to hide her laugh behind her cup.

"Alright, ready," I say, and Callie snorts next to me.

"You both can find your own way if you like?" Adam's vein on his forehead looks like it's about to pop. God, the temptation to delay this even more is so great, but Callie steps up, slinking her arm through her brother's.

"Alright, we're sorry. Come on, I'm freezing my freckles off. Let's get walking." Callie turns Adam around with her to face the crosswalk just as it flashes a "walk" sign. "Look at that! Perfect timing!"

For the rest of the walk, I'm positive it's Callie leading the way. Something tells me if Adam did really leave us, we'd be just fine finding the place on our own. Something also tells me that I need to be careful because that idea shouldn't sound so damn enticing.

Chapter 4
Callie

"So, those are the two apartments currently available," Christi says, setting her keys on the kitchen counter.

"And we can move in right away?" Adam asks, and I immediately start to tune them out. As much as I would love to have input on this, I know it's going to be Adam's call. And frankly, I don't think I can listen to the sales pitch for another second. My focus is shit as is, but hearing something for the third time? Yeah, my listening has gone out the door.

Despite the delay, we made it to the apartment complex with time to spare. Christi took us through two fully furnished apartments where the guys simply nodded as she went on and on about the layout and furniture included. In regular professional sports fashion, the place is nice, but Adam's never been one for the overly flashy penthouse type. During the season they're barely home anyway, so what's even the point?

I'm not sure if that's what Christi is overcompensating for or if it's just her personality, but half of the time during the tour I had to bite back, "They're guys, they don't care." I know Adam is going to take one of these apartments. The stuff he had on his list was "move-in ready" and "fully furnished." I can't say what Will will do, he's only nodded and grunted half responses since we got here.

I can't seem to make heads or tails of him. I'm not ashamed to admit that Will is exactly my type. I might have kept an extreme distance from the team in Seattle but I'm not blind—dude's hot as hell. He's a starting pitcher and it shows—lean but not lanky, chestnut brown hair that he usually hides under his ball cap, and don't even get me started when he turns it around backward. He did that on the plane ride over here and I was half tempted to take a picture for future spank bank.

Too bad he's a baseball player and I've sworn them off for good. But looking when they are as attractive as Will isn't off the table. Looking is harmless.

"Perfect, I'll get the paperwork drawn up for these two." Finally letting Christi's voice stick in my brain instead of sneakily eye-fucking Will, it seems like decisions have been made and I missed them.

Damn, I hope Adam picked the other apartment down the hall. It had such a prettier view than this one. "I'm sorry, I spaced out. Where am I living?"

My question is directed to Adam, but Christi answers first. "Oh, I didn't realize you needed a place as well." Her voice is so high pitched, it's like I just told her it was Christmas.

"Oh, she meant—" Adam tries to cut in, but Christi pushes through.

"You are so in luck because there will actually be another apartment opening up right next to the one down the hall next week. The one with the view you loved so much." She winks. "The only issue is it's only one bedroom and partially furnished but the rent is lower than these two."

Well, wait a minute. Lower rent? Not live in the same space as my type-A brother?

"She's good to stay—" Adam tries again, but this time it's my turn to talk over him.

"Hold up, how low are we talking?"

With the salary the Blues offered me I know I can move out of Adam's place eventually, but I hadn't talked to him about it yet. I didn't even know it was an option right now, but hell, I'll jump on the opportunity now if I can swing it.

At this moment I've made Christi's whole day. "Let me grab the paperwork to be sure, but it would be the perfect space for you. I'll be right back."

As she walks out the door I let a squeal escape. "I could have my own place!" The idea is so exciting. I've never lived on my own before. Now that the thought has entered my brain, I can't think of anything else. I can decorate with so much color. I can mismatch anything I want, and no one can say a word because it's going to be mine.

"Adam, my paycheck doesn't come in until the end of the month, but I can pay you back. Please, please, please, help me this last time and then I'll be out of your hair."

"Am I that bad to live with?" Adam huffs.

My sweet brother knows we have the same, yet completely different personalities. We both have a more positive outlook on things, but where Adam's rays of sunshine are in a perfect circle, my rays are manic with heat fluctuations and constant color changes. But despite our differences, we've grown closer since I moved in with him.

"Of course not! But I could actually have my own place. I've never had that."

Adam crosses his arms like he wants to say no, but I know better. "I got the first month's rent, then it's all you."

I let out another squeal with small jumps up and down. "Thank you, thank you, thank you! And we'll be neighbors!"

Adam opens his mouth to speak but Will beats him to it. His tone is flat as he says, "Actually, *we'll* be neighbors."

Well, this ought to be good.

It's done. My apartment is ready and it's perfect. It took about a week for me to move in and since my place only came partially furnished I had quite the list of supplies to get. But I didn't mind. This place needed the Callie touch.

By the end of the week, I had boxes and bags piled so high in Adam's living room I thought he was going to break into my place just so he could get the clutter out.

But once the keys were in my hands I was just as eager as he was. It's only taken me two days to get everything where I want it. Granted I'm working on a budget with the little I have in my savings, so it wasn't exactly a ton of stuff. I've filled the whole place with color and it's wonderfully chaotic.

Mismatched patterned pillows on the couch. Mixed antique kitchenware and cutlery from at least five different thrift stores. A lot came from thrift stores honestly, and I won't apologize for it. What's that saying? "One man's junk is another man's treasure." That pretty much sums up my apartment. I did draw the line at thrifted bedding and towels. Those I bought brand new. But everything else is my treasure.

Folding my last throw blanket and tossing it in one of my baskets I collapse on the couch. I'm pooped. My eyes shut for a minute before there's a knock at my door. "Cals, it's Adam. Let me in."

"I think it's open," I holler back. I went this morning to get tea from the shop two blocks down and I'm pretty sure I forgot to lock my door. I was so focused on letting my tea fuel me putting the finishing touches on my place that the thought of locking my door never entered my mind. I'm sure I'll get a comment on it, but eh, who cares? The lobby is locked, and Christi talked for a solid ten minutes about the building's "low crime" rating.

Shutting the door behind him, Adam plops on the couch next to me. "Place looks nice. Too bad someone will steal it all because you leave your door unlocked."

Hard eye roll. I knew it. "At least the robbers have good taste." As I breathe in, the smell hits me. "Get off my couch! You're all sweaty and you smell!"

I'm pushing him to my best ability to get his nasty ass up, but he puts all his weight against me. "Ugh, what are you doing here anyway?"

"I just left the gym, I'm not even that sweaty." Still fighting against me, he laughs. "After all I've done for you, this is how you treat me?"

"Years, Adam. I've had years of your catcher's gear smelling up everything. Please don't ruin my new couch."

"Alright, alright." Finally standing up, he relents. "But me leaving comes at a cost. We're all going out with the new team tonight."

"Noooo, I want to stay in my apartment. Leave me be, you Social Sally." Reaching for one of my pillows I swat it at him before readjusting to lie down. A nap is calling my name, not socializing with a bunch of baseball players.

As soon as my eyes shut my pillow gets ripped out from under me. "Hey!"

Adam holds it over me and only holds it higher when I reach for it. "Not up for negotiation, Cals. These people are our co-workers now. I'll drag you and Will out, kicking and screaming."

"Will's not been home in days." Probably shouldn't be something that I can say so confidently, but it's true. I haven't seen him since he moved in, and I've been in my new place for two days and haven't heard a peep.

"He was visiting his family in Rowley, but he just got back, so no excuses. Be ready at six." Adam throws the pillow back at my head.

"Dick," I grumble.

"When I come back at six your door better be locked," he calls as he walks out.

Chapter 5
Will

Why do I keep letting Adam drag me places? I barely made it in my place before he was knocking on my door telling me we were going out tonight.

There was no way I was going. None. I was ready to fight him on it, and I started to, but when he mentioned he was forcing Callie to go out too, my arguments weakened. We're not really going to dwell on that fact or that I've drank a chai latte every day this week.

Finding a place to park my bike, I'm a half hour later than when Adam told me to be here. The Blues were in charge of getting our vehicles sent over and I didn't trust them to drop off my Indian Motorcycle at the stadium for whoever to sign for it. So, I had them drop it off at my mom's. Going to get it from her place gave me a good excuse to see my family...and get some space from my new neighbor—who I definitely haven't thought about doing the lame "Hey neighbor, got any sugar" bit just to see her.

I head into the bar where Adam texted me to meet them. While this wasn't exactly at the top of my list of things to do tonight, I get what he's doing. We might know the major players on this team already, but we don't know them as teammates, and if I want to make this no-trade clause work I fear it's going to involve a little more effort than Olsson let on. I don't think small talk during practices or in the locker room will cut it.

Walking in, the bar is packed but you can still hear the cracking of pool tables off to the side and one fiery redhead's laugh.

"Damn, Callie, I didn't realize you were a hustler." Beck Daines, the Boston Blues star first baseman, stands off to the side with a pool cue in hand.

"I might know my way around a pool table," Callie says, leaning back down to take what looks to be her final shot. "Eight ball, corner pocket."

With a simple tap of her cue the ball goes right in. That soft smile plays on her lips as it goes in, and once she stands back up, it breaks into a full-on grin. "I believe I'm the winner."

"I call for a rematch," Beck says as I walk up. "Well, well, William fucking Anderson. How are you, man? Welcome to the Blues."

I've always liked Beck. He's a solid player and seems like a stand-up guy, a little too personable for me, but I'm trying.

"I suppose I could have been traded to a worse team."

"I believe it's what they call trading up, actually." Beck laughs and places his cue on the table. "You've got perfect timing because Little Reyer here just kicked my ass in pool."

Placing her cue down, Callie finally looks my way. Her red hair is pulled back with a loose braid, with strands framing her freckled face.

"I was about to place bets that you bailed on us, Will."

My smirk comes naturally in response to her playful tone. "It was debated, but then I thought Adam might burst a blood vessel and I couldn't put you through that."

She gives me a small chuckle as she puts her cue down. "Thanks, I appreciate that."

A small blush creeps up her face, and she tucks some of the loose stands behind her ears before pulling at the sleeves of her sweater and crossing her arms. In Seattle it felt easier since she kept her distance, kind of out-of-sight, out-of-mind, but she's so effortlessly beautiful that I don't know how all this time with her is going to go. It's barely been over a week here and I've already felt like she's been on my mind more than any potential friend should be.

"So, where's everybody at?" I look around absent-mindedly.

Beck claps my shoulder. "We've got some booths in the back."

I follow them through the bar and feel a little proud of myself that I didn't check Callie out the whole way back.

"Hey, look who finally showed up." Adam stands to let Callie slide in beside him. Next to her is the Blues' shortstop, Mateo Keener, who I know is happily married with a baby on the way.

Adam shakes my shoulder to get my attention. "Did you get lost or something? I was about to send out a search party."

"I might have taken a detour on my bike."

Adam takes his seat, and I reach for the empty chair behind me, pulling up to the end of the booth. Taking a glance around, it seems like the majority of the starters are here with some other players I've seen but can't recall their names.

As for my table there's Mateo, next to Callie, then Adam. Across is Beck and our third baseman, Tripp Pierce.

"Hey, Will." Mateo gives me a nod. "Ellison decides to retire and then you two get traded. What, were the Mavericks thinking they needed a lineup change?"

"Who the hell knows?" I toss back. "Maybe Olsson just wanted some World Series players on his team again."

"Fuck off," Tripp jokes as he reaches for his beer. "You're on the Blues now. That World Series trophy didn't travel here with you."

"Nah, just my annoying ass catcher who barely let me have a damn bathroom break."

"Hey!" Adam tosses his hands up. "I got us here, didn't I? You probably would still be in Seattle getting hit with late fines if it wasn't for me."

"And Callie," I add. I could tell from the plane ride over here that she's way more capable than either of them lead on.

Callie perks up just a smidge at the mention of her name. She might not have thought that anyone had noticed her tuck her head down and let the conversations just happen around her, but I did.

Being more on the loner side in Seattle was my preference, but I know this industry. I know how to be social when it's required of me, but I don't think Callie does.

"And speaking of Callie," Beck starts, turning to her. "Who knew our new team photographer was a damn pool shark."

Callie rolls her eyes but smiles. "Self-taught during my college years. Which reminds me, I believe the winner is owed some mozzarella sticks."

"Coming right up!" Beck slides out of the booth and he shakes my shoulder. "What are you drinking, Anderson?"

This is always a fun question. As professional athletes the majority of us don't typically go crazy at bars anymore—minus special occasions—but I don't drink. Period. And I don't do follow up questions about it either. "Don't worry about it, I'll grab something in a minute."

"Alright, suit yourself."

Letting out a sigh of relief, I feel some piercing green eyes on me. As tempting as it is to see if I can count all the freckles on her face, I ignore her completely this time.

Which proves to be quite difficult because I can feel her studying me.

"I think I might say hi to a couple other players," I say, sliding my chair back.

Adam's eyebrows pinch together. I know he expected me to sit my ass in this chair all night until I left, and I'm tempted to, but I've got my limits on socializing. Even if this attraction to Callie made tonight's outing a little more appealing, I'm not sure I should feed into it.

Forcing myself to interact for another hour, I get mostly hung up with the other pitchers on the team. The Blues have been known for having great pitchers, but with their starter, Dex Larsen, retiring this year and the general manager change, I'm curious how our lineup will play out. Starting pitcher was discussed with my agent during the trade but I know not to hold much weight in anything I don't see in writing.

Feeling like I've made enough of an effort I decide to call it a night. Glancing around the bar, I can't help but look for a certain redhead. I tell myself it's just to make sure she's okay and to see that she's having fun, but she's not to be seen.

I know I'm not overlooking her because I easily spotted her multiple times tonight. Part of me wants to check in with

Adam to make sure he at least knows where she is but *he's* her brother. I just need to let him do his job of taking care of her.

Weaving through the crowd a couple people stop me, asking about the season and the trade. I keep my answers light and short. My social battery is beyond dead, and I can't get caught up in a drunken fan's strategy for a new pitch.

Keeping my head low, I walk out the door and reach for my keys in my pocket. Finally outside, I look up and come to an abrupt stop at the redhead shivering in front of me. "Callie? What are you doing out here?"

Turning around slowly, she's got her phone in her hands. "Escaping," she replies under her breath.

"Escaping from what?"

"My brother." She shrugs as she shakes from the cold. "I'm exhausted and maxed out on socializing. Please don't rat out my attempt at the Irish goodbye. I swear I'll text him once I'm in an Uber home. That is if I can ever get one to show up."

She looks down at her phone again before letting out a small curse under her breath.

I should tell her to go back inside and wait for one to pick her up. For her to tell her fucking brother that she wants to go home, and he should go with her so she doesn't have to take an Uber by herself. Those should be the words out of my mouth, not, "Come on, you can ride with me."

"I can wait for a ride," Callie clips, but runs her hand against her arm to try to warm up.

"Okay, you have two options: ride with me or get your butt back inside where it's warm and tell your brother to take you home."

Fidgeting again, she slides her phone in her back pocket.

"No, I have three options. I can not ride with you, not tell my brother I'm leaving, and just walk home. It's what, ten blocks or so? I can do that."

"Callie." I sigh, pinching the bridge of my nose. If living with three women my entire life taught me one thing, it's that if she's made up her mind, me telling her what to do will only make it worse. "I'm going to ask you one time. Will you let me take you home? We're both going to the same place, and this way you can avoid telling your brother you want to leave and freezing to death while waiting for a ride." And for good measure I add, "Please?"

She bites at her lower lip while still rubbing her hands up and down her arms. When a cool breeze comes through, she caves. "Alright, fine."

"Thank you, now come on." I lead her over to my bike and pull my sweatshirt over my head.

"What the hell is this?" Callie stammers a good five feet away from my bike.

"Your ride," I say as I walk up to her and with no hesitation, pull the sweatshirt over her head.

"Will!" She tries to fight me on it, but this is nonnegotiable. Pulling it down, she refuses to stick her arms through and if looks could kill, this one would do me in.

"Go ahead, leave your arms in there if you want to be stubborn about it, but you're going to have to hold on somehow."

Callie narrows her eyes at me. "You know most guys try to get the girl's clothes off. I don't think I've ever been forcibly clothed."

"Yeah, well, it's the only thing I'd forcibly do." I chuckle with a small smirk. She's wittier than I thought, but then the implication of what she says registers. "Hold on. Care to expand on that for me, Callie? Has anyone forcibly done something to you?"

Swallowing, she mumbles, "No, just an observation." She slinks her arms through the sleeves. "I also didn't see why it's necessary."

She finally takes a few steps closer as I get my extra helmet off the back. "It's necessary because you're cold and it will be colder on the bike."

I motion, asking for silent permission to put the helmet on her and she nods. "What about you?"

"I have another helmet."

"No, about your sweatshirt. Aren't you cold?"

"I'll be fine. It's like you said, only ten blocks." It's very much not ten blocks, but I'm not about to tell her that. "There's comms in your helmet, so I can hear you when we get going."

"Okay," she mumbles. "You won't go fast, right?"

"I'm going to go the speed limit," I reply, putting my helmet on next.

"How many drinks did you have tonight? Maybe I should just wait on an Uber. The wait time might be down by now."

She reaches for her phone and some out of body experience takes over. I reach out, taking her hand in mine. "Callie, I haven't had a single drop of alcohol tonight. I won't go fast. I won't take sharp turns or weave in and out of traffic. You are perfectly safe, okay?"

"I've never rode on a motorcycle before." She keeps her voice low. All night, Callie's shown nothing but utter confidence, but right now, she seems scared.

I take a deep breath. "I was six when my dad got me my first motorbike. Every weekend, he'd take me out to this dirt track, and we'd ride for hours. And if you tell any of the guys this, I will deny it, but for years I wanted to go pro in motocross, not baseball."

That gets a small snort out of her. "Could I wager a picture of Little Will in his motocross outfit to get me on this motorcycle?"

"No, but I'll wager that Adam's probably going to come looking for you in about three minutes, so your call, Callie."

I gesture to my bike, and she hesitates for a moment, before letting me help her on. "God, please don't let me regret this," she whispers. I'm pretty sure she's forgot I told her I would be able to hear her through the helmets.

In my mind I know she means regret getting on a bike in general, but when her arms wrap around my waist, I just hope she doesn't regret me.

Chapter 6
Callie

It's a normal response to be attracted to the hot baseball player on a motorcycle. Perfectly acceptable to want to hold onto him instead of any other possible spot. What shouldn't be a normal response is how much I want to rub my hands up and down his torso while we ride. I can practically feel the six pack through his t-shirt.

"You okay back there?" Will's voice comes through my helmet. Definitely forgot he said they could do that.

"Yeah, I can't say this makes me want to go pro in motocross though."

I feel Will's stomach tighten like he's holding back a laugh. "Want to see how fast this thing can go, keep talking."

"Sorry, I'm not a dream crusher. I didn't mean to offend your passion."

Will shakes his head before revving the engine as he starts going a little faster. I let out a small squeak and involuntarily held on to him tighter.

"Not funny," I snap as he slows back down.

"I disagree and completely fair. I warned you."

Thank God he can't see me, the smile on my face is downright cheesy.

"Come on, you can't tell me you're not enjoying this even a little bit." Maybe it's the translation through the comms but I think Will might be flirting with me...I don't hate it and I kind of want to flirt back. But then I remember that not only is he Adam's teammate, but he's also technically my co-worker. The irony of my new job being for a baseball team despite my disinterest in being around any player that isn't my brother isn't lost on me.

Being attracted to Will is harmless, but flirting with him is dangerous.

"I think this ride will hold me over for a while." I bite on my lower lip while I wait for his response.

"We're almost there," he says flatly, then doesn't speak for the rest of the ride.

I, on the other hand, open and close my mouth at least fifteen times. I hate silence. It gives me too much time in my head. Do I need to apologize for something? He disappeared after Beck asked him about a drink and it felt weird to me that he didn't come back to our table at all. Even when more of us got up to play some pool, he stayed firmly in his seat.

Maybe if I talk about something else it will be less weird, but now it feels like too much time has passed. We're just stuck in this awkward silence now.

Pulling up to the doors of our apartment complex, Will stops in the unloading zone. "I don't think you can park here?"

"I'm not." He gets off with such ease but doesn't turn the bike off. "I'm letting you out here. I'll park in the garage a block down. I don't want you to have to walk that far."

He holds out his hand to help me off but avoids all eye contact.

"I don't mind walking."

"I mind," he says, and I can't tell if it's out of care or to get me out of his hair.

Slightly bummed that this night seems to be ending on a weird note, I take his hand and let him help me off. I'm not entirely sure my pride would recover from busting it on the concrete. Once I'm sturdy he reaches for the helmet, and I let him do it.

"Did you bring your lobby key?" he asks.

Is he implying something here? Yeah, my door might not have been locked again when Adam came to pick me up. I might be forgetful, but I'm not helpless. "Yes, of course I did."

"Good. I just wanted to make sure Adam didn't tell you to leave yours since you were supposed to be with him."

"Oh, right." I'm not going to willingly admit that Adam had one hundred percent suggested that before we walked out of my place.

"Um, well, thanks for bringing me home."

"Yeah, no problem," he says dryly before sliding back on his bike and pulling his helmet over his head.

I hold my eye roll until I've turned to walk toward the entrance when a cold breeze whips by. Then it dawns on me. "Oh, I almost forgot." I turn back to him to find him watching me as I start to take his sweatshirt off.

"You can give it back to me later." He doesn't give me any time to argue as he slides his visor down and drives off, leaving me confused as hell on the sidewalk.

I overanalyze the last half hour of events in my head until I'm back in my apartment. How can it feel like something happened between us, but nothing changed at the same time?

I'm overthinking this, I'm sure of it. I hyper fixate on everything, and it's so draining. Everything about tonight was just a simple favor. A guy taking his friend's little sister home. Him being neighborly, eco-friendly really. So tell me why I've replayed our conversations in my head a million times? Thought of ten different things I should have said and twenty different ways to start the conversation with him next time we run into each other?

My brain is exhausting.

Walking into my bathroom I rip Will's sweatshirt over my head and throw it on the floor of my bedroom. I take off my makeup and comb the knots out of my hair before putting on some pajama shorts and a cami.

In my mind I walk to my couch and plop my butt down to watch some bad reality TV until I pass out.

In reality, I stare at Will's sweatshirt on the floor for a second too long and now it's the only thing that sounds remotely comfortable right now. Damn it, why did it have to be so soft and warm? I swear, when he pulled it over my head in the parking lot it smelled so freaking good.

What was that smell? It was a softer scent, definitely wasn't any of those typical guy smells. Maybe I need to smell it just one more time, to get the scent right.

Picking it back up I impulsively put it back on, convinced it's the best way to decide what the smell actually is.

Vanilla? It's almost beachy...cedarwood? No, it's sweeter. Bringing the collar up again, I take a deep breath in. Coconut! Oh hell, I might love him for this.

Satisfied with myself in figuring it out, I don't think twice about leaving it on. It doesn't mean anything. It's warm and smells like one of my favorite scents. It's only weird if I think too hard about it and I'm in my own apartment. Who's going to know?

As I walk into my living room there's a loud knock at my door and suddenly it dawns on me—Adam. I ditched him without saying a word and totally forgot to tell him that I made it back here safe. He's going to chew my butt out.

A loud knock comes again, and I swing the door open with my apology ready. "Adam, I'm so sor—Will?"

Why is he here? Why is he staring?

Jolting like he's coming out of a glitch, he stammers, "I... uh, I wanted to make sure you made it inside okay?"

"You brought me here. Did you hit your head on the arm bar in the parking garage or something?"

A surprising chuckle rattles out of him. "No, I just realized that I drove off before I saw that you made it into the building okay."

"Oh." I don't know what to say. I'm rarely rendered speechless, but this was not at all what I was expecting.

"Clearly you managed fine." There's a sly smile forming on his face as he looks down my body. "Sweatshirt looks good on you, Callie."

I look down, hiding my blush at the fact that he's aware I put it back on because I'm clearly not in my jeans anymore. By the time I look up, ready to spit out the first excuse that comes to my mind, he's already walking in his door.

Fuckity, fuck, fuck.

Chapter 7
Callie

The next morning, I do not put Will's sweatshirt back on. As appealing as the idea is, I need to set that boundary. Granted, all morning I've done nothing but think about putting the warm sweatshirt back on as I'm having one of those days where I hate everything I try on. My clothes feel itchy and unnatural, but I know that's just my brain hyper fixating on the fact that while it was embarrassing getting busted by Will last night, it also felt really good to see him checking me out.

I've thought about it all morning and while there are many things about my brain that just piss me off, the top one is my lack of impulse control. Which has now led me to the predicament I'm in now.

"Calliope Reyer, I can't even begin to express my disappointment in you right now. A *photographer* for a *baseball team*." My father's angry voice booms through the speaker and I wince.

I know I should have looked at who was calling before answering but I was off in Lalaland thinking about Will's sweatshirt. My phone was ringing, I answered it. Threw it on speaker as I'm cooking the classic bitch-on-a-budget meal of ramen.

"Dad, please, let—"

"And to hear about it from *his* family? Are you kidding me? How could you do this to us?"

I pinch the bridge of my nose, not sure if it's to prevent an oncoming headache or crying. I hate the words coming out of my dad's mouth right now. I hate that I've disappointed him, but the life he wants me to live will end up killing my soul in the long run.

"Dad, if you would just listen to me—"

"No, you listen, Calliope. I let you have your little temper tantrum with your let-down of a brother. No more. You have till Wednesday to get your ass home.

Tears prickle at my eyes but I shove them down. It's always been this way. "Calliope, do this." "Calliope, sit still." "Calliope, Calliope, Calliope!" *I hate that name.*

Before my debacle with my ex, these mean words and demands would have had me caving. Doing whatever I was told to keep the peace, but I can't go back there. Not without some sort of olive branch at least. To show that they can see my side of things...is that so hard?

Swallowing down my emotions, I take a deep breath. "Dad, I'm not coming home."

I can see it now. The great Harrison Reyer too stunned to speak by the actions of his children. I count to five in my head, like clockwork.

"Calliope Elizabeth Reyer, you will come home. I'm tired of you constantly disrespecting this family's name. You and your brother both. After everything I've done for you, this is how you treat me? How you treat this family?"

I try to blink back the tears, but I know this time it's pointless. I hide behind my hands as his reign of terror continues through the speaker.

"You are such a little ungrateful brat. You're probably out whor—"

The phone clicks off at the words I know I'm thankful I won't hear again, but I didn't turn it off...

Slowly looking up, Adam is looking at me in shock, my phone in his hand. I hadn't even heard him come in. I must have left the door unlocked again.

"I promise I'll be better at locking my door." I sniffle, because I'm trying really hard not to break down right now.

Adam sighs as he shakes his head. "Cals."

"I..." I don't even know how to explain this to him. Adam hasn't spoken to our parents since he got drafted into the minors. Dad never raised his voice at me until the day he moved out.

My big brother wraps me in a giant bear hug, and I honestly couldn't tell you the last time I got a hug like this. A true, let-it-all-out hug.

"I didn't do anything, Adam. I swear," I cry.

"I know, Callie, I know." And he does. Adam was always the victim of Dad's verbal lashings growing up and then some. I don't blame him for not thinking about me becoming the next target. Adam was nineteen when he left, and I had just turned twelve. I was still "Daddy's little girl" at that point.

"Does he talk to you like that often?" I open my mouth to answer, but he stops me. "Actually, I already know the answer. Damn it, Callie, is this why you moved in with me?"

Adam danced around this question from the moment I knocked on his door. I'm not sure if he was too afraid to ask or if the guilt of leaving me behind was too much for him.

While he cut off our parents completely, he still reached out to me. But we never talked about family. Period.

"Partly." It's not a lie. Every time I spoke with my parents, my breaking point grew closer. Surprisingly, they weren't necessarily the straw that broke the camel's back.

Finally releasing his hug, Adam puts his hands on my shoulders and levels his face with mine. "Never answer his phone call again, Callie. Never speak to that man. Never talk to either of them."

"But they're our parents, Adam..."

"Biologically, sure. Parents who give two shits about their kids? No." He shakes my shoulders gently as tears fall down my cheeks. "But I care about you, and I'm telling you, cut them out."

I know he's right. Not talking to my parents over these past few months has led to a lot less emotional turmoil. I don't feel like shit every morning when I wake up anymore, but I'm still holding out for a moment when they might actually be willing to hear me out. Sometimes I just want to shake my father and scream, "Please, just listen for five minutes!"

"Promise me, Cals."

I nod slowly. "I promise."

"Good." Releasing my shoulders, he sighs again. "I came over here to talk to you about what you were doing for Thanksgiving on Thursday. Now I know what you won't be doing."

"Yeah." Wiping the tears from my cheeks I try to shake off this awful feeling of self-doubt. Before my dad's call, I hadn't made a final decision on if I was going home for the holidays this year. This season was always a big deal in the Reyer household. It's a time to wine and dine the rich and politically powerful.

"What do you usually do?"

Adam shrugs before turning to the stove, clicking it off and moving my boiling pot to the side. "It was always different. Usually just ordered take out, went over to Jett's a time or two. Do you want me to call him? I'm sure Wyla is planning something."

As much as I would love to see her and cry with her over wine, I know I can't. "No, this is their first holiday season as a family. I don't want to take that away from them."

I'd kill for a real Thanksgiving meal and with Wyla being a southerner, her comfort food is unmatched. Maybe she'd send me some recipes.

"What if we just had it here? I can try to cook. It might be the saddest sibling Thanksgiving ever, but..." I kind of lose my train of thought at that. Why does this idea sound so sad? Two kids who are no longer welcome at their parents' house.

Adam chuckles, looking at the ramen on the cooktop. "You cooking? Can it be something other than ramen?"

I can't help but laugh. "I promise no ramen."

"Alright, sounds good, Cals. Sad Sibling Thanksgiving it is. Text me some stuff to bring. The easy shit, though."

"Yeah, yeah. I won't push you out of your comfort zone of meat and potatoes." I kick my leg out, tapping him on the shin.

Adam shakes his head. "Sounds good. Now come on, let me take you for an actual lunch."

"Meat and potatoes?"

"How about actual ramen?"

Chapter 8
Will

How can one person make so much noise? It's Thanksgiving morning and it sounds like Callie's remodeling her kitchen. Are our walls really that fucking thin or I am just more apt to her chaos? Like a damn dog whistle, only I am sensitive to the sounds coming from the redhead in the apartment next to me.

Another crash comes through the walls, and I can't decide if I want to chuckle or bang on the wall to tell her to keep it down.

Maybe I should go over and check on her? Another loud clunk noise comes through. I mean, really, how can you make this much noise?

That thought is quickly interrupted because I hear a loud "fuck" come through the walls. Heading to my door I step out into the hallway just as the smell of smoke hits me. I'm at her door in a single step.

"Callie," I semi-yell while banging on her door.

"Fuck, fuck, fuck," is all I hear back. Twisting her knob, I find she's left her door unlocked.

"Callie! What the hell?" Smoke fills her apartment as she frantically looks at her stove.

Racing over, there are flames growing rapidly, fueled by a box of stuffing mix. Grabbing the top of the box, I toss it in the sink, flipping the faucet on before returning to the stove. I turn the burner off and take a rag to smother the small flames remaining.

When it seems like it's under control, I turn off the water and turn to Callie. Her hands are stuck to her cheeks with a look of horror on her face. My first instinct is to yell, "What the hell happened!" but she speaks first.

"Oh my goodness...I almost burned down my apartment." Her voice trembles and her hands shake as she brings them away from her face.

"Hey, it's okay." Letting my hands take the same spot on her cheeks, she looks up with watery eyes. "I'm going to open the windows to let some of this smoke out, okay?"

She nods slowly. "Okay."

I let go of her face and walk over to the windows. "Let me know when you're ready for questions."

"Questions?" she asks just barely above a whisper.

I push one window open then go to the next. "Yeah, I got three whenever you're ready."

"Can you ask them nicely? Because I'm not sure if I'll cry or cuss you out if they're mean." Her voice is still shaky and low.

Honestly, the face of pure terror she had a moment ago was enough to kill any anger in me, so yeah I can ask them nicely. After opening the last window, I walk back over to her. "First question."

"I didn't say I was ready yet," she mumbles.

"Callie, are you okay?"

Almost stunned, she blinks once, then twice. "Am I okay?"

"Yeah, there was a fire in your kitchen, and you could have seriously hurt yourself. So, my first question is 'are you okay?'"

Folding her lips in a thin line she pulls at the sleeves of her Yale crew neck before crossing her arms. With a deep breath in and out, she nods. "Yeah, I'm okay."

"Good. Okay, question number two. Why didn't your fire alarm go off?"

"Well, last night the one in here was beeping and I couldn't sleep." Shrugging, she uncrosses her arms to move her hands while she talks. "I tried calling the super, but no one answered. So, I might have stacked my small step stool on a chair and took the batteries out myself."

I follow her hand gesture over by the wall behind her where the chair with a pink step stool is still stacked on top.

Don't give her a lecture. Do not give her a lecture.

"Okay." I sigh. "I have some fresh batteries, I can fix that. Final question, what are you doing that it sounds like you're remodeling in here?"

Huffing she throws her hands in the air. "I just wanted to cook some food for Thanksgiving, but I've already broken a plate while unloading the dishwasher and concussed myself from opening a cabinet and all of my Tupperware falling on my head. Then I accidentally knocked my sugar off the counter and thought I would try to start boiling some water while I cleaned it up, but I turned on the wrong burner and nearly burned this place down! And now my box of stuffing is ruined and I—why are you smiling?"

I'm smiling? Shit, I was just imagining how her morning played out then thought what if I had been here to help her and, in that daydream, she's wearing my sweatshirt instead of this worn out Yale one.

"I'm sorry, I was just amazed that one small person could create so much damage."

That was the wrong thing to say.

Burying her face in her hands she cries, "I just wanted to make some food for mine and Adam's sad little Thanksgiving, and I...I—"

"Hey, hey, it's okay." I know I shouldn't, but I pull her hands away, wanting to wipe her tears myself. It's an out of body experience, but right now I want to be the reason she stops crying, not starts.

"I guess crying was my answer." She half laughs then looks at me with her glossy green eyes. I know at this moment I'll do anything she'd ask me to.

"I don't have to leave for my mom's for a couple hours. Let me help."

Her eyebrows furrow with a sputtered laugh. "You want to help?"

"I'm not too bad in the kitchen. Plus, someone's got to keep the blaze under control."

Rolling her eyes. "You put the fire out already."

"I was talking about you."

And just like that, the fire ignites in her eyes. Her hands circle my wrists and pull my hands down. "I might have cried first, but I'll still cuss you out."

I take a step back and smirk. "Oh, I'm well aware, Blaze."

After running back over to my place to grab some batteries, I come back and immediately make my way over to her chair-stool combo and sigh. She could have seriously hurt herself. As I move the stool over, I can't help but notice the tension shift. Neither of us has said anything yet and the silence is starting to feel thick.

An extra layer of tension gets added when we catch each other staring. I might have been busted first...I couldn't help it. She was pulling her long red hair up in a ponytail. She's a fucking blaze, alright. It's like I've been caught up in her flames and I can't find any oxygen.

I catch her looking when I started to replace the batteries in her fire alarm. I could have gone down to the super's office and made someone else fix it, but call it caveman of me, I wanted to be the one to fix it for her. Maybe this is just me being able to fill the void of taking care of someone again. Back in Seattle the most I got to do during the season was send money back to my mom and sisters, but I like doing stuff like this. I like being the one to take care of things...and the people I care about.

"You know, I'm pretty sure I'll lose my job if you fall and can't pitch this season." Callie leans on her elbows on the small island in her kitchen. She's holding out a box of Velveeta Shells and Cheese, pretending to read the instructions, but I've noticed her eyes darting to me a few times.

Sliding her alarm back in place, I laugh. "Please don't even get me started on the setup you had here." I step off her chair and slide it back in place at her small dining table. My eye catches on her pink stool again. "Scared of riding on my bike but makes makeshift ladders and climbs them in the middle of the night."

Callie stands up straight. "Hey, it worked out just fine, didn't it?"

"I feel like 'fine' is up for debate."

She scoffs. "Hey, a fall from that would have hurt my

pride more than anything. A fall from your motorcycle would likely kill me."

"You were perfectly safe with me, but I'm not saying anything else at the fear of being cussed out."

Rounding the corner of her island, Callie hums with a tight-lipped smile pulling at her lips. "Listen, I know I seemed like a hot mess this morning."

When I raise my eyebrows and nod in agreement, she hits my shoulder. "Will!"

"Okay, okay. I'm sorry. Please continue."

Rolling her eyes, she huffs, "I was just saying I was a little overwhelmed, and I appreciate your help, but..." She trails off as her eyes lock with mine. This is the second time I've seen Callie nervous, and I can't decide if it makes me feel good knowing I get to see this other side or if it makes me feel like shit that I'm the one making her uncomfortable.

"I can leave if you want me to, Callie." I let any playfulness I've had in my tone from earlier leave my voice. I don't understand much about this attraction to Callie, but I would rather die than make her uncomfortable.

Breaking our staring contest, she crosses her arms. "I just thought I could do it myself, that's all."

Ow, that hurts a little bit. It shouldn't, but it does. "Okay, the fire alarm is working now, so I'll head out."

Callie's mouth opens, then shuts. Not wanting to make things worse, I walk out without another word.

Chapter 9
Callie

I am the dumbest girl in all of Boston.

I had one of the hottest guys I've ever seen in my apartment fixing stuff and wanting to help me cook and I sent him away. Why? Why did I do that? I mean, really, who would it have hurt if Will stayed?

The thought of Will in my kitchen...shirtless... Okay, I know he wouldn't actually be shirtless, but this is my daydream, so whatever.

It's probably best that he left. I'm not interested in dating another baseball player. And this meal is about me and my brother. He's done a lot for me over this past year, and I want to prove to him—and myself—that me showing up on his doorstep a few months ago wasn't a bad thing.

Turning back to my kitchen I'm more determined than ever to actually cook this fucking food. It might not be the extravagant meal our personal chef would make growing up, but it would be good. Wyla sent me recipes. I can do this. I can do hard things!

Getting everything out on the counter I think I'll start with the mashed potatoes. The idea seems simple enough. I put a pot on the stove to boil—turning on the right burner this time—then go back to Wyla's text. Step one: peel potatoes. Fuck.

I don't have a peeler here. I didn't think to buy one. I'm pretty sure I'll lose a finger if I use a knife.

We're off to a great start here, Cals.

Ugh, okay, maybe something else will be better. But as I look around it becomes abundantly clear that my kitchen is not prepared to cook this meal. Can opener? Don't have one. Measuring cups and spoons? Not one. Apparently, I only thought about buying pretty things and basic necessities.

Fuckity, fuck, fuck.

I could go to Adam's and cook it in his apartment. His came fully furnished so it should have everything. But then that puts me back at going to my brother to rescue me. And I don't have the time or the money to get all of this stuff right now.

Swallowing down every bit of pride I have I walk out my door to go knock on the door of the only other person I know that has a fully stocked apartment.

The knock feels full of regret. He's going to tell me no, I'm sure of it. Why did I even think this was a good idea?

I'm halfway into my turn to run back to my apartment when Will opens the door. "Callie?"

Shit.

Turning back, I try to cover the fact that I was mid ding-dong-ditch with an overly happy, "Hi!" Ugh, can I crawl in a hole and die right now?

"Hi?" Will leans against his door frame and it's annoying to me how sexy that is for no damn reason.

"Hi." Damn it, I've already said that. "I...uh...well, you know how I said I wasn't a hot mess?"

The corners of his mouth tug into a smile ever so slightly. "I don't hear your fire alarm so I'm assuming this mess isn't life threatening?"

God, I'm a disaster. My shoulders slump and I don't have the willpower to fake positive right now. "I just want to make some food for me and Adam. I wanted to prove that I could do it without any help, but my apartment didn't come fully stocked like yours so I'm missing things I need. I know I could ask Adam, but I've asked him for so much this year. I just wanted to do it, because damn it, I can do hard things. But I just..."

I look down at the floor as I trail off and wait for the door to slam in my face, but instead, Will laughs. "What do you need?"

Looking up I try not to show too much schoolgirl happiness. "Something to peel potatoes, some measuring cups... and spoons. Oh, and a strainer and mixer!"

Leaning off the door frame, he smirks. "Anything else? Kitchen sink, maybe?"

"Honestly, maybe." And with that small joke a smile spreads over Will's face. Damn, he should do that more often.

"Head back to your place. I'll bring everything over."

Holding back a hug, I decide on a simple, "Thank you."

Well, he's not shirtless, but Will still looks damn good in my kitchen. He brought over everything I asked and besides the small jokes in his doorway, he came with no more snide remarks or judgmental stares. Not to mention, he's let me do the bulk of the cooking, only helping when I ask.

I fully anticipated him coming in here and taking everything over, but he's let me take the lead from the start. I didn't know how much I needed it to be that way until he said, "Okay, tell me what to do."

One small part of me really wanted to make a joke asking if he takes instructions this well in bed, but I will absolutely not go there. There must be boundaries if we are going to be friends.

Because that's what we are...right?

Will pulls the rolls out of the oven as I finish whipping the mash potatoes. "Okay, I've got about twenty more minutes before I've got to get to my mom's. What do you need next?"

"Oh my gosh, Will, I completely forgot you have an hour drive." I feel like such an asshole taking up his entire holiday. "Please, go ahead. I can finish—"

"Callie. What do you need next?" The look on Will's face tells me not to argue, and I honestly don't want to. I've liked having him help. It's almost as if he's calmed my chaos down.

Earlier when I was too preoccupied in making the marshmallows pretty on the yams, he had already preheated the oven and cleaned up the mess I made with the brown sugar.

"Could you possibly get one of the nicer bowls out of that cabinet?" I gesture to the tall one behind him. "I can get the chair-step-stool combo if you'd like, though."

Shaking his head with a small chuckle, he turns around to do as I asked. "I feel like I'm going to need to get you a life alert necklace anytime you think you need to climb to reach something."

"Help. I've fallen and I can't get up," I mock, and that smile is on his face again when he brings me the bowl. Dear Lord.

"What?" he asks, snapping me out of my stare.

Shit, I blink out my daze. "Nothing. I...um... So, your mom's? What do you guys do for Thanksgiving?"

Rounding the island to the opposite side, Will shrugs. "Nothing too crazy. It's typically me, my mom, and sisters. We don't have a lot of extended family up here. Most of my extended family lives down in Florida."

"Really? And you don't travel down there for the holidays?"

"Eh, my mom isn't really into the idea of big family functions. We went down a few times growing up, but honestly, I like it better just the four of us not cramming into a way-too-small beach house where my grandparents insist on keeping the A/C set to seventy-five."

"Oh, yup. I can see that." I half laugh because that does sound a bit like torture, but then again, it seems more normal than any holiday I've ever had.

Picking up on my mood shift, Will speaks softly. "So, your parents..."

I look at him as he trails off. I'm not sure if he doesn't know what to say or is waiting for me to finish the sentence but I don't really know how to.

"We might not have spent much time together, Callie, but I've been Adam's teammate for five years. It might not seem like it, but I pay attention. I know he doesn't speak to them anymore. I just wasn't sure if that extended to you too."

Swallow your tears, Callie. You've been entirely too emotional around this man today alone.

"It didn't always...it does now. But it's fine." I look around my kitchen at the small meal on my island. "I know it might seem like the saddest Thanksgiving meal ever, but it will be the first one I get to enjoy in sweats and not cocktail attire making small talk with snooty rich people." *Or get the small unnecessary touches from the sleazy husbands.*

"Your dad's in finance, right?"

"Yup," I say, popping the p. "I hate even saying it, but the Reyer's are old money rich. My great-great grandfather started the company and each generation's grown it since. Frankly, his story wasn't exactly rags to riches. It seems a silver spoon was shoved in his mouth too."

When Will doesn't say anything, I can't help the word vomit. I haven't talked about my family in so long and as I'm staring at this food, I just get angrier.

"At about this time, I'd probably have heard at least three 'Calliope, sit still,' probably six 'Calliope, smile more,' and ten 'Calliope, why don't you let me talk?' I have a fucking master's degree from Yale but can't be trusted to have a conversation with the women of the DAR or the slimy husbands who look me up and down before speaking."

I angrily reach for the rag on the counter, wiping my hands, still on a fucking roll. "Then after the dad's got a good look, my mother would have dragged me around introducing me to all their equally touchy sons who only like to talk about themselves. So, yeah, this meal might be sad, but at least it's not that."

Sighing I throw my rag on the counter feeling like I got this elephant off my chest. I look up and Will's staring at me with an emotionless look on his face. Oh my goodness, I've completely lost it. Why did I just word vomit on him?

Forget being a hot mess, I've been a dumpster fire around him today and now he's just staring at me.

"I'm sorry, I got carried away."

"Don't," he snaps.

Rolling my shoulders back, I'm a little stunned at his tone. "Excuse me?"

"Don't apologize. The words 'I'm sorry' should never come out of your mouth to excuse someone else's actions."

My mouth opens but no words come out. I hadn't really thought of it that way. Apologizing almost feels like second nature to me. I trauma dumped on him—thankfully excluding the issue with my ex—and just gave him way more than he asked for.

"While we're at it"—Will walks toward me—"don't apologize for men's actions, the unwelcomed ones, in particular. Don't say you're sorry for voicing your opinions or not smiling when you don't feel like it. And don't you ever let anyone talk for you."

He's angry...but not at me. Will's angry *for* me. Angry *with* me, actually. Well, there's that need to hug him again.

"You know what they say about habits."

Will's hand lifts, hovering for a moment as if he wants to touch me but stops before he brings it behind his neck.

Holy fuck. He was going to touch me but stopped because I was talking about men's unwelcome advances.

I hadn't intended it to be a new boundary that also applied to *him*. Will has never made me feel uncomfortable in a way that has me questioning my safety, but he was listening so intently to what I was rambling on about that it affected him.

Fuck it, I'm hugging him anyway.

Not allowing myself time to chicken out, I wrap my arms around his waist. "Thank you," I whisper.

I count one then two before his arms finally hug me back. "You're welcome, Callie."

Chapter 10
Will

"Chai latte!" a girl behind the counter calls.

Stepping up, I grab my drink and take the first sip to prepare for the heavy snow that's been falling for days now.

"Oh, excuse me, sir?" The girl behind the counter walks back up with a bag in her hand.

"Yeah?" She blushes as I turn and face her.

"You're friends with Callie Reyer, right? You live in the same building?"

"Uh, yeah...we do." I'm not sure if I should be alarmed by these questions. I'm used to being recognized, but not exactly for my affiliation with a fiery red head.

"Great! She called in a ginger tea, but our delivery guy just left and forgot her order. Could I trust you to bring this to her? I sealed it up and gave her a coupon for next time. I could wait for him to come back. I didn't want her—"

"I'll take it to her," I say, cutting her off. I probably should've hesitated, given I've been avoiding Callie over these past few weeks. After our...hug...moment on Thanksgiving, things have been a little awkward.

We ran into each other in the hallway the next day and we tried to have a conversation, but it was like neither of us knew what to say. She's my teammate's little sister. My neighbor and co-worker. And that's all we will be, so my first plan in making sure it stays that way was avoiding her. But here I am again bringing her this tea because I can't stand the idea of her having to travel out in the snow to get it or hell, waiting on the delivery guy to come back.

Taking the bag from the girl she thanks me incessantly, which isn't necessary. She doesn't realize that she asked me to do the one thing I've been dying to do for three weeks now—take care of Callie...as her friend.

The walk back to the apartment only confirms my decision to bring this drink to her. I know if they would have called and asked if she wanted to wait, she would have tried to walk in this mess. Thick snowflakes have been falling all morning. It's actually kind of beautiful, that is until the wind chill hits. I can hear her now saying she's freezing her freckles off. I can't have that.

As I reach her door, I can hear the Christmas music playing so I knock a little louder to make sure she hears me.

I hear some shuffling around, then the music turns down a bit, then more shuffling right before I hear, "Shit!"

"Callie?"

She opens the door with her hair piled up in a bun and freckles not covered up by any makeup. This is my reward in itself.

"Hey, Will. What's up?" Her voice sounds off as she favors her right leg.

"You okay?"

Scrunching her nose, she pouts. "I just rammed my toe into my coffee table." She stands up straighter trying to come off strong. "I'll survive though. Is everything okay? I was kind of hoping you were my ginger tea."

I hold up her bag. "This one?"

Her eyebrow quirks as she takes the bag and walks back into her apartment leaving the door open for me to come in. "Was the multi-million-dollar contract not enough? Had to take a job as a delivery man?"

I chuckle. "Only for you." That came off stronger than I intended. "I was at Spilled Tea this morning and the girl behind the counter knew we were friends so she asked me to bring it to you. Apparently, the delivery guy forgot yours."

That soft smile tugs at her lips. "You went to Spilled Tea?"

"I like the chai lattes, okay?" I admit. "You were right, it's better than coffee."

She lets her smile grow slightly before taking her first sip.

Not wanting to stare, I look around her place and notice the absolute disaster state it's in. "What the hell is going on here?"

It looks like Santa threw up and didn't stick around to clean it up. There are tangles of lights piled on the floor, three boxes of what looks like different sets of ornaments, a box of stuffed Christmas decor, then one long box which I'm assuming is the tree.

"Okay, I know it looks like a mess." Callie walks to the edge of her living room looking at everything on the floor. "I'm going to get it all up, I just got a little overwhelmed with the lights being in a giant knot. But now that I have my tea to start my day properly, I can try again."

"Do you need any help?"

She turns to me with a look on her face that's hard to read.

"I...um..." This is a bit of how our conversation a few weeks ago went. Started out normal then sputtered out about halfway in. Already preparing to leave, I'm taken back when she says, "Yeah, actually, I do."

Thank fuck.

"Okay, what's up first?"

Callie looks at me and my heart clenches in my chest. Back in Seattle I only knew her as overly positive from a far, but now, I see that when she's around crowds or strangers. And right now, in the comfort of her own home, I'm seeing her soft smile with genuine excitement in her eyes.

"The Christmas tree!"

Callie walks in her living room and gestures to the box. "You should have seen me dragging this thing in yesterday. Adam didn't answer his phone, so I decided to lug everything in myself. While the feminist in me was proud, I'm positive the surveillance footage is highly comical."

I snort a laugh at my situation. I thought my pull to be around Callie came from the desire to take care of someone again. But at the same time, I like that she's independent.

"Well, since you did all the heavy lifting to get it up here, why don't I put it together?"

Callie takes a sip of her tea. "I'm going to take you up on that, but I would like to acknowledge that I *can* do it." She laughs.

I set my drink down and pull off my coat. "I know you can, Blaze, but let's not let the fire get out of control when dealing with flammables."

Callie scoffs like she's offended but there's a touch of her true smile there. "We never joke about fire safety, William."

I can't help but let a full laugh escape. I don't remember the last time I did that with anyone but my family.

After assembling her plastic tree, I join her on the floor to help untangle the giant ball of lights. We've made small progress and have it separated into two parts.

"Callie, please tell me when you thrifted this giant mess of lights, that you made sure they worked."

Biting her lip, she hums. "Well..."

"Cal—"

"Hear me out, okay?" She shoots up on her knees dropping the tangle that was in her lap so she can use her hands as she explains herself. "It was one giant ball, and I didn't know where each and every end stopped and started."

Knowing she's not done defending her thinking, I rest my head on my hand, listening intently. I should probably tell her she doesn't have to explain herself, but I let her continue.

"But!" She holds her finger up ready to dive into the full story. "I did find one end, so I plugged it in, and one strand definitely lit up. I also asked the nice little old lady working there and she said that they were a new donation. So, I was hoping that maybe it was the knot that made the people throw them out because, I mean, look at it, I might have thrown them away too."

"And we can't throw them away now because...?"

Rolling her eyes, she huffs, "Because if they do work then I got a bunch of lights for five dollars and that's a bargain!"

I try to hold back my laugh, I really do.

"Will! Stop laughing! Here, look we got some more ends out at least, why don't we test those now?"

"Oh, let's." Standing I take mine over to an outlet on the wall. "And so help me, if even one of these doesn't work, I'm going out and buying you all new Christmas lights."

She scoffs as she stands bringing her tangle with her. "You will not."

"I most certainly will. I'll even buy the most expensive ones just to spite you."

"Well, that's not going to happen because they are all going to work." Callie shoves her bundle against my chest. "Go on, light 'em up."

I'm pretty sure something has already been lit by Callie Reyer, but I can't tell if it's going to go out or fully ignite anytime soon.

Kneeling down by the outlet, I plug the first one in and it immediately lights up with a warm glow.

"Ha!" Callie claps her hands in excitement.

"Okay, that was one. You've got three more to go."

"Yeah, yeah, hurry up. You're wasting detangling time."

Plugging in the next one Callie does another small victory dance when it lights up the same as the first. Her dance gets a little bigger at the third, but as I reach for the last plug, I can already tell it's a different plug from the others. Oh, please God let this one be a dud so I can buy her non-knotted ones.

I plug it in, and it immediately lights up...in multicolor.

"Alright, I win. I'm going to get new ones." I stand back up ready to head for the door, but Callie shoots in front of me.

"You are not! You didn't win! Excuse me, but that looks like it's working to me." Callie gestures back to the multicolor strand on the floor.

"I can see that, but it's a completely different type of light, Callie. Those two colors are probably all mixed together, so half of them you won't even use." I try to step around her, but she follows me.

"Who says I won't use both! Maybe I want to mismatch the lights. Have you looked around my place before?! It's all mismatched! And just so we're clear, you said that you would buy new lights if one of them didn't work and they all do."

"Callie, they're in a giant knot. Will you please let me buy you new ones?"

And here we are again, every emotion shown on her face. Her smile disappears and the light in her eyes dim. "No, I bought these. I'm going to use them. You don't have to help me. I can do hard things, Will."

She steps to the side and walks back over to pick up her lights before plopping down on her couch with a sigh.

Well, shit. I know she can do hard things, but what's the harm in me taking care of something so small like buying her new lights?

I guess that's not really the point though. Didn't I just say I liked her independence too?

Sitting on the opposite end, I hold out my hand. "Give me one."

Looking up, she wants to argue, I can see it. "But you—"

"Callie, if I can't do it for you, then I'm going to help you, so give me one."

"Okay," she mumbles, tossing one to me.

She looks down at the mess, starting to unknot what she can then huffs. "Look, I get that this is annoying to undo, and I know that I should just buy new ones, but I like the challenge. I like that these are something I bought, and I don't know, it feels like it's more fun this way."

"You don't have to ex—"

"But I want to." She shifts facing me on the couch with her legs crossed. "I want to explain. All my life, Christmas was done for me. People came in and decorated the whole house with these extravagant lights and fancy decor that I was never allowed to touch. Our Christmas trees were quite literally perfect, nothing out of place. No ugly ornaments that we made in school, only classical Christmas music, and never ever did we have mismatched lights. So, yeah, this might be annoying, and it might not look amazing, but it's mine. I did it. And that's why I want to sit here and fight these damn knots."

Well, I think I fucked up here. "Callie, I'm sorry."

Shrugging, she leans back on the arm rest. "It's okay, I get what you were trying to do. It's just…Christmas is also my birthday, and I guess I've always resented it a little."

"Hold on. Your birthday is on Christmas?"

"Yuppp, it kind of sucks, honestly. My parents always said we would 'float' my birthday out so I could have a party when it wasn't the holidays, but that never really happened. I guess I just thought since I'm not going back home this year, I could try to reclaim both. That's why if you look under the box with the snowman and reindeer pillows there's also old curtains that I want to DIY into streamers. And I picked up a bag of balloons from the dollar store next to my thrift shop. So, I know I didn't mean to buy multi-color lights but it kind of works."

Oh, so I *hate* her parents. "So, let me get this straight. You never got to decorate for Christmas and then you never had an actual birthday?"

She shakes her head. "Nope."

"And Adam never said anything growing up?"

"What was he supposed to say? We were both stuck at those miserable parties. At least he would actually tell me

'Happy birthday,' but there was nothing else he could have done."

That's the part I don't get. I would never let my sister's birthdays pass without doing something. "That's bullshit and you know it."

Letting out a breath, Callie pulls out one whole strand from the pile in her lap with a smile. "I could look at it that way, I guess. Adam had his own stuff with our parents, and it affects him more than he lets on. But I can't change what happened. What I can do is decorate my living room in the tackiest Christmas-slash-birthday party combo you've ever seen."

"And I'll help."

Chapter 11
Will

I should have said no to working out with Adam today. In theory, it seemed like a good plan, but after learning new information about Callie's family, I kind of want to punch him.

I guess it's the brother in me. I didn't know much of what happened between them, but to leave Callie to suffer there alone after he left... Callie might not be holding it against him, but I can't seem to understand how he left her without a second thought.

"Beck says we're getting a new pitching coach this season," Adam says as he puts some of the weights back up. "Supposedly it's Dex. Have you heard from him yet?"

"No." I've heard the rumors that Dexter Larsen will be joining our coaching staff. It seems a little surprising considering he just retired, but that's not really my business.

"Dude, calm down. Your excitement is overwhelming."

"I'm just not in the mood to chat." I shrug. It's not a complete lie. I can't say that I don't want to ask him why he left Callie like that, but I don't, because then I would have to explain that I've been hanging out with his sister and that might lead to questions I don't know how to answer.

We hang out and kind of flirt with each other, but don't worry, we're just friends.

"Clearly." Adam grabs his water then tosses me mine. "Look, one last thing and you can grunt back in response if you feel like it, but it's Callie's birthday on Christmas. I know you'll probably be with your family on Christmas day, but if you happen to run into her could you possibly manage the words 'Happy birthday, Callie'?"

Oh, I could manage that. "Uh, yeah, I'll tell her."

"Thanks. Our parents never really did anything, so I was going to try to get her a cake or something, but it's three days away, and every bakery I've called is either closed for the holidays or won't take last-minute orders this close to Christmas."

"Why don't you and Callie come to Rowley with me?" Fuck me, the thought entered my brain and just decided to come out. This is Callie's doing. I'm not usually one to say whatever I'm thinking, but here we are. Now Adam's looking at me like I have two heads.

"I...my...um..." I clear my throat. Dear Lord, this recovery is going terribly. "One of my sisters loves to bake. I'm sure she could throw a cake together, and Christmas isn't really a big deal at the house anyway. Just my mom and sisters will be there."

"Okay, you've said a total of twenty words max to me this morning and now you're inviting me and my sister over to your family's house for a major holiday?"

"I could uninvite you?" If it were up to me, I would just ask Callie to come but I know that this will only work if I invite Adam too. From the look he's giving me, I know he feels something is off. "Look, Callie and my sisters would get along great. Lucie could easily bake her a birthday cake and Reagan's creative and shit, so she could do some birthday decorations or something."

"So, you're inviting us for Callie's birthday?"

Fucking hell. "I—"

"Because that would be great, actually. Callie's never really got to celebrate it, so if you're serious about this, I'm going to take you up on it."

Well, this morning has done a complete one-eighty. I don't know how to respond to him. *Am I serious?* I started out that way. Of course I want to do something for Callie's birthday, but I wasn't expecting Adam to straight up agree with this idea so quickly.

"Uh, yeah. I'm serious." There's this tightening in my chest that I don't really understand. Maybe it's the fact that this will be the first girl I've brought home—ever. Reagan and Lucie are going to have a fucking field day.

"Okay, man. Thanks!" Adam reaches for his duffle bag to leave. "Callie will love this."

The tightening intensifies. "She will?"

"Her first birthday party? Yeah. I know you haven't been around her much, but Cals can be a little emotional. She's going to fucking lose it, in a good way." He shrugs casually, where I feel like I'm having a heart attack.

Adam cocks his head at me unintentionally rubbing my chest. "You okay?"

"Yeah," I sputter, dropping my hand. "I'll call my sisters and they'll handle the bulk of it, I'm sure."

"Whatever the cost, man, just let me know and I'll pay it." He smacks my back as he walks out.

Did I really just offer to throw Callie her first birthday party? Fucking hell.

Walking back up to my apartment from the gym, I shoot a text off to my sisters. Maybe if I'm nonchalant about it, they won't ask many questions...

> Hey, I need to throw a birthday party for my friend on Christmas. Do you mind helping?

REAGAN

A FRIEND?! What friend? I didn't know you had those.

LUCIE

On Christmas? That's three days away!

> Just a friend. Will you help, yes or no?

LUCIE

I'm going to need more information. I'm assuming you want me to bake the cake, so what flavors does he like? Should I make a baseball-themed cake?

Ah, fuck, here we go.

> Definitely not baseball. I'll ask her brother about the flavor.

LUCIE

Shut the front door. HER!

REAGAN

I have so many more questions now.

I won't answer them. She's a friend. I'll cover the cost, just tell me how much you need.

Lucie has changed the group name to: *Will's Love Elves*.

REAGAN

Elves?

LUCIE

It's Christmas, we must be festive.

Change it back.

Chapter 12
Callie

Well, this is twenty-six. Sitting on my couch, still in my Christmas pajamas with a hot cup of peppermint tea to really set the mood.

I've been lazy so far today. I don't usually like to lay around for hours, but today I didn't get out of bed till eleven. I put my phone on Do Not Disturb and just snuggled in my bed until I finished my current read. I can't tell if that sounds sad or not. I only missed a "Happy birthday" text from Adam and a call from Wyla and Stevie, so it's not like I had much else going on.

Pulling out my phone I click on Wyla's name, Face-Timing her back.

"Hey, it's the birthday girl!" Wyla answers. "Stevie, Auntie Cals is on the phone." As soon as the words are out of her mouth, I can hear the pitter-patter of Stevie's feet barreling to her mom.

"Auntie Cals! Merry Christmas-Birthday!" Stevie giggles as she takes the phone from Wyla. Her blonde hair is pulled up in her favorite "fun buns" with some red bows pinned in.

"Thank you, Stevie Bug. I sure do miss you." Sometimes FaceTiming these two bums me out a little. It reminds me how much I miss having their close friendship. There was never a dull moment with Wyla and Stevie, and here I only really have Adam...and Will, oddly enough.

"We miss you too." Wyla forces Stevie to share the screen so I can see her too. "We're about to head over to my parents for Christmas lunch. What are your big birthday plans?"

"Oh, it's going to be a real rager. I rotted in bed all morning, and now I'm going to rot on my couch until Adam comes over. He's supposed to be bringing whatever takeout that's open on Christmas, and I'm going to see how many Hallmark movies I can get him to watch before he loses his mind."

"Oh, my girl, please calm down." Wyla laughs.

"Hey, not everyone knows how to party like Wyla Bennett."

Wyla scrunches her nose. "I haven't partied in a long time, thank you very much."

"Yeah, it was...what? How old are you again, Stevie Bug?"

"Four!" Stevie yells. "Almost five." She smiles so proudly.

Wyla shakes her head. "Then add nine months before that and then you've got the last time I partied. Maybe you're right. Stay home."

"Hey!" I can hear Jett yell off screen. "Best night of my life. Go have a one-night stand, Cals."

Rolling my eyes, I take a sip of my tea.

Stevie looks up at Wyla so sweetly. "Mommy, what's a one-night stand?"

And now I'm choking on my tea, trying to fight off the laughter.

"Jett! Look what you did!" Wyla sighs.

I'm about to make a smart-ass remark when my door swings open and Adam bursts in.

"Happy birthday!" With that loud announcement and the pop of a confetti tube, I scream and nearly spill my tea on the carpet.

As the confetti falls, Adam reaches for another tube. "Adam, don't—"

The loud pop cuts me off as my room is blasted with more confetti. "Get up. We've got to leave in thirty minutes."

Shaking the tiny pieces of paper out of my hair, Stevie's little voice comes through the speaker with so much concern in her tone. "Auntie Cals, are you okay?"

"Yes, Stevie, I'm fine. Adam was just being insane! And making a mess in my new apartment." With the confetti now in my mug, I cut him some major side eye, but he shrugs me off.

"It's Christmas and your birthday. Did you seriously think I wasn't going to do something special? Also, because it's your birthday, I'm not going to make a comment on the fact that I got in here because your door was unlocked *again*."

Rolling my eyes, I flip him my middle finger out of the camera frame so Stevie can't see.

"Hey, Stevie, Auntie Cals gave me a silent bad word." Adam squats behind me, leaning on the back of my couch.

"You deserved it," Stevie says very matter of fact. That's my girl.

"Rude," Adam mumbles while I laugh at her sass.

Wyla rests her head on Stevie's. "Alright, little miss. Tell

Auntie Cals 'happy birthday one more time then let's let her get to her partying.'"

Stevie gives me a big, toothy grin. "Happy birthday, Auntie Cals! Oh, and Merry Christmas!"

Wyla takes her phone back. "Happy birthday, babes. We love you."

No tears on your first actual birthday, Callie.

"Thank you. Love you big."

The moment I hang up Adam jumps over the back, crashing beside me on the couch. "Nice, pajamas. You know it's like noon, right?"

"Okay, one—leave my Christmas jammies out of this. Two—I thought our plan was to have another sad sibling dinner."

"Not this time, Cals. Go get ready. We're going to actually celebrate this holiday properly."

Properly? "What the hell does that mean?"

"It means go get dressed before Will leaves to go have Christmas with his family without us."

Will? Wait, Will's family? Damn, that shouldn't make me feel all warm and fuzzy inside, but it does. However, knowing that Adam has been invited too kind of helps dull those feelings. He probably remembered how sad our Thanksgiving was and felt bad for us.

"We don't really have time, but can we talk about the absolute chaos that is your living room?" Adam looks around at my half-Christmas, half-birthday decorations.

The warm and fuzzy feeling comes back as I look around. My Christmas tree is full of warm lights and colorful ornaments. My Christmas pillows make it officially annoying to try and sit on my couch now. On the far wall I have the colorful lights worked in with the old curtains I ripped to shreds to make fun streamers with balloons tied in on the ends.

All of it Will helped me put together.

Chapter 13
Will

I wasn't entirely sure how this day was going to go. My sisters have hounded me incessantly, asking questions about Callie and begging for there to be something more than a friendship there—much to their disappointment when I insisted there wasn't. My mom didn't ask any questions, which is even more annoying because I know what she's doing—she's waiting to see Callie and I in person before assuming anything. I guarantee I won't even make it to the kitchen before she stops to ask me questions.

I get their curiosity, I do. I've never brought a girl home. But what they fail to remember is that my teammate, said girl's brother, is also joining us, so I feel like that should really cover the whole "do you like her" question that they keep asking me.

Even though it doesn't really answer it for me.

My old teammate always said he fell in love with his girl the moment he saw her, but I know this isn't that. I would have to be a complete idiot not to find her attractive, but now it's like I've added endearing and intriguing to that list.

Waiting outside on the curb for them in my new Audi SUV, I turn up the heat knowing Callie will likely be cold. Back in Seattle I didn't have much need for a car. I had my bike and when I couldn't drive it, I would use rideshare because off-season was spent back at my mom's, and during season I didn't really care to do anything but play. It wasn't a necessary purchase there, but here I know I'll be driving back and forth to Rowley a lot, and my bike definitely isn't suitable in this snow.

Without warning, my back door opens and Callie slides into the back seat. Her long red hair is down in loose waves and her cheeks are rosy from the walk from the building to the sidewalk.

"Hi," she greets with that soft smile.

"Hi," I parrot back, taking her in through the rearview mirror.

I don't get to look long because as quick as Adam shuts her door, he hops in the front. "I almost didn't believe you when you said you bought a new car."

"And yet it's true. Are you guys ready to go?" I click my seatbelt and wait for them to follow before pulling out on the road.

"Um, Will?" Callie's voice travels up from the back. When I glance at her from the mirror, she has the tea I got her in her hands. "Is this for me? It's hot, but I don't want to assume."

"Uh, yeah. I went by Spilled Tea and got their holiday special." Picking mine up from my cup holder, I gesture to the other one for Adam. "Spiced cranberry green tea, I think. I just ordered three of them."

Adam raises his eyebrow at the cup. "They were open on Christmas?"

Well, shit. I was really hoping they wouldn't question it. "Yeah, half a day or something," I lie, hoping Callie doesn't pay close attention to their signs inside.

The truth is I went in yesterday before they closed and talked the owner into letting me get the tea bags so I could make their holiday special. My only intention was to get Callie a tea, but the fact that I actually made this tea for her is something I can't let Adam know, so I got enough for all of us.

With a simple nod, she sits back in her seat, taking a sip of the drink. "Oh, thank you."

I breathe a sigh of relief, but I also want Callie to know that I got this special for her. "It should be low in caffeine. They said they mark that on their cups somewhere."

Picking up her cup she turns it slowly, and I try my best to keep my eyes on the road, but I want to see the look on her face.

The soft smile returns as she sees the *Happy Birthday, Blaze* note I scribbled on the side of her cup.

"Yeah, here it is. That's perfect."

I put my focus back on the road, feeling a lot better about my plan when Adam clears his throat. Shit, what now?

"I think you have something to say to Callie?"

"Adam, knock it off," Callie grits out through clenched teeth.

Unable to stop myself from looking in the rearview mirror again, her cheeks are rosy still, maybe even more so.

"Happy birthday, Callie," I tell her, then turn down the heat as if that's the reason her cheeks are red.

I looked in my rearview mirror a lot this drive because I wanted to be aware of my surroundings. A safety precaution when driving in the snow, really. The fact that I could catch glimpses of Callie each time is really a moot point.

But if it wasn't moot, I enjoy Callie's company—there's nothing wrong with that. Plus, I know how much she loves to talk, but she's been oddly silent for this car ride. Maybe that's why I keep looking back. I'm concerned for her...as a friend.

As we pull into my mom's driveway I steal another glance. She's wearing a big cream sweater with a light blue scarf that she's wrapping back around her neck in anticipation of the cold.

Her green eyes flash my way, and we exchange this charged eye contact that I pull away from before I get shocked. "We're here."

"Great, I'm fucking starving," Adam says as we all get out.

"When are you not?" Callie laughs as they both come around the front of the car.

Adam gives Callie a playful shove forward to her smartass response, but considering the guy is huge, the light shove sends her flying.

On instinct, I step up to catch her before she hits the ground. "Whoa, hey, I got you," I say as her head hits my chest.

It's a total of two seconds that I appreciate how nice it is to have her in my arms. Thankfully, Adam brings me back to reality as he pulls her toward him to help her stand back up.

"For fuck's sake, Cals. I barely touched you." He laughs.

"You asshole." She punches his shoulder. "What did you expect? You're practically a bear of a man—I'm just a girl."

"Okay, ow." Adam looks down at her with shock, and now it's my turn to laugh. "Where did you learn to punch like that?"

"Up until this trade I've taken kickboxing classes since I was twenty." She shrugs, wrapping her arms around her body with a shiver. "I think you'll survive, but I won't if we stay out here much longer."

"Come on." I start to place my hand on Callie's back as I lead the way but pull back immediately. Callie talks a lot, and I hang on every word she says. No matter how many times we hang out, I refuse to be one of those guys she talks about with the unwelcome touches.

Starting on the path to the front door, when we reach the porch Adam falls behind, checking his pockets and sighs. "Shit, I left my phone in the car. You head on in, I'll be right there."

"Alright, the door will be open," I holler, before turning to Callie. "You good?"

She fidgets with the tassels on her scarf while shivering of course, but those emotions are threatening to show. She doesn't have on her over-the-top smile, and she's avoiding eye contact.

"Yeah, I...uh...I don't know." She shakes as if a chill went through her body before she finally looks at me. "Is it weird to be nervous?"

"No," I reply immediately. Hell, I'm nervous. I know this first greeting is going to be a little much, but once my sisters calm down, I know they'll love Callie.

I reach for the doorknob but turn back to her before

opening the door. "It's okay to be nervous, but I assure you there are no father-son asshats that will make you uncomfortable."

Her lips press together, seemingly holding back something she wants to say. I turn back to the door, but Callie grabs my shirt sleeve.

"Will, I, um, wanted to let you know that you aren't one of those guys. It's okay for you..." She trails off for a moment as her cheeks blush slightly. She shuts her eyes briefly and lets out a small breath. "You don't make me feel uncomfortable."

It's below freezing today but now I'm sweating standing out here. I'm pretty sure the sentence she trailed off at was going to finish with "for you to touch me," and while I know what she means by it, the idea makes alarm bells go off in my head and blood rush to my dick.

Her hand drops from my arm as she stares at me sheepishly, waiting for me to say something.

Hell, I'm waiting for me to say something. What should I say? *Oh, good because I find myself wanting to touch you impulsively, but in a caring way so that makes it better.* I can't fucking say that.

The silence is deafening. I should just say thank you, right? There's nothing misguided in that. But as I open my mouth, and her eyes gleam in anticipation, I see her brother coming up the stairs.

"What are you guys still doing out here? I thought Callie was going to freeze to death." Adam slings his arm around his sister. "What a horrible way to go—and on your birthday, nonetheless."

With one more look my way, Callie turns to her brother, letting all her sass come back to her voice. "I just wanted to wait on you. If Will's actual plan is to kill us on Christmas, I'd rather not go alone."

"I don't plan on killing you on your birthday, Callie," I deadpan. Christmas has been an afterthought for most of the day honestly.

The smirk that crosses her face melts away all the tension in my body. It shouldn't, but it does. It's short-lived as the front door swings open.

"Why are you all just standing out here?" my sister Reagan says. The little shit starter has probably been looking through the peephole the entire time. She motions for Callie and Adam to come in first and gives me a shit-eating grin as they pass by.

"Adam forgot his phone in the car," I mumble.

She hums quietly. "How nice of you to wait on him."

I don't remind my sister of the friend status I've practically beaten over her and Lucie's heads already.

"Yay! You're here!" Lucie cheers, greeting everyone with an involuntary hug. "Hi, I'm Lucie."

Sliding in front of both of my sisters, I step closer to Callie for introductions. My sisters exchange a smile that sits with me the wrong way causing me to immediately retract my step. "These are my sisters, Reagan and Lucie. Reagan, Lucie, this is Adam, and his sister, Callie."

"We're so excited you all came! You know, Will's never brought any of his teammates to visit before." Reagan's eating this up. She turns to look at Callie again. "Or a friend, for that matter."

"That part still may be true," Lucie snickers under her breath.

"Okay, is lunch ready?" I ask, eager to get this party going, but then my mom comes strolling in.

"Oh, you made it!" She clasps her hands together and sighs in relief. "I'm so happy you all came." Stepping forward she goes to Callie first for a quick hug then to Adam. "Hi, I'm Catherine. Will's mom."

"Thank you for having us, Ms. Anderson." Adam nods and shakes Callie's shoulder. "I'm sure my sister is especially grateful that she doesn't have to endure my cooking or slave over her own birthday meal."

"First, please call me Catherine," my mother chastises as sweetly as she can. "And yes, Callie! Will said it was your birthday! Happy birthday, we are all excited to finally meet some of the people Will works with."

"And potentially loves," Lucie whispers to Reagan.

Thankfully I don't think anyone else hears it, but just to irritate her I undo her claw clip and drop it on the rug.

Doing Lucie's version of cursing, she hits my shoulder and whisper-shouts, "Wi—"

Cutting her off and stepping in front of her, I play it off by greeting my mom with a hug. "So, is lunch ready?"

"Yes, it's ready." My mom gestures down the hall. "Reagan, Lucie, why don't you guys lead the way."

Great, here we go. My sisters start and Adam and Callie follow behind them, but when I go, my mom holds me back. *I knew it.*

"She's really pretty," she whispers with a smile.

"I'm not doing this with you too." I sigh. "We're friends. Her brother is my teammate."

My mom nods her head, but her facial expression tells me she doesn't believe me at all.

"I'm serious, Mom," I huff.

"Mm-hmm, I believe that you believe that. She might

even believe it too." She pats my shoulder with a smile. "I don't believe that."

Before I can even think of how to respond to that mess, she just walks away.

"Mom," I whisper-shout after her, but she makes it to the kitchen first.

"Okay!" she cheers. "Birthday girl gets to go first!"

Chapter 14
Callie

I don't know what it's like to have a sister, but if I could be Lucie and Reagan's third sister but not be related to Will, I'd sign up immediately.

Well, there is one way that's possible.

Ope, too far. But I think I could argue my case for some sister adoption program. Reagan has this dark brown hair that matches Will's; she also seems to be the more outspoken one, while Lucie's blonde hair matches their mom's and she is more bubbly and light. And here I am, a redhead who just wants to complete her dream of becoming the real life Powerpuff Girls.

Okay, maybe I've had enough eggnog.

I set down my empty drink, focusing back on Reagan as she tells the table about Will calling his teacher an asshole in high school.

"I stand by what I said." Will pushes out his empty plate and looks at me to explain. I try to tell myself that he's looking at me more than Adam since I'm in the middle of them, but my heart does beat a little harder when it's more eye contact than a quick glance. "Mrs. Clancy was an asshole, not a bitch. An asshole who hated me specifically."

"Who then hated me by extension!" Reagan exclaims.

"She liked me." Lucie shrugs.

"Everyone likes you," Will and Reagan both say at the same time. Their bond as siblings is clearly strong. I love Adam, but we don't have this. We don't have funny stories to look back on or stories from going to the same school.

Maybe it was the age difference and the fact that our parents sent us to a prep school that kept boys and girls on separate campuses. But I'm jealous of the Anderson siblings right now. They're all relatively close in age, with Will being the oldest at twenty-eight, Reagan just slightly younger than me at twenty-five, and Lucie at twenty-three. They all went to the same schools and from what I can tell, actually spent time with each other with no obligations or strings attached.

"Okay." Will's mom clasps her hands together. "Before we start the long, drawn-out debate of why everyone is nice to Lucie, let's decide—games or dessert next?"

"Games?" I ask, almost too excited at the idea. I'm down with some good healthy competition. Family game nights at the Reyer household included charades with "sophisticated" topics only. You try acting out King Henry VIII and having a good time.

"Birthday girl gets to pick." Catherine smiles at me before turning to Will. "Will, do you mind helping clear the table?"

He nods, taking my plate first and stacking it on his.

Adam stands up, reaching for some more plates to take in the kitchen.

"Thanks, man," Will tosses his way as Adam heads out.

Will stacks some more stuff on top slowly. "Hey, don't let Reagan talk you into Monopoly. She's a sore loser."

Reagan scoffs. "Don't listen to him, Callie. He's terrible to play with! He'll start sweet talkin' deals and taking all your money. He's a con man when he plays. He's trying to con you into playing now by placing blame on me."

Peering up at Will, I can see this light on his face that's been there since we all settled down to eat. He seems so comfortable here. He seems so happy.

"Oh, I think we need to play Monopoly," I say, and Will winks at me in response before taking the dishes out.

I know there's a blush creeping up my cheeks and I can feel his sisters' stares. If they plan on asking if there is something going on between us, I honestly won't know how to answer them. There are moments where our friendship definitely teeters on the flirty side of things, but I genuinely enjoy his company. I like being his friend and call me crazy, but I think he likes being my friend too...maybe more?

Maybe I'm reading too much into it, and I swore I would never date a baseball player again. But there are exceptions to every rule, right?

After clearing the table, we broke out Monopoly and let me tell you, I don't think I've ever laughed this much. Like genuinely laughing with people I just met. It's arguably one of the best days I've ever had and the fact that I haven't heard from my parents today is something I'm oddly okay with.

Monopoly was the best decision I could have made. I thoroughly enjoy the sibling arguments, negotiating when rent couldn't be paid, and rules—the rules in the Anderson Monopoly Playbook—that are apparently more like suggestions.

Lucie was the first one out, which, according to Reagan,

happens every time. To which Lucie replied that her and Will's competitiveness stresses her out. Then Will buys out his mom, much to Reagan's protest. Catherine says she refuses to play past an hour, because it raises the stakes. Which it most certainly did because soon after Adam's out and I'm surviving on community chests and chance cards.

My properties have all gone to Will in trades to stay alive and I can't help but feel like my stakes weren't ever as high as the others.

My luck is running out as my little dog lands just one short of "Go" on New York Avenue, which happens to be Will's most valuable property.

"No," I fake whine, and Will tenses next to me. I haven't got shit to offer him and I know I'm screwed. "Welp, I'm out."

At this point Adam, Catherine, and Lucie have all abandoned us to go watch holiday specials in the living room, so I scoot out my chair to join them.

Will grabs the leg of my wooden chair pulling it back in. "Hold on—"

"Oh no, no, no," Reagan stops before he can even get another word out. "Sorry, Callie. But she doesn't have shit to offer you. If you want to keep her here, so you can keep looking at her every five seconds, then ask her to stay until you lose because she's out."

Will's jaw clenches and his hand lets go of my chair. Tension fills the table, but I don't think it's because of the game. I'm honestly on cloud nine about it because a hot guy stealing glances—um, go me—obviously is good for the self-esteem. But I don't think Will wanted me to know he was looking...or maybe he didn't even realize he was doing it?

A timer on someone's phone blasts from the living room

and while Reagan and Will have their little stare down, everyone files back into the dining room.

"It's almost like clockwork," Lucie says as she comes up behind her sister. "Two hours on the dot and you two are fighting at the end of the game. We may have to set the timer for an hour and a half cutoff time now."

Catherine chuckles as she leans over, sliding the board to the opposite end of the table. "I should have warned you, Callie, that I also have to set a timer for the game to end, or I fear Will and Reagan may kill each other."

I chuckle lightly. "It's okay, Adam and I would never be able to do this with our family, so this was a nice change in the holiday."

Adam shoots me a sympathetic smile then squeezes my shoulder.

The tension that was coming off Will seems to dissipate as he stands from the table. "How about dessert?"

"I'll help," Adam says, releasing my shoulder to follow Will out, leaving just us girls at the table.

I start organizing the extra monopoly money on the table and hand it to Lucie while Reagan picks up the properties. "I wanted to thank you guys for letting Adam and I crash your holiday. Things have been tense with our family for so long, it's nice to see how much fun Christmas can be. I hope we didn't impose too much."

"Oh, nonsense." Catherine waves her hand, brushing off my words. "We're happy you're here. Will was practically on autopilot when he lived in Seattle. It's nice to see this trade has brought you all closer together. I like seeing my boy smile for a change."

The tug those words have on my heart is stronger than I expected.

"Did you and Will hang out in Seattle?" Lucie asks, putting on the lid to the game and sliding it to the end of the table.

"No, to be honest, I think I was on autopilot too for this past year while living with Adam. I never hung out with him while he was with the team and left his games right after they ended. I've been holding a bit of a grudge against base-ball players for a while now. Bad ex, he kind of put a bad taste in my mouth for dating baseball players." And when I realize how that sounds, I add, "Or being around them for that matter."

Reagan and Lucie give each other a quick glance but I don't really get a read on if it's a good or bad telepathic message they've sent each other. It seems silly to care, but I want them to like me.

Behind me, I hear the start of the birthday song. Turning my head, I see Adam walking in with a round cake in his hands and Will trailing in behind him. Everyone around me starts to join in singing and when Adam sets the cake in front of me, the tears pool in my eyes at the realization that this was actually planned for me.

On the top it reads *"Happy (first) Birthday, Callie."* Beautiful icing flowers decorate the sides, and it even has a "1" candle lit on it.

When the singing stops, I have to wipe the escaped tears from my cheek before blowing out the candle. My wish is to pull myself back together because I'm about to look like a mess if I can't get my emotions in check—but I'm pretty sure I'm already failing.

"Adam, you didn't have to get me a cake." I chuckle through the happy tears.

Much to my surprise, Adam replies, "Oh, I can't take credit for this, Cals."

Lucie raises her hand slowly. "I made it, but it was Will's idea. He said you like chocolate cake with chocolate buttercream filling. I hope that's okay."

Will did this? This was his idea? I turn to him slowly, but he doesn't meet my eyes.

"Adam told me the flavor, but—"

"It's perfect, thank you." I don't let the fact that he won't make eye contact bother me. I can't, because then I look back at this cake and no matter who did what, it means so much to me.

I pull out the candle and lick the icing off the bottom. My word, it's good. "Since it's my 'first' birthday, I want the piece with my name on it."

"Coming right up." Reagan picks my cake back up and carries it back to the kitchen.

When Lucie gets up to follow behind her she leans down next to me. "Happy birthday, Callie. Please don't take this the wrong way but you have a little mascara under your eyes."

Great. Kill me now.

"Mine and Reagan's old rooms have a Jack and Jill bathroom. We crash here a lot so there's tons of stuff that we leave in there. Use whatever you want."

"You angel," I whisper. "Thank you."

Fucking mascara. I try to wipe a little out from under my eyes as I excuse myself upstairs, but as I reach the top, I realize that Lucie didn't specify a door. I go for the first one on the right, and I'm pretty sure I've just walked into Will's old room.

There are some baseball and motocross posters on the

walls and medals and trophies that take up almost an entire bookcase. I check the back of his door because finding a poster of a girl out of a *Sports Illustrated* magazine would make my fucking day, but it's bare.

I'm dying to snoop, but I know I shouldn't. Shutting his door, I decide on the door across the hall and find a room filled with bright colors—this one has got to be Lucie's.

After quickly freshening up, I tell myself to go straight downstairs, but impulsive me takes control of my body and somehow my hand is twisting the doorknob to Will's room again.

Walking up to the bookshelf first, I see a mix of baseball and motocross everything. Baseball medals, motocross trophies, pictures of him throughout the years in both. I feel like I can say confidently that his mom set all of this up and he never argued.

"Sneaking away from your own party?" Will's voice makes me jump back from the shelf.

"I got a little confused finding my way back," I blurt out the obvious lie.

He walks up next to me with a quirked eyebrow and one corner of his mouth tugs up at my ridiculous excuse. "Okay, Callie, whatever you say."

Knots start to form in my stomach. I should be embarrassed that he caught me snooping but I don't think he cares. He almost seems happy that he found me up here.

I don't even know how to begin to express how much today has meant to me. This was everything I ever wanted out of this day. I didn't need the big parties or any presents, I just needed someone to show that they actually cared.

I open my mouth, unsure of what will come out first, but

Will holds up a little ornament. It's a frame made with macaroni noodles and extremely worn stickers.

"I'm sure this wasn't the present you were expecting, but you said that you were never allowed to have those shitty self-made ornaments on your tree, and I thought maybe this could be your first one."

Will hands me the ornament, and my mouth is still open but there are no words coming out of it. I'm freaking speechless.

My fingers tremble slightly as I take it from him. Looking at the picture in the ornament, I see it's a smaller version of one I just saw on the shelf.

"It seemed only fitting that you get your picture of me in my motocross stuff since you rode on my bike."

He's giving me this ornament...that he made himself... because I talked about wanting them on my tree. And the picture that's in it is a picture I talked about a month ago.

I can't tear my eyes away from the gift. I'm in complete shock.

Will runs his hand through his hair. "If you don't like it, you don't—"

Impulsive me is still very much in control because before he can finish that sentence, I move up on my tiptoes and place my lips to his.

The kiss is soft and quick...but nice... As I slowly move back to my heels, I feel how stiff Will's body is, and I already want to run and hide.

I just kissed him. My only real friend here and I kissed him.

"Sorry, I—I," I stumble over my words. I don't even really know what to say, but I need to fill this silence. "I shouldn't have done that. We're at your family's house, my brother's here, you're a player on the team. I just—I'm sorry."

Maybe I was in the wrong by taking control like that. Maybe I crossed a boundary that we should have talked about before. I had gone on and on about unwelcome advances and here I was doing exactly that tonight.

And what am I doing, really? Do I like Will or am I just caught up in all of the sentimental aspects of this day? No one has ever thrown a party for me before or given me such a heartfelt gift, but maybe I'm misreading this whole situation. I mean, I do overthink things. Is this just normal friend behavior? Wyla has been my only real friend and she's only gotten me gag gifts before.

Will continues to look at me with this unreadable look on his face, and I should stop talking, I really should, but I count two whole seconds of deafening silence before I start again.

"That was a mistake, I shouldn't have—"

"A mistake?"

Chapter 15
Will

I breathe out the question, cutting her off. She thinks that was a mistake?

Fuck, my brain feels like it's in slow motion. The word "mistake" isn't exactly what I'd use to describe what just happened, but now I'm not sure what to do. We're friends, that's what we've always been, right?

Callie shuts her eyes briefly almost like she's trying to process her next words. I can't tell if it's out of regret or embarrassment, but the anguish on her face feels like a punch to the gut and my brain finally catches up—I can't let this ruin her birthday.

"Callie," I say calmly. "It's okay. We're friends—why don't we head back down for cake?"

Callie shakes her head lightly. "Friends, right. I just, um—"

"Hey, it's okay," I reply, placing my hands on her shoulders, hoping it softens her guilt from the blow of the rejection she's giving me.

Is it a rejection, though? Yeah, we've flirted, but I haven't exactly made my intentions clear either. Mostly because they haven't been. But then she kissed me, and I think I really want to kiss her again.

Callie stills as she looks down at my hands resting on her shoulders and when they make their way up to my face I swear they pause at my mouth.

She doesn't move, and I can't bring myself to either. I'm tempted to pull her back in and kiss her for real this time and find out if the word mistake really does fit here.

My hands tighten on her shoulders lightly as I track the freckles on her beautiful face. She told me I'm allowed to touch her, right?

But then the sobering voice of her brother comes from the hall. "Callie?"

Callie jumps back. Ice water being thrown on us would have been less of a mood killer.

Callie glances at my shut door and calls back, "Coming," before turning back to me. "I—"

"Let's just head down, okay?" I say softly, and she nods.

I hold out my hand to let her go first. The moment she walks out my door my whole body stalls. Fuck—I need a minute.

Callie kissed me. Callie fucking kissed me, and I just stood there. Why didn't I kiss her back? It just took me by surprise, and I don't know—I panicked.

But now, all I can really think about is kissing her. I like Callie. And based on the effort I put into this party for her... fuck, I think I like her a lot.

Suddenly, the words I heard Callie say to my sisters come screaming back to me.

I've been holding a bit of a grudge against baseball

players for a while now. Bad ex, he kind of put a bad taste in my mouth for dating baseball players.

I didn't think much when I overheard it, but now I have a million and one questions. Is that why the kiss was a mistake? Does that mean she doesn't want to date *any* baseball players? Is it the reason she never spoke to anyone outside of Adam and Jett on the team? How bad was this ex exactly? Is he why she showed up at her brother's in the first place? She's talked about the guys in her past not respecting her boundaries.

Or was it the lifestyle? If this trade has taught me anything, it is that everything can abruptly change at any moment. Maybe if she knew I have the option to get a no-trade clause for my next contract...

I make my way down the stairs cursing this new revelation and find Callie sitting by my sisters, smiling as she takes the first bite of her cake. I did so much to make today happen. I don't regret it, seeing Callie's reactions made every doubt about setting this up go away. And yeah, that kiss might have been small, but it didn't feel wrong.

Friends. Why did I say that? Fuck!

But I've given her no indication that I want anything more from her either so here we are—in the fucking friend zone.

My brain is still trying to process everything that's just happened, and I know if I don't pull my shit together my sisters will get suspicious. I refuse to let my fuck up interfere with her day.

I take a deep breath and take a seat next to Adam.

Be cool, it's not like you kissed his sister...oh, wait.

"Hey." Adam nudges my shoulder. "Thanks for today. She needed this."

I take another look at Callie as she laughs at something my sisters said. "Yeah, I think she did."

The drive back to Boston was nearly identical to the ride up here. Except the stolen glances back to Callie held more meaning. How do I take back my friends comment without sounding like a total ass? Do I even have a fighting chance with her "no baseball players" revelation?

Making our way up the elevator and to our floor, Adam pulls Callie into a hug. "Happy birthday, Cals."

"Thank you." She smiles. "Best one yet."

Adam shrugs and grips my shoulder. "Eh, I can't take the credit. Thanks for throwing this together, man."

Stealing a quick glance to Callie, her smile falters for a moment before her eyes find mine and she plasters the smile back on. "Right, thank you. It was perfect."

It was almost perfect.

"I'm happy you had a great time." I shove my hands in my pockets and rock on my feet. Do I wait for her to walk to our apartments together? Do I ask her about the kiss? Fuck, now I even sound like her with all the questions.

Turning, I decide I should give her space. Maybe that's what we need. Maybe it was just today that has our emotions all twisted...or mine at least.

"Will," Callie says softly, as I reach for my doorknob. "Hey, um... I didn't—I mean—"

I watch as Callie shuts her eyes again as she looks for the words to say. This should be my moment to clear up my feelings. I should tell her that I think I like her more than just friends, but it's her birthday. I shouldn't force my feelings on her today. Maybe tomorrow.

"Callie, we're good," I say as normal as I can, because it's true in theory. We are good, I just think we could be great. "I promise."

Callie's lips come together in a thin line for a moment as she nods. "Right, you're right. Um...thank you. I mean, thank you for today. I know it seems like a small thing but today meant a lot to me. I've never had a day like today and I was worried about moving here—away from Wyla and being closer to my family. I don't know. I just didn't expect this friendship between us..." Callie trails off with a sigh then looks at the ground. "This is the first time I've actually felt like I belong somewhere, and I don't want to ruin that."

Is that what is really going on? She's afraid she's going to lose me?

Before I can respond, Callie steps around me and walks right into her unlocked apartment door.

Shit. Resting my head on my door, I feel my phone buzzing in my pocket.

Will's Love Elves

LUCIE

So, did she love her party?!

REAGAN

Please tell us you've pulled your head out of your butt and realized you like her.

> She said she loved it. Thank you for helping.

> We are still just friends, so will you please change the fucking group chat name.

REAGAN

> You're delusional if you think you two are friends.

LUCIE

> I think it's romantic! It's very "When Harry Met Sally" of him.

Lucie has changed the group name to: *When Will Met Callie*.

Will has left the group chat.

I look at Callie's closed door one more time before stepping into my apartment. Shit, this is my fault for not figuring out sooner that what I felt was more than platonic, but what am I supposed to do now? How could I force my feelings on her when she's scared of what a relationship could do to our friendship? I guess I'd rather have some of her than none of her.

Chapter 16
Callie

Mistake. Ugh, I want to cringe at the word. Why did I use that word to describe what happened last night? I know that it technically was a "mistake," just typical me, making every impulsive action that comes to my head. Damn it, why can't I ever just think things through?

Having rotted—and ruminated—long enough, I roll out of bed and prepare to start my day. Thank goodness the tea I ordered should be getting here any minute.

Friends. Of course, we're friends, but do I want more? Kind of...I mean, I think I might have wanted more from Will for a while now, but the fact is, I enjoy his company. I do...ugh...enjoy his friendship. I don't want to lose that. No matter if it's friends or more—I do care for him. He makes me feel safe. No guy besides my brother has ever truly made me feel safe. Not to mention Will doesn't seem bothered by any of my quirks or rambles. Hell, he listens to them! No one's ever paid that much attention to what I've had to say before.

And telling him that I want more than a friendship leads to so many unknown outcomes. I mean, we work together and we're neighbors. And he's my only true friend here. This could get complicated so quickly if it went south. Being friends is better than nothing, I suppose, but why does it also feel so annoyingly wrong?

Walking to my closet, I flip through it and my eyes immediately find Will's sweatshirt. I know I shouldn't put it on. It will only make me feel worse. But I almost don't want to feel better... I kind of want to wallow over what I can't have.

How did I let myself fall for another baseball player?

Ripping the sweatshirt off the hanger I pull it on and take a deep inhale of the lingering coconut scent. Damn him for smelling so good.

After pulling on a pair of clean sweats and fuzzy socks, I tell myself I'm allowing this small weakness of putting on his sweatshirt as an ode to what could have been.

Walking into my kitchen there's a knock at my door.

"Perfect timing," I mumble to myself.

Now with my tea here and cozy clothes on I'll stop thinking about my "friend" and lose myself in some bad reality tv.

Whipping my hair up in a quick bun before opening the door, I'm taken back to find *my friend* standing on the other side.

When Will does a quick glance down my body, the realization hits me. Damn it, this is the second time I've been busted wearing his clothes.

A blush creeps up my cheeks as I fiddle with the hem involuntarily. "I was cold, and it was on top of my laundry." It's not at all true, but he doesn't have to know that.

Will chuckles softly and holds up the bag with what I'm assuming is a tea. "Margaret gave me your delivery order, so the tea should help warm you up too."

He brought me my tea again? Invisible strings pull at my heart. "Thanks. Does this mean I need to give you a tip?" A small bit of flirtiness appears in my tone.

"Eh, a dose of that Callie charm should cover it." Will smiles, and I'm tempted to feed into the flirting but then he adds, "I mean, what else are friends for?"

Right. Friends. How many times are we going to say that word now? I feel like it's beginning to lose all meaning.

"Yeah, well..." I start, losing the flirty undertone, "it was really great yesterday, so I thought I would get another order."

I reach for my door and pull it closed behind me. As much as I want to invite him in, impulsive me is in timeout. Maybe space is what we need. I don't want to keep pushing Will on the idea of being more. Him and Adam are all I really have here—and my job, but that's not the same.

"Thank you for bringing it."

Will rocks on his feet and for a moment I swear I see regret cross his face, but then he nods. "You're welcome, Callie, I'll see you around."

Chapter 17
Callie

I curse myself for not grabbing my umbrella as I sprint through the rain around the building to the front of the complex. This is my first time at this training center, so when I told my Uber driver to drop me off at the first door I saw, I never expected to find it locked.

Cold rain hits my face, and I squeal at the feeling. I'm rather thankful Adam got me a new, fancy, waterproof backpack for all my camera stuff. It was his late birthday gift to me. I think he felt bad letting Will do all the grunt work for the party.

It's the end of January; shouldn't it still be snowing? Here's my thing—if it's going to be this cold, I need to see pretty snow. Winter rain is the worst and instead of being able to hide away from it in my cozy apartment, I'm racing into the Blues training facility because today is my first official day as the team photographer. And boy, is it going to be a busy one.

It's shocking how little I've paid attention to this sport. I know the rules and how to play from watching Adam, but all this background stuff has thrown me for a loop. Apparently, this is Mr. Olsson's first year as general manager and the changes he's been making haven't exactly settled well with the fans.

A few days after the new year, Mr. Olsson called a meeting with me and his assistant, Shannon, to come up with a marketing strategy, from brand deals to an all-out media campaign.

I let Shannon take the lead on organizing the brand deals. I can lend a hand in the photos, but all that corporate stuff is what I ran screaming from earlier this year. I volunteered to run the Blues' social media and revamp the website. I'm shit out of luck in the love department so might as well fling myself into my job.

I let out a sigh of frustration as I make it inside the complex. I take off my backpack, strip off my wet rain jacket and gently dry my face with my hands. So much for trying to wear my hair down today. I pull my frizzy strands of red hair into a bun.

I hear the door behind me open and I turn, thankful that someone can show me the way and I won't have to call Adam who headed over here earlier. "Hi—"

My words die off at the sight of Will.

It's been nearly a month since my birthday, and I think we've spoken less than a hundred words max to each other and that's extremely concerning for me, considering my penchant for monologuing. Will would deliver my tea a couple times during the week, but the timing just never worked out for us to hang out. He'd bring it by and he'd either need to head off to practice or I was headed to a meeting with Shannon and Olsson.

"Hey, Callie. Did you jump in some of the puddles?"

His tone is soft and there is a hint of a smile on his face. Will takes his hood off and runs his hand through his hair. "I can take your bag if you want."

He reaches for it at my feet, but I scoop it up first.

"I got it," I snap, but flinch at how snippy it sounded. "I mean I don't mind carrying it."

He gives me a small nod. "Okay. I think we're starting in the main room in the back. It's this way."

I let him lead as I press my lips together. I've been a little anxious about how working together might go. Do you know how hard it is trying to stay in the friendzone with a guy who does boyfriend shit? To Will, delivering my tea is nothing. Just a neighborly gesture. But to me? To me, it's a *boyfriend* gesture—a small thing like bringing your girlfriend chocolate because you know she likes it. Same goes for carrying my bag. If we're going to be friends, then I'll be carrying my own things.

"If you have something to say, Blaze, just say it." Will glances back at me with a small smirk.

"No, nothing to say. Just trying to remember where we're going, so I can find my way next time."

He hums quietly in front of me. "Are you going to be here all day?"

Do you want me to be here all day?

"Um, yeah. It's my first day on site. I haven't been around the full team since that night at the bar, so I'm a little nervous." The vulnerability comes out before I can stop it. I'm known to ramble and have no problem engaging in conversation. But never about my insecurities. Except with Will.

He stops abruptly, causing me to run straight into his muscular back that's still wet from the rain. "Will," I squeal.

I take a small step back as he turns to me and places his hands lightly on my shoulders. "Hey, it's okay to be nervous. But everything's going to be okay. I'll"—he lightly shakes his head—"Adam will be here if you need him."

"And you?" My question takes us both by surprise. Weeks—it's been at least three weeks since we've truly been around each other. Maybe we just needed more time to find some common ground.

"Yeah, Callie. I'll be here too." His sighs and just when I think he's going to say something else Shannon walks up to us. I'm honestly surprised I missed the clicking of her heels approaching us.

"Oh, Will...Callie. You're still out here? I was afraid I was going to be the last one here."

Will's hands drop from my shoulders and he takes a small step back.

I'm still trying to decide if Shannon likes me or not. There are times when I think she might but more often than not, she's treating me like a child who can't function on her own. I get that she's older than me and has been in this industry longer, but I'm also not an invalid.

Will glances at his watch. "We're still ten minutes early, so no worries. We can all head in now."

"Actually, you head on in." The smile she gives Will causes knots to form in my stomach. "I need to run some stuff by Callie before we get started."

Will simply nods. "See you in there, Callie."

Listen, I'm a girl's girl, I swear. But him leaving Shannon out of that little line made all those knots come undone. Even if we're sticking to this friend status.

When the door closes and we're completely alone, I turn to Shannon, mentally preparing for whatever tasks we need to discuss. The condescending look on her face tells me this likely won't be work related.

"A little FYI, there's no sleeping with the players. I thought Mr. Olsson made the importance of our standards for this team pretty clear but to reiterate, that won't be tolerated."

"Hmm, well, thank you for the reminder." I put on my best fake smile for both her and my sake. I knew image was a big deal to Olsson, but I didn't really think about this being an issue. It wasn't ever brought up during my onboarding, but I could have zoned out during that part. I guess I should be grateful that it gives me a reason to shut the door on the idea of a relationship with Will. But why does it also feel like my heart is in my stomach?

"I'll be sure to keep that in mind. Mr. Anderson and I were just talking about today's agenda. I have no interest in fraternizing with the players."

...Kind of.

"Great!" Her nose and eyebrows crinkle for a moment at my dramatic response. Maybe I'm in the wrong here, but it wouldn't have killed her to choose her wording differently. A simple, "Hey, as employees we're not allowed to date the baseball players on this team. Just wanted to make sure we're all on the same page since this is your first day." But no, this is precisely what I mean. Condescending.

"Should we go in now?" I ask.

Blinking away her snarky facial expression, she smiles politely. "Yes, I'm glad we cleared the air."

"Me too!" I say at an usually high pitch. We're off to a great start.

Letting Shannon go in front of me, I take a deep breath to mentally prepare myself for this day one last time.

I can do this. I can do hard things.

We walk into the massive space with black turf flooring. In the back, large nets are pulled out to form batting cages. Off to the side there is an area that mimics a bullpen, then there's this big open space that has lines and bases—as if this were a real field—where all of the players are warming up now.

Finding Will out of the twenty-six players is easy. Not because I'm looking for him, but because he's warming up a good ten feet away from everyone else. Okay, I might have been looking for him. A little. His gaze connects with mine, so I turn away quickly, looking for a good place to set my stuff.

Up first on today's agenda is getting some good behind-the-scenes content for our social media and photos for our website. I've spent the past two weeks deep-diving fun ideas and researching ways to make the fans feel more connected to this new team.

"Hey, look who's here." Beck's chipper voice comes from behind me.

"It's almost like they pay me to be here." I chuckle. The cocky first baseman appears to be a flirt, but really I think it's just his M.O. to be personable and happy. Plus, there's no real attraction there between us. With his red hair, he looks more like my brother than Adam does.

"It's about damn time we hired someone decent for this position. We needed another redhead on the team."

Playfully rolling my eyes, I sit down on the turf and pull my bag in front of me. "Especially one without your ego."

"You wound me. Here I was thinking this special connection would get me extra publicity time."

"If anyone's getting extra time, it's me," Adam says as he comes up, plopping down in front of me.

"I'm pretty sure that would be grounds for nepotism." Tripp comes to the other side of Beck and now all three are sitting across from me.

I start pulling out all of my stuff to get organized. "Okay, you guys know I'm not the team's publicist, right?"

My brother cocks an eyebrow. "Aren't you, though? You've been researching ways to make our online presence more appealing. I've barely gotten you to look up from your computer for three weeks."

Okay, that's fair. "My job is technically just to take photos of you guys. The website and social media are part of that, but it stops there. You guys can talk to Shannon about any extra media time."

"But talking to you is way more appealing," one of the team's new rookies says as he sits next to Adam.

Adam smacks his shoulder. "Um, hello, she's my sister."

I want to say the rookie's name is Charlie—left fielder, maybe. This is his first season in the major leagues if I'm placing him correctly. I've tried to remember the roster, and I think I have the "starting nine" nailed down but some of the guys I still get confused.

"It was a compliment!" possibly-Charlie responds.

"Does this mean we can't talk to your sister, Reyer?" another player says walking up. "Can't you separate work from personal life?"

"Doesn't matter. You guys are all wasting your time. Cals and I have this connection. I'm going to be getting the most camera time." Beck smirks and gives me a wink.

I fear my eyes might roll out of my head today—fucking

men. Looking around, I see I'm surrounded by them. More than half the team is now circled around me—sitting and standing, and all talking about me.

"Callie knows what the people want. Let her decide who's best for the fans."

"I'm her brother, she'll take the best pictures of me."

"Can we hire her for personal sessions?"

I try to tune out the guys and start rifling through my bag pulling out my things, so I'm not exactly sure who's saying what at this point. I know they are all just messing with Adam and the comments aren't necessarily making me uncomfortable, but I would be lying if I didn't say this was a little overwhelming. I came over here to get ready and get my nerves under control, but now I'm drowning in testosterone.

I feel a tap on my shoulder, and I turn to see Shannon. Oh great, am I getting another "you can't sleep with any of them" speech?

"Callie, there's a delivery guy here with a drink for you."

A delivery guy? "I...I didn't order a drink?"

"He said your name." Shannon shrugs.

I turn back to the guys for a second and they're all still talking away. Pushing off the ground to stand up, I start walking toward the front where Alex, the delivery guy from Spilled Tea, stands with a sealed bag in his hand.

"Hey, Callie. Got your lavender tea with honey."

He holds out the bag and I reach for it slowly with creased brows. "Thanks. Don't judge me, but I don't think I ordered this. If I did, I don't remember and if that's the case, don't tell me."

Alex gives me a small chuckle. "No, you didn't—"

"Hey, Alex," Will says casually as he walks up to us.

"Hey, Will!" Alex looks elated. He even gives Will that weird handshake-hug thing guys do. What is going on? "I put yours in the same bag. I think it killed my mom a little to ice your green tea. She won't admit it, but I'm pretty sure she froze green tea ice cubes last night because she couldn't bear the thought of it being watered down."

Will smiles while he laughs and then if things weren't weird enough, he starts asking Alex how his changeup is going. What is happening right now? Has he been giving pointers to the teenage delivery guy at the tea shop?

I watch this interaction with complete amazement because Will doesn't socialize. This man was just standing ten feet away from his teammates two minutes ago.

"Listen, thanks for bringing these. I know this was out of your delivery range." Will hands the kid some cash, but he doesn't take it. Alex is downright starstruck right now.

"Are you kidding? The team is literally right there! This was a freaking dream come true. Please, call the shop anytime and I'll bring whatever, wherever."

"I will. I'll see you Thursday." Will holds the tip out again for Alex to actually take this time. Alex nods eagerly and looks around again like a kid in a candy shop before walking out.

Will turns to me shaking his head, reaching for the bag with our drinks.

I move it out of his reach. "Oh, I have *sooo* many questions right now."

Will takes his focus off the bag and his warm brown eyes meet mine with a small smirk on his face. "I know you can talk fast, so rapid fire them, Callie. I think Olsson just got here and I want some of my drink before we start."

Ugh, why is this man—who I can't date even if he did

want to date me—so cute? Maybe some of his answers to my questions will help bring down my need to beg this man to put a ring on my finger.

"How are you on a first name basis with the delivery guy at Spilled Tea?"

Will shrugs. "I go there. A lot. Alex's mom owns the tea shop. She talks while I wait, and she said her son pitched for the high school team."

Okay, nothing too crazy there. "Why will you see him Thursday?"

"I offered to help him one-on-one with some of his pitches before the season starts." Will tries reaching for the bag again, but I pull it out of reach again.

"You're coaching him?" I'm swooning. This is a real-life swoon.

Will sighs like he's annoyed but there's a small smile there. "You can call it that if you want. Can I have my drink now?"

"One more question. Why did he say one of the drinks was mine?"

Will pinches his eyebrows. "Because one is yours. You love their tea, you're the one who got me hooked on the damn place to begin with. I thought you might not have time to get one this morning, and lavender tea has no caffeine and it's good for nerves."

"You know what it's for? How did you know that?" My mouth gapes slightly.

"I might have made an assumption about the nerves, but it seemed like a safe bet. I remember you saying that there were different benefits with tea, so I looked it up." He shrugs. "Any more questions, Blaze?"

Are we sure about being friends?

"Um, no." I hold out the bag so he can get his drink out.

"Anderson! Callie! Come over here," Mr. Olsson calls. "We're getting started."

Chapter 18
Will

The start of the new year is typically my cue to get back in the groove for the season. After one of my many tea runs, I somehow roped myself into coaching Alex with some pitches. The kid is good, and I did get some added perks out of it. Much to my dismay, Alex has been my only distraction lately.

Over these past few weeks it seems like time's been against me, and seeing Callie was nearly impossible. Despite our small run-ins that always result in her making delivery boy jokes, I've barely seen her.

I told myself if she wanted to be friends, I would be the best damn friend she ever had. But then she asked if I was going to be there for her today, and, respectfully, fuck being friends.

Not being able to spend time with Callie over these past few weeks did absolutely nothing for me other than making my life feel a little colder without her blaze. She's afraid to lose me? Not possible, and I'll prove that.

No matter what it was in her past—I don't care if it's

from her parent's or whatever it was with her ex—I'll prove I'm better. If her rule comes from the fear of this schedule, then that's no longer an issue because our schedules are the exact same. If anything we'll have too much time together. And if it's the fear of being traded then those fears can be put to rest because I'm doing everything in my power to get this no-trade clause.

"Alright, gentlemen, unless your name is Daines, Reyer, Kenner, Pierce, or Anderson, you're free to go." Olsson claps his hands together. "Great job today, I'll see you guys next week."

As the other players filter out my eyes catch on Callie while she talks to Shannon and Olsson. She's been floating all over today taking pictures. It was very noticeable that every player's effort went higher when she was around, mine very much included. When she was around, my pitches were touching a hundred miles an hour. And this wasn't even a strict practice, more conditioning, but who cares. I'll show off for her—we all will.

Most of the team looked at her like a shiny new toy in the toy chest, but oddly I wasn't jealous. Callie's gorgeous, it's just a fact. I don't blame the guys for looking because I'm just as guilty. The difference is that I know who she really is. And ogling from a distance isn't going to get them anywhere with winning over *my* Callie.

Olsson makes his way over to us while Shannon talks to Callie. I'm hoping it's not about her calling it a day. I selfishly want to be in her space a little while longer.

"Okay, so as you know, we completely gutted the workout room in this facility over break and worked out a deal with Life Fitness to get all new equipment. They elected you five for brand photos. Life Fitness was supposed to send one of their photographers for the pictures, but something came up. So, in order to keep our agreement and not have it interfere with the season, they have agreed to let Callie take the pictures. I'm going to hand all of this over to Shannon and Callie. They're in charge, but I'll be in my office if they need me."

"I'm sure we won't," Shannon says, walking up with Callie a step behind her.

Callie's hair never came down from her bun, but a few strands have come loose. She tucks the ones around her face behind her ears then fidgets with the rings on her fingers.

"Okay, boys!" Shannon's voice hits a weird high as she claps like this is a team huddle. "Life Fitness sent some clothes for you to wear. The bags are labeled with your names by the door. After you change you can meet us in the weight room."

"Maybe I will get a private session with Callie after all!" Tripp shoots up and wraps an arm around Callie's shoulder.

Now, looking I don't mind. Touching? Touching, I mind. Next thing I know I'm up on my feet. I don't know what I'll say, but I want his arm off her.

"Listen, hotshot." Callie takes his hand and pulls it up so she can step away from him. "The only private session you'll be getting is with one of the batting coaches. If I'm remembering correctly, you missed a few in the cages earlier."

A collective "ooo" comes from the guys and I fail to hold back a laugh.

Adam grips Tripp's shoulder and gives him a little shake and if I was a betting man, I'd say his grip is harder than necessary. "Come on, leave my sister alone. I can say on good authority that she knows how to pack a punch."

Adam pulls everyone back to the small locker room. I try

to hang back and check in on Callie because she's fidgeting with her rings again. She's nervous, I know she is. It doesn't help that Shannon has hovered over her all day. Hell, I don't even know if she got to enjoy her tea because it seemed as if Shannon was constantly there.

I'm not really sure what the dynamic is there, but Shannon pulls her away again saying they need to go into the weight room to scope out the lighting.

When she passes by me her eyes find mine and she mouths a very dramatic *"Save me."*

I let out a small laugh and shake my head. It's rather tempting to blow this whole thing off, but I know I've got a lot of ground to cover with her and this shoot is the perfect opportunity.

Walking in the locker room Adam tosses me my bag. "This one's yours."

"Thanks." Pulling open the drawstring I pull out a pair of shorts and see there's nothing else in the bag. "Did someone get in my bag? I don't have a shirt."

"I didn't get one either," Mateo adds, but as the rest of the guys all pull out shirts he laughs. "Ha! Guess Anderson and I have just officially been deemed the best built by our new brand reps."

"Here, Will. You can take mine." Tripp holds out his shirt, but there isn't a chance in hell it fits me.

"Knock it off, Tripp. You know that's a dead end," Beck scolds and damn right it is. "Callie isn't going to give you the time of day anyway." Couldn't have said it better myself.

"You were flirting with her too, Daines," Tripp retorts.

"Yeah, to fuck with Adam. Callie knows I'm not being serious nor am I stupid enough to act on it."

"Listen, the comments could end now, if you don't

mind," Adam says. "My sister isn't interested in any of you guys, so just let her do her job."

Well, that hurts my confidence a bit. I knew this was a possibility, that a genuine interest in me just isn't there, and if anyone knows Callie best, it's Adam. Can't say that didn't suck to hear.

She's not interested.

After changing we start heading to the weight room. I tell the guys I'm going to run back up front for some water—some air, mainly—so I can shake off the doubt Adam's comment has placed.

"Will?" Callie's voice comes behind me as I make my way down the hallway.

Turning around to face her, the best thing happens—Callie checks me out.

Her steps slow as she walks up, and her eyes drag slowly from my face down my torso. "D-did you lose your shirt?"

"Nope, didn't get one." Do I slightly flex my muscles a little bit? Maybe.

Her eyes dart up and down again. "No shirt?"

I love this shoot. "No, is that a problem?"

"N-no." Callie clears her throat and blinks a couple times. "No, I was just looking for the kitchen. I'm thirsty and Adam said you were headed that way."

At the mention of Adam's name, I remember his comment but now it's seemed to lose a lot of its validity.

"I am, need an escort?"

"Um, yeah," she mumbles.

As we walk back up to the front Callie starts to fidget with her rings again.

"What's up? You seemed pretty comfortable taking pictures earlier. Did something happen?"

She sighs. "No, I just didn't anticipate taking branding pictures today. I was told I was supposed to get behind-the-scenes and fun content of the shoot. But now..." She groans as she trails off.

"Now you're running the shoot."

"Ha! If you think Shannon is going to let me run anything, you're very much mistaken."

"Yeah, she does seem like a hoverer. But Olsson wouldn't have you take these pictures if he didn't think you were capable."

"I guess." She shrugs.

Opening the door to the small kitchen I let her go in first. "What do you mean 'you guess'? Come on, Blaze, don't tell me you've let your flames die out over these past few weeks?"

Pulling out two waters from the fridge, she snaps up. "I have not. I just get nervous sometimes. Something I tell you often for some reason."

Walking back to me she shoves my water at my stomach. Seems I touched a nerve.

"Callie, I told you I'd be here all day with you. I know you get nervous. I got the lavender tea because of it. But if you're nervous then let me provide some comfort. I know without a shadow of doubt that you'll nail these pictures." I brush some loose hair behind her ear and my hand lingers for a second as I repeat the phrase I've heard in her rambles a couple times. "You can do hard things, Callie."

Callie sucks in a breath and her lips immediately move into a thin line. Her green eyes dart down to my bare chest briefly before coming back to my eyes. And for a second, I swear they look at my mouth.

My hand still lingers on her neck. It would be so easy to

pull her in and make my feelings perfectly clear. I can still touch her...I think.

"Cal—"

"Will," she whispers. "We should probably head back."

Dropping my hand, I fight my disappointment with a smirk. "Yeah, you've got some pictures to take."

The "take it easy" memo was lost on all of us during this workout. Whether it was showing off for the camera or the girl behind it, we were all dripping sweat by the end of it.

Shannon's been talking to us for a minute about some follow-up things Life Fitness might want but I'm only half listening. Callie's sitting off to the side looking through her camera with a small smile on her face.

I should probably be more concerned with whose picture she's smiling at, but honestly, I think she's just smiling because she can see how good of a job she's doing. Shannon might have tried to take control, but Callie ran this show. She spoke up when something wasn't working and gave us stern but clear directions because, let's face it, we're ball players not models.

So yeah, I don't care if she's not smiling at my pictures, I'm so fucking proud of her.

"Okay, that's all for today boys." Shannon claps, pulling my eyes from Callie. I hope someone else was listening to what she said because I sure as shit wasn't.

"Hey," Adam says next to me. "I have something I need to float by Coach Olsson. I think you'd be good for it too. You got time to hang back with me?"

"Is it going to take a long time? I'm supposed to be heading up to Reagan and Lucie's place tonight for dinner."

"Nah, it shouldn't. I'm going to give Callie money for an Uber so she doesn't have to wait for me then a quick shower. So give me ten minutes."

Adam doesn't wait for my answer before heading over to Callie. Well, I thought I might get another minute with her before she leaves but standing around waiting for her to finish with Adam and Shannon who is still hovering might come off a little desperate.

So I head to our small locker room for a quick shower and put on some clean gray sweats and a hoodie. Knowing Adam won't be too far behind I decide to make my way to Olsson's office, but it seems I won't be waiting alone.

"Hey, what are you still doing here?" I ask Callie as she leans against the wall fiddling on her phone.

"Told Adam I didn't mind waiting." She smiles at me while sliding her phone in her jacket pocket. "Thanks for earlier, I needed to hear that."

"No need to thank me, Callie." I lean next to her on the wall. "It's what I do." *For a select few*.

Her smile falters for a second and I'm not entirely sure why, but she recovers quick. "Well, I appreciate it."

"Okay, are you ready?" Adam asks, hitting my back.

I hadn't even heard him come up, so no, I'm not ready. I'm working with small windows of time with Callie, and I need more. I don't even know what this meeting is about, but I know I can't say, "I'd rather stay out here and talk to your sister."

"Yeah," I reply, pushing off the wall.

Adam turns to Callie. "And you're good to wait? I'll keep it quick so Will can make it for dinner."

"Dinner?" Callie parrots as she looks at me with a raised eyebrow. *Is my girl jealous?*

"Dinner at Reagan and Lucie's place. Reagan's girlfriend is in culinary school so we get to reap the benefits."

Callie pushes off the wall with her soft smile. "Tell everyone I said hi."

She was totally jealous.

I give her a nod before following Adam in Olsson's office. Olsson hardly looks up from the papers in front of him when we enter and gestures for us to sit. "So, what's up?"

"An old teammate of ours called me asking if the Blues might be able to spare a few players for this spring training fundraiser he's running. I thought it could be a good PR opportunity for us as the proceeds go to the animal shelters in South Carolina."

Is he talking about Jett? I knew he was moving back to South Carolina after he retired. Jett was like me in that he wasn't an outwardly social guy, but he was close with Adam.

Finally looking up from his desk, Olsson raises an eyebrow. "You know Spring Training starts in two weeks, right?"

Adam gives him a quick nod. "I'm aware. It would be the week before, but only for three days. They have other players from the league coming in so they don't need many of us and since Will and I played with Jett for years it would make the most sense."

So it is Jett. He was also the only other player in Seattle who Callie would talk to, but I think that was only for his girlfriend and daughter. She'd probably love to go down with us if we get this approved—and I would get more time with her.

Sitting up a little straighter in my chair, I run with that

idea. "Callie could get some great pictures. It would be really great publicity for us and the team. And we would still be getting some good warmups in."

Olsson drops the paper in his hand and leans back in his chair, sizing us up. "Who's covering travel?"

"We are," Adam responds.

"You know, as pitcher and catcher you guys are due in Florida for Spring Training before everyone else."

"We know." I nod. Shit, is he actually going to agree to this?

Olsson sighs. "Alright. I'll excuse you both from practices that week and if you guys are so much as even five minutes late to report, I will—"

"We won't be, sir. You can count on me," Adam says. His need to be punctual probably just screamed at the thought of ever being late.

Olsson taps on his desk. "Alright, I'll hold you to that. You guys are good to go. Callie too."

Fuck. Yes.

Chapter 19
Callie

Today, we are going to sit our butt down and edit some pictures. I've had this mindset all week but zero motivation. At this point it's straight ADHD avoidance. I have nearly two thousand photos downloaded onto my laptop and every time I've turned on my screen and seen that number, I slam it shut and tell myself I'll do it tomorrow.

But there are no more tomorrows. I need to get started if I want to have everything edited before we leave for Aster Creek on Monday. To help, I set little daily goals for myself. Today I need to comb through the photos, making notes of my favorites and deleting the unusable ones. I've played around with my presets enough that each picture won't need heavy editing, and most can go into files for a later date, but realistically, I need to get this number of photos I have way down.

Setting my tea bag in my mug to steep, I reach for my laptop. Work—we are going to work.

As I pull everything up, there's one other major reminder of why I've closed my laptop for the last five days. One sweaty, muscular, shirtless Will with these incredible abs and long arms. Damn it, why did we have to take brand photos of Will with the workout equipment? The brand photos I need of Will should be for cleats or a cereal box— literally anything other than having to take pictures of him shirtless lifting weights.

I'll never be able to explain this because I've never considered sweat to be sexy, but seeing Will all sweaty felt like it unlocked some kind of weird ass kink for me because hot damn. How I did that shoot with the level of profession- ality I had was practically an act of God.

Is it wrong to be jealous of metal? Because anytime his hands would grip on the weights I'd have to shove the mental image away of him gripping on to me in any way he wanted.

Maybe I'm foolish to think he was being a little flirty at the training center, but maybe I missed him more than I thought over this past month.

I thought we'd get our footing on the" friends" front this week, but our schedules still aren't matching up. I've unfor- tunately been trapped at the stadium all week taking photos for our new virtual tour, while the guys are still practicing at the training center. Adam's talked about Will being at prac- tice so I know he's been around. On the neighbor front, I've barely heard a peep come from his place.

I guess I should stop fixating on him. Even if I did do something about my feelings there isn't much we can do about it. I *can't* lose this job...but I can't seem to let this idea of Will go.

"Okay, Callie, we're just going to add these to his album and move on," I say aloud to myself. I can't afford to get caught up in Will's muscular thighs. I. Have. To. Work.

Clicking on a chunk of Will's photos, I add them to his

album. One thing I did do in my procrastination state was create different folders for every player and team photos.

Reaching for my tea, I decide it's entirely too quiet and if I'm going to keep happening upon Will shirtless, I need some calming—dare I say sad—music to counter his hotness.

"Okay, let's do this." Again, I say to no one.

I push through for a good hour. My tea is now gone and my set up on the couch has officially become uncomfortable. Groaning, I stretch out my arms and roll my neck.

Surely, I made some good progress. I tried sticking to quick decisions, keep or trash, then immediately into the folder. According to the math in my head, I went through roughly five hundred. I did feel like I saw a lot of pictures of Will, but maybe that's just because he stands out to me more than the rest.

I move my workspace to my small dining table, telling myself a change in scenery will help. I have to keep going. I'll feel so much better if I can check this off my to-do list for today. I set a timer on my phone for another hour. One more hour, then I can treat myself.

Looking at my screen, I groan and shake out my hands. "Just focus, Callie. For all that's holy, focus."

As soon as my hand clicks on my mouse pad, my phone rings. "Oh, thank God." Reaching for my phone I see Wyla's name at the top.

I answer so fast it's silly. "Could you sense my cry for help all the way down in South Carolina?"

Wyla snorts. "Eh, it's more Jett took Stevie with him to the gym today and I so desperately needed some adult conversation that doesn't involve any mention of or a sound from a child. So maybe we were both sending vibes."

Gladly scooting my laptop to the side I prop Wyla's Face-

Time up against my now empty mug. "You overstimulated, Momma? I'll be there to help in a few days. I could definitely use the distraction."

If pictures of Will are enough to get me this worked up, I'm a little worried about us having to spend almost every day together when the season starts.

Wyla dances her eyebrows. "Oh, a distraction from what? Please, let it be interesting. My soul is dying for some super dramatic girl talk! I'll even take gossip about people I don't know."

I laugh. "Gossip about people you don't know is the best gossip."

"Right! Okay, so tell me. What's distracting you?" Wyla settles in on her couch, wrapping a throw around her shoulders. "Please don't spare any details!"

I glance at my computer knowing I should give her the quick version and get back to it...but once I open my mouth, I know this is about to be a short story told long.

About twenty minutes in, I'm finally nearing the end. "And now I have to edit all these pictures of him, all gorgeous and sweaty. It's not fair." I pull my laptop over, clicking it on to check the numbers I haven't wanted to see. "I've sorted roughly five hundred photos. On average, each player right now has about fifteen to twenty pictures in their folder...Will's has over fifty."

I can see Wyla trying to hide her laugh.

"Don't laugh at me! Wyla, I even had to skip over of the branding photos because the number of pictures with him in it were overwhelming!"

Wyla tries to stifle her laugh again.

"Wyla!"

"Hey, I get it. I'm partial to the pitchers myself. They're very good with their hands."

I'd bet good money that Will's fantastic with his hands. If he isn't, I know how he listens, and he'd be great at taking directions. Fuck. "You're not helping! Did you miss the part where I said we're not allowed to date?"

Wyla rolls her eyes and waves me off. "Yes, I heard you. That's a stupid rule. You clearly like him, Callie."

"Of course I do! But it doesn't change anything. We're not allowed to date and even if we were, he agreed that we were friends."

This time Wyla actually does laugh. "That man does not want to be your friend."

Her response, much to my chagrin, makes me feel all warm and fuzzy on the inside.

"It doesn't really matter. Even if I wanted to call his friend bluff, we couldn't have anything more than a secret fling." And I don't think that's something I could handle with Will. I have one too many emotions involved already, and Wyla can clearly see that.

"Okay, well, babes, what are you going to do? I'm not saying you can't wallow in your crush a little bit longer, but you still have to live your life."

"Says the girl whose boyfriend fell in love with her after one night."

"Okay, but that's my point! Thank you for proving it. Yeah, everything worked out, but we lost a lot of time because I was scared. Whatever you do next, Cals, is up to you. Take the risk and try a fling with Will or move on. You never know, maybe your one-night stand will fall madly in love with you too. Just make sure you use protection."

I snort a laugh. "Says you."

"Shut up." Wyla rolls her eyes and settles deeper into her couch. "Maybe Will's not your Jett and maybe he is, but as your best friend, I can't let you trap yourself in your apartment to be sad over a man."

Ugh, Wyla's tough love hits me deep. Is she right? Should I move on? Things with Will seem like a dead end, even though I wish they weren't...

"I'm sorry." Wyla's tone softens. "I just love you and want you to be happy."

"Ugh," I groan. "You're right. Go enjoy the rest of your quiet time. I'll see you in a few days."

"See you soon, Cals." Wyla blows me a kiss before hanging up.

Laying my phone face down on the table, I try to fully process what Wyla said. I mean, she is right. I've been hiding out in my apartment for a month essentially moping over Will. Maybe I should just get back to work and answers will come to me later.

And by later I mean in the next fifteen minutes because I can't get Wyla's speech out of my head. Am I over Will? Most definitely not. But what am I supposed to do? Even if I did tell him my feelings, I can't say he'd return them with the same confidence Wyla did. And then what? We're not going to be able to date, so I'm just supposed to put my heart on my sleeve and say, "Oh, but don't worry, we can't date anyway."

Sighing, I push through another hour of work...kind of. Somehow, I ended up on a website for Boston's top wine bars. Was going out alone my safest move? Probably not, but Wyla's right—I'm rotting in here. Maybe a night branching out will be good for me.

Chapter 20
Will

Throwing on a black Henley and some jeans, I curse Adam for forcing me into tonight's outing. He made it clear that this team bar crawl to kick off the season was nonnegotiable. And the best part of it? Since I don't drink, I'm one of the appointed designated drivers.

I'm tired of driving. If I'm not at the training facility, I'm driving back and forth from my sisters', trying to help them get situated after not one, but two water pipes burst in their apartment. Their landlord wanted to be a real dick about it and claim that the damage didn't fall under their contract as something he has to fix. Which is complete bullshit, and since I'm the one paying for the place, I've been up there trying to get it sorted out. It's been a fucking week and I hate that I haven't been able to see Callie at all. The one bright side is that it's a team outing so Callie should be coming and I've been clinging to that hope all fucking week.

Waiting in my living room I pull out my phone to check the time and see I've been added back to the dreaded group chat with my sisters.

Lucie has added Will to the chat: When Will met Callie.

LUCIE
What are you doing tonight?

I'm going out. Do you need something?

REAGAN
Nope, can't we just check in?

Is Callie going?

I don't know. Maybe.

LUCIE
What's the plan? Are you dressed nice? Girls always appreciate a guy who can dress.

I put on clothes.

REAGAN
See, this is why I'm dating a woman.

LUCIE
Are you this glowing of a conversationalist with Callie? This might be your problem.

Ugh, fucking sisters. A knock comes to my door and I shove my phone in my pocket. Opening it I hope to find a fiery Callie, but unfortunately Adam's alone.

"Hey, you ready to go?" he asks.

Not exactly. We're missing someone.

"Yeah, yeah. Ready to babysit." I grab my keys off the hook and step out into the hallway.

"I knocked on Callie's door for her to hurry up, but she's still not out yet." Adam walks back over to her place, and I'm fucking relieved.

Adam reaches for her door handle. "I bet the first round that her door is unlocked."

I'm about to tell him I don't make stupid bets, or drink for that matter, but I don't get the chance because Callie swings her door open and jumps back when she notices us. "Shit, what are you guys doing out here?"

"We're waiting on you," Adam replies, which thank goodness, because I'm at a loss for words.

Callie looks beautiful. I mean, she's always beautiful, but tonight she's got this gorgeous short brown dress on and her hair is pinned back half up, bringing all the attention to her freckled face.

"Adam, I told you I wasn't going tonight," Callie shoots back, and all my hopes of spending time with her tonight die.

"Yeah, I thought that meant you didn't want to go, not that you couldn't." The question comes to me the moment it does to Adam. "Where are you going?"

Callie's eyes dart quickly from her brother to me before looking down at her boots. No, just no. I need her to say that she made some new girlfriends and she's going out with them right now, because—

"I'm just going out," she mumbles.

Fuck me.

"Out with who?" Adam continues, completely unaware of how much I don't want to hear this.

A date? A fucking date.

Callie's eyes dart up toward me and for a brief moment, I think I see regret in her eyes.

Damn it, I want to walk her back into her place, lock her

fucking door for once, and fuck this whole "friends" idea out of her. Fuck her date. Fuck her ex for putting this whole "no dating baseball players" bullshit in her head. And fuck me for even thinking I only wanted to be friends to start with.

"It's not a big deal, Adam. I'm going to a wine bar. I've already shared my location with you and Wyla."

I'm so beyond tempted to demand she share it with me also, but I know if I have it, I'll be checking it every five minutes and the need to go find her and pull her away from her date might not be something I can hold back on.

Adam pulls out his phone, clicking on her name to double check that he can see her location. "I know you don't need my permission to go, Cals, but I have to at least ask the questions." Adam shrugs it off as he shoves his phone in his pocket like it's nothing and to him, I guess it is. But, damn it, would it kill him to be the asshole brother just one time? Tell her no. There's no telling who this guy is and what could happen. She doesn't need to go on this date with whatever dickhead she met. She should come be with me instead. Maybe I should tell her that?

But as she looks at me and bites at her lips to keep from talking, I know I can't say any of that. As much as I want her to be mine, the fact is she's not and I have no right to tell her what to do.

"Right." I nod, swallowing down everything I wish I could say. "Call us if you need us."

"Sure," she whispers. "I forgot my jacket, but you guys can head down. My Uber should be here in about five minutes."

She doesn't wait for us to answer before shutting her door and disappearing back into her place.

Adam pats my back. "Let's go, first round's on you."

"Dude, I'm the designated driver, and I don't drink."

"Well make your drink whatever you want, your money still spends just the same."

Annoyed already, I pull out my phone in the elevator and against my better judgment, I text my sisters.

> She's going on a date tonight.

REAGAN

Bet you wish you would have pulled your head out of your ass a month ago.

LUCIE

Don't kick him while he's down Rea. Sally and Harry both dated before they got together. There's still hope.

> This isn't a movie.

LUCIE

You always have to act like you're the main character anyway. So, what are you going to do?

> I don't know yet.

REAGAN

Well you better figure it out soon!

LUCIE

Might I suggest the grand gesture?

Fuck this night.

Chapter 21
Callie

Fuck this night. Oh my goodness, this was a horrible idea. I wanted to change my mind immediately after closing the door on Will. Seeing him made it perfectly clear that I'm not ready to move on. So now, instead of sitting at home in comfy clothes and wallowing, I'm now sitting at the bar wallowing in non-comfy clothes and heeled boots that are pinching my toes. And the worst part—this tool won't leave me alone.

"So, I'm just saying when Prez tells you to go long, you go fucking long even when it's a beer can," Kyle drones on. The moment my butt hit the bar stool he appeared in the empty seat next to me and hasn't stopped talking about his glory days in his fraternity.

Kyle continues to go on despite the many times I've told him I'd rather finish my glass of Merlot alone. I look down at my glass—there's at least half left—but I need to get out of here or I'm going to lose my mind.

"Right." I fake laugh and slide out of my chair. "Kyle, if you'll excuse me—"

"Where do you think you're running off to?" he snaps as

looks me up and down. "I thought our night was just getting started."

Shit, I don't like his tone at all. I know I owe this asshole nothing and I should tell him to fuck off, but this guy screams "I have roofies in my wallet." I need to play this smart.

"I just have to use the bathroom, that's all." I smile but then he clocks my purse in my hand. "I need lady things in there." Oh yes, let's confuse him with lady business because I need to take my coat too. "And actually, I think I put my tamp—"

"Just take whatever you need, dollface. I don't need the details."

I smile, what a pussy. But as I step toward the door, he stops me. "I think the bathrooms are back there."

Fuckity, fuck, fuck.

"Thanks," I mumble and I make my way through the crowd. I don't know if there's a back exit, but I'll sneak out the bathroom window if I have to.

Searching for my escape I don't even see the waitress coming. With a small bump I'm knocked to the side, and I see a girl who looks about my age with long black hair. "What the—" I start but she cuts me off.

"Hi, I'm sorry, that was a little harder than I intended. I am one of the bartenders, and I couldn't help but notice you seemed uncomfortable, so I just wanted to check in, but I didn't want to raise suspicion by outright stopping you."

Thank God. I exhale. "Your girl-dar was right, I'm very uncomfortable. Is there another way out of here by chance? He caught me when I tried to sneak out the front and I don't want to deal with any confrontation."

"For customers, technically no, but this qualifies as an

emergency. Come on." She motions for me to follow her back through the kitchen and I try to stay as close as possible so I'm not in the way of any of the other staff.

"Listen, I really appreciate this. What's your name?"

She laughs. "It's Jensen. I know, it's an odd one for a girl."

"Ha! Try having the name Calliope."

As she opens a black door she turns back to me. "Ah, are we weird name twins?"

Oh, I like her. "Calliope and Jensen? We sound like an old crime duo."

"Damn straight." Walking out the door, we enter a dark alleyway where some of the employees are smoking off to the side. "Okay, the main sidewalk is just up that way and you're home free, my girl."

Unable to help myself, I give her a quick hug. "You're a lifesaver. Here let me give you cash for my drink and a tip. Goodness knows that dickwad is a horrible tipper." I start to rifle through my purse but Jensen smacks at my hand.

"No way, this is tip enough."

"Well, I need to give you something." I pull my coat on and it comes to me. "Oh, here." Pulling out one of the business cards Shannon made me order, I hand it to her.

"If you ever want some tickets to one of the Blues games let me know."

"Wow, I definitely will! Have a good night, Calliope."

"Call me Callie!" I shout back as I head down the alley. It's really quite sad that this dark alley feels safer than sitting at the bar. That should really tell Kyle something, but he wouldn't be able to understand that even if I got the frat house president to explain it to him.

When I get back to the sidewalk I'm not entirely sure

what to do next. I could call a car and head back home, but I'd rather not wait out in front of the restaurant. I glance at the front of the building and note the number of windows. Yup, I want zero chance of Kyle seeing me in my escape, so heading left it is.

After a block or two I think I'm in the clear, so I pull out my phone to call a car, but I can't help but overhear a group of girls dropping names that make my ears perk up.

"I'm telling you, that's Beck Daines!"

"Holy shit, and Tripp Pierce!"

"I think the whole team is here! I've been dying to introduce myself to the new players."

And with that last one, I march my butt right in the bar they are standing outside of. I truly have no reason to be jealous right now. I was just trying to move on—unsuccessfully, might I add—and I have no claim on Will. As much as I wish I did, I don't...and can't.

Skidding to a stop in the middle of the bar, that reality hits me hard. Those girls have every right to want to talk to him, which sucks but it's true. We're *just* friends. We're only allowed to *be friends*.

Maybe I should just turn around.

"Ahh, look who it is!" Beck says way too loud. "Callie's here!"

Welp, no turning back now. I guess this is some sort of punishment from the universe for me being so dumb tonight. I make my way over slowly and more of the players start to greet me...but I don't see Will.

"Hey, guys," I say and pull out the empty seat next to Beck. "I barely made it through a glass of wine, and it looks like you've already lost some players."

Beck pats my head, clearly teetering from buzzed to

drunk. "Don't fret, Callie Bear, everyone's here. Some of the guys are just in the back playing darts." And as if I can actually see the thought entering his head, he exclaims, "How was your date?"

"Callie was on a date?" Mateo chimes in next.

"No, Cals, you were supposed to be with me." Tripp places his hand over his heart dramatically.

Oh, great they're all walking that line.

Rolling my eyes, I sigh. "It wasn't a date; I just went out. But I did have to make friends with a bartender to sneak out the back from a pushy asshat."

"You ditched your date?" Mateo asks, too drunk to hear me say "wasn't a date." Clearly, I'm going to have to stick to shorter sentences.

"Yes, I ditched a guy. Don't judge me."

The table erupts in laughter.

"Shut up, this is great," Beck chokes out while laughing.

"What's great?" I hear my brother say over my shoulder and as I turn, I see Will's a step behind. An involuntary sigh comes out when I don't see any girls on his side.

Adam's eyes get wider as he realizes I'm here. "Hey, little sister. What are you doing here?"

He gives me a bear hug from behind in my chair. "Okay, I see you're at about the same level as the rest."

Beck shakes Adam's shoulder. "Reyer, Anderson, you guys are going to love this. Callie was just telling us how she snuck out of her date."

"You what?" Will slides into the seat across from me. God, it's so good to see his face.

Adam finally lets me go and comes around to my side. "You stole my seat, scoot over."

I try to scooch over but my brother is huge. "Adam, go find a new seat."

Adam and I push and elbow each other to get the chair, until Mateo snaps. "Okay, children, enough. We need the story, Cals."

I huff and give up, letting Adam take the larger portion of the chair. I'd really rather not talk about my fuck up of a night, but it doesn't seem like they are going to let this go. "There's not much to tell. This guy was awful and kept talking about his glory days in his fraternity. Halfway through a glass of wine I couldn't handle it anymore, so I bailed."

Beck boos next to me. "Come on, Callie Bear, paint us a picture. How'd you escape the bastard? And do we need to hunt him down and teach him a lesson?"

"He probably needs one but not from doing anything to me. I saw the warning signs with flashing lights." I spend the next five minutes recapping my exit from my not-a-date, and everyone gets a good laugh when I tell them about my "lady stuff" excuse. Well, everyone but Will. Will only stares at me with this blank look.

I tell myself it's because he doesn't have the same emotions toward me as I do him, but deep down that doesn't exactly feel right. I know I haven't made up these moments between us—I couldn't have.

Not that it matters now, I keep forgetting the whole point here—we date, and I lose my job. And at that my heart sinks into my chest.

With my arrival the guys agreed to let this bar be the end of their crawl so, according to the time on my phone, we only stay another hour tops. It felt a lot longer with the cold shoulder I was getting from Will. I tried to not pay him any mind, but I'm not that strong yet.

With him being one of the DDs, he had to take some of the guys home. Thankfully, Mateo's wife, Avery, said she would come get him so I could ride with Will. Dropping off the three other players only added to the eternity of this night, but now we are finally riding up the elevator to our floor and we only have one drunk catcher left.

Getting out my spare key for Adam's place, I get his door open while Will leads him inside to the couch. As his head hits his throw pillow he's practically out already.

"Is he going to be okay here?" The sister in me wants to stay here and make sure he's okay, but Will nods.

"He'll be fine. The morning might be another story, but sleeping it off is what he needs."

"Okay, well..." I grab one of the throw blankets and lay it over top of him. That helps my conscious a little bit.

"Come on, Callie, he's good. I promise." The softness in Will's voice feels like a weight off my chest. Maybe it was the crowded bar that was keeping him quiet.

I follow him out, hitting the lights, and locking the fucking door. Goodness knows I would never hear the end of that one.

Will shoves his hands in his pockets as we make our way down the hallway. "So, the date?"

Ugh, it wasn't a date! "Going out was a mistake. Definitely one I don't intend on repeating."

Will nods slowly.

I don't know what to say. How do I explain to this man

that I don't want to date anyone else but him, but I can't date him because then I would lose my job? And at the same time not come off as crazy because he's agreed before that we're friends. Now here I am walking down this dreaded hallway, and I don't know what to say or how to act because not a single thing about this makes sense to me.

"Callie," Will says softly as we reach my door.

"Yeah?" God, I need him to follow this up with some sort of sign because I'm going to go insane.

He sighs. "Good night."

Soul shattered.

I force a big fake smile on my face. "Right, good night. Thank you for the ride home." Spinning on my heels I reach for my doorknob and let that smile fall with the twist of the knob because, yeah, I didn't lock my door again. I'm hoping to get in my place quickly and put this whole night behind me.

Swinging my door closed, I don't look back until I hear a loud thud and next thing I know, Will's stepping into my apartment. "Fuck, Callie. I need to know what's going on in that head of yours." He shuts the door behind him and closes the distance between us until he's just a small step away.

Too stunned to speak, I manage to sputter out, "Wh-What?"

"Because you are the only damn thought in mine, Callie. I hate that you went on a date tonight. I hate that I've barely spoken to you in weeks. I hate that I haven't gotten to hear your rambles and long-winded explanations. And I fucking hate the idea of only ever being just your friend.

"Listen to me, I know you've got this thing with baseball players, but whatever it is, forget it. Whatever it was, take it out of the equation, because right now I'm not the Blues' pitcher. I'm your neighbor who is sick of being in the friend zone because I've never wanted someone as badly as you. So please, Blaze, tell me what's going on in your head, because that's what's in mine."

"Will..." My heart is beating out of my chest and all other words seem to be lost to me.

Will's eyes track down to my mouth. "Callie, am I still allowed to touch you?"

Swallowing, I nod, and in that instant Will's hands thread through my hair and his lips find mine. Holy hell. Will's kissing me.

Chapter 22
Will

Kissing Callie adds major fuel to the fire with how badly I want her, but when she starts kissing me back...I decide I want to be lost in her blaze. Let it suffocate and consume my whole being.

Her hands wrap around my neck as I move mine from her hair to the back of her legs. I pick her up and set her on the edge of the island, hoping her legs stay locked around my waist.

One hand goes to her back while the other cups the back of her head. Callie lets out a little moan when my tongue glides against hers. She pushes back for a second, taking her coat off, but I don't want to stop this so I follow her retreat, bringing my lips back to hers and helping her remove the layer.

Another small moan escapes her and fuck if I don't give one in return. She tastes like everything I've ever wanted and as I kiss her again her hands go through my hair, gripping tight when my hands meet the bare skin on her thighs where her dress slid up. I don't want to push her too far, but feeling

Callie is reviving my soul. Fuck, we were never meant to be friends.

"Wait, Will." Callie's hand pushes back on my shoulders. Both of our chests are heaving from that amazing kiss, but the look on her face gives me pause. "We can't," she pants.

"Callie, whatever it is, I'll fix it." Cupping her face, I choose my next words carefully. "I heard what you said about not wanting to lose this, but you won't. I want this. I want you. And before you even argue—I heard what you said to my sisters about not dating baseball players because of an ex, but I'm not him. I don't know if it was something he did or the schedule, but that doesn't matter now. Hell, if it's the fear of being traded I'm playing by Olsson's rules to get a no-trade clause in my contract."

Tears pool in her eyes. Fuck, maybe it's not the baseball thing at all, maybe it's just me.

"Baby, please don't cry. If you don't want this, it's okay."

"No, Will, that's not it," she cries, pushing me back so she can hop off the counter. "How could you possibly think I don't want this? I've wanted this since my birthday, but we can't. As in, we're not allowed."

I want to interrupt with at least ten questions, but she's starting to use her hands while she talks and I've only ever had the strength to interrupt her one time and I'm starting to think that might have been the real mistake.

"I didn't go on a date tonight—yes, I went out, but not on a date, just to breathe for a second. For months, all I've thought about is you! I've been fighting this idea of friends for weeks. The idea of what we could be consumed me and I thought maybe a night out would show me that I could let this fantasy go but damn it, it sucked! Being stuck as your friend sucks! That kiss that you just gave me should have been our first kiss, not the one on my birthday. And I was going to tell you that that night. I wanted to tell you that I didn't mean for our first kiss to be that way, but then you said 'friends' and I didn't want to lose you. You listen to me. You threw me my first birthday party and brought me tea when you knew I would be anxious. You fix things for me, but somehow still let me hold some control. I can't even begin to express how much that means to me.

"And that damn brand shoot not giving you a shirt, it was torture! But then the real icing on the fucking cake. Shannon tells me that because of my job—the first job that I've actually enjoyed, the job I need more than anything to prove I'm not some fuck up—it means we're not allowed to date. The guy I can't get out of my head I'm not allowed to date."

No, no, no. That can't be a fucking rule. Sighing, I run my hands over my face.

"So, unless you want to lose that no-trade opportunity"—Callie's voice starts to tremble—"and I lose my job...we can't. And I don't know about you but, I don't think you could ever be this one-night fling. Getting you out of my system didn't work before this kiss, I don't think I'm strong enough to walk away so easily if it were more."

Motherfucker. Callie wipes a tear off her cheek, and I can't stand to see her upset. Stepping to her slowly, I cup her face and let my thumb wipe away another tear. "Tell me what you want me to do, Callie. Tell me how to make this better because if it's within my power, I'll do it."

She looks up at me with those glossy green eyes. "Can you go back in time and make us just acquaintances again?"

I let out a forced chuckle. "No, baby, I can't do that. Nor do I even want to. For what it's worth, I might not know where this thing between us could go, but I know you could never just be a fling. So, if you want me to go bang on Olsson's door and tell him fuck his rule, I'll do it. If you need me to walk out the door right now and have us go back to being friends, so be it. But I never want to go back to how we were in Seattle. Call me a pyromaniac but I need you, Blaze, in whatever capacity I can get."

Callie breaks eye contact as another tear escapes. Wiping it away, I take the hint, not that I blame her. When I saw that smile she had looking at the photos she took I knew what this job meant to her.

Letting her go, I sigh. "Listen, I understand, Callie. But do me one favor. Lock your door for me, or I might come back over here and beg you to change your mind."

Those damn eyes find me again as she sucks in a breath and if I keep looking at her, I'll start begging now. Each step to her door feels heavier and heavier, and I'm so fucking tempted to turn around but I reach for her doorknob anyway.

"Don't," Callie stammers, and I fucking freeze. "Will, did you ever want to just be friends?"

I turn back to face her but don't close the distance yet. I'm not entirely sure where this answer I'm about to give will take me...but it'll be the truth.

"Yes and no. We might not have talked in Seattle, but I knew exactly who you were. The attraction has always been there, but when you first opened your mouth on that plane something felt different. I didn't need a damn thing from the convenience store, but I bought that fucking crossword so you'd have an excuse to get a charger. When you mumbled something about wanting to go into Spilled Tea on the second day, I only went in because I was so tired of seeing you shiver, and I needed to do something to warm you up. I blamed a lot of stuff at the beginning on this idea that we were friends and I just wanted to take care of someone again after being away from my family for so long.

"I don't know what it was, if we're being honest. I just knew that I kept seeking you out everywhere I went. I kept looking for any excuse to be near you—hung onto every word you said. I even went to Spilled Tea and practically begged Margaret to show me how to make that holiday drink because they were closed on your birthday. So, yeah, I guess—"

"Wait, you made that tea?"

"Well, yeah. How I got away with that lie was beyond me, but..." I trail off as she walks up to me. I'm damn near holding my breath waiting for her to say something.

She looks up at me and the silence feels palpable in this moment but then she whispers, "Why do I feel like I should be the one begging?"

It takes less than a second for those words to process and for me to haul her cute ass flush to me. Her hands fist my shirt as I kiss her again and I lose it at the sounds coming out of her.

Her hands pull around my neck and I bring her thighs back around me. Pulling her lips back for a moment she rests her forehead on mine. "Will, I still don't know where this can take us, but I—"

"Hey, let's just focus on one day at a time, baby. We'll worry about all the other shit later, but for today—for right now—I need to know where you want me to take you because I've been dying to exercise my right to touch you."

Chapter 23
Callie

"My bedroom is back there," I tell him, and a shiver runs down my spine at the anticipation of him.

Should we be doing this? Is it the healthiest decision to be making? Probably not. And will future me feel a whole lot of heartbreak when this inevitably has to end? Oh, most definitely. But I don't care.

I was holding on so strong. I was going to let him walk away, but I needed to know when it had changed...I didn't expect to get that answer. I knew I couldn't let him walk out the door after that. I don't know what tomorrow will look like but for now, I want this. I want him.

One thing is for sure—Will is a damn good kisser. He carries me back to my room all while his mouth never leaves mine.

Mouth, not lips. Will has somehow managed to get the perfect balance of kisses, tongue, and small nips with his teeth in between. Fuck, and I thought his hands were going to be the stars of the show. If this kiss is any indication...damn.

When we get to my bedroom Will lays me down and stands at the end of the bed. Feeling even more turned on by the way he's looking at me, I can't help arching my back a little while teasing at the hem of my dress.

"Look at you," he rasps before picking up one of my legs and pulling my boot off. "Raise your dress, let me see you."

Mm, communicating already. I love it. "Hey, Will," I say as I pull my dress up ever so slowly. "I want to get on the same page before we get started."

He drops my other boot then his eyes glide up my entire body. "Tell me, Blaze."

"I'm going to focus on tonight for now, but before we start—first, I'm clean. I haven't been with anyone in over a year and I'm on birth control. But I also have condoms in my nightstand drawer."

A small smile tugs at his lips. "I'm clean too. It's also been over a year for me, but you shouldn't have to provide condoms, Callie. I'm supposed to do that."

"Oh, I never count on a man to be prepared, but that rule applies in everything."

Will shakes his head with a laugh, then to my surprise he wraps his arms around my legs, yanking me to the edge of the bed before getting on his knees. "What's second?"

"What?" Going up on my elbows I gulp. Fuck, he looks good like this.

"You said first earlier, which usually implies there's a second." Will spreads my knees further apart but even though he's level with my pussy he keeps his eyes on mine. "Tell me what's second because I'm fucking starving."

Oh, fuck.

"I-I," I stumble because how could I not after that. "I like to communicate in bed. You talk, I talk. I'm not exactly quiet."

"Oh, I'm well aware." He smirks and I can't be mad at the comment when he slides my dress up to my waist. "Now, is there a third thing?"

Goosebumps prickly my skin and I can't say it's from my newly exposed skin. I swallow and shake my head slowly.

"Oh, don't go silent on me now." Will plants a kiss on my inner thigh. "Where'd that communication go?" His mouth trails small kisses down my right thigh and I damn near hold my breath waiting for him to reach my center but then he moves to my left side. "Talk to me, Blaze."

"N-no, there's not a third," I sputter and as the words leave my mouth, his finally comes to my panties. "Fuck. Will," I hiss.

I immediately want to protest as he backs away but he smiles and taps on my hips for me to lift them so he can pull my underwear down. "There's my girl, let me hear you. I told you I missed hearing your rambles."

That shouldn't come off so sweet in this moment, but I swear it heals a little part of me that was constantly told to be quiet no matter the setting.

However, the sappy moment in me is immediately shut down when Will's mouth starts licking and kissing me again. I fall off my elbows and run my fingers through his hair. "Oh my...damn, and I thought your hands would be where your talents lie."

Will's tongue flicks my clit. "Been thinking about me, baby?" And because Will has always been an excellent listener the next thing I feel is his fingers teasing me as his tongue starts again.

My back arches at the new added sensation and a moan

rattles out of me. "I tried not to but—" My next words get caught in my throat as Will inserts one of his fingers. "Fuck, don't stop."

I swear in that moment, a small bolt of an orgasm shoots through me and Will fucking moans. Why is that so incredibly sexy? My toes curl at the thought of hearing that moan again.

Will continues to work his finger in and out but then lets his thumb start to work over my clit. "God, woman, I've thought about you constantly and this view right here puts every fantasy to shame. You are so fucking beautiful, Callie." He places a kiss to my hip that makes me shiver. "Tell me what you need, because I'm nowhere near done."

As his thumb gets replaced by his tongue again, sounds pour out of me. In between my moans and curses Will dutifully follows every plea.

"Faster."

"Another finger."

"Don't stop."

My legs start to shake, and I feel like my body is on fire. I've never been afraid to orgasm before but this one building up feels like it may alter my brain chemistry. The jump to get there feels too terrifying and I don't know what will push me over at this point until...Will moans my name while devouring me.

And I jump.

My orgasm tears through me in the most agonizing and pleasurable way. My legs shake and I grip on to my sheets to ground me. "Fuck, Will," I cry out and that only spurs him on. He laps up every second of my climax until my body relaxes.

Laying boneless on my bed, Will kisses my thigh one last

time before standing up slowly. "You're a fucking vision, Callie."

I preen under his praise and my body slowly starts to come back to life under his gaze. But in taking him in, I realize he hasn't taken off a single article of clothing yet. Finding the willpower to move, I scoot up to my cushioned headboard and smirk. "Strip for me."

Holding my eyes, Will pulls his shirt over his head first. God, those muscles. I want to drag my finger—and tongue—through every outline. "Keep going."

Will hums quietly. "I'm going to need that dress first."

"Alright, fair is fair." Sitting up I grab the end of my mini dress that's still bunched up around my waist and pull it the rest of the way off.

Will keeps his eyes locked on me and when I lean back raising an eyebrow, he shakes his head and undoes his jeans. "If we're talking about fairness, then I believe you have to take the rest off."

Stepping out of his jeans my mouth goes dry at the man in front of me. Fucking hell, and in Calvin Klein boxer briefs.

Getting up to my knees—my bed isn't exactly big enough for a whole crawl moment—but I do my best to look as sexy as possible.

"Fuck," Will groans as my fingernails graze his skin to pull his underwear down.

Pushing them as far as I can, Will kicks them off the rest of the way and I go back down on my hands to kiss his abs. "So, do you have any firsts or second thoughts for me?"

Moving my mouth lower I peer up at him while wrapping one hand around his length. He hisses, "No."

I glide my hand slowly over his shaft, fuck he's a good

size. Part of me is a little anxious for how well I can actually do this with him, but I want to at least try.

Finally looking down, I lick off the bit of precum on his tip. Will's hands jump to my hair, threading his fingers through and using the gesture to pull my hair back.

"Go on, show me how else you use that mouth of yours."

Peering back up at him, I hold eye contact as I take him in as far as I can. I use my hand in tandem with my mouth but since I'm having a little trouble reaching it's not exactly wet.

I start to pull back so I can remedy this little issue, and as if Will can read my mind he looks down and spits on my hand. Holy hell.

"You liked that, didn't you, Blaze?"

I do my best to murmur something along the lines of "yes," because, fuck, I loved that.

"Yeah, that's my good girl." Will gathers all of my hair into one hand and his other slides down my spine to my bra and unsnaps the clasps. "So fucking perfect. You like communication in bed, Callie? Does that mean you like the praise or degradation talk with it?"

Will's hand holds my head, pushing in a steady rhythm, so I'm not entirely sure how to answer him, but I kind of want to see if he can talk his way through the answer. Peering back up at him I push myself a little deeper and a growl vibrates out of him.

Pulling my head back by my hair, he curses. "I know which one it is. You love the praise which is good because I intend on worshiping you."

Getting off my hands I slide my bra the rest of the way off as I smile. "Then please, take me to church."

Chapter 24
Will

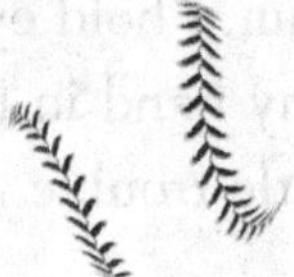

Picking Callie back up, I need to feel her body against mine. Her legs wrap around my waist and with one arm holding her up steady, I cradle her head with the other to bring her back in to kiss her.

Everything that's happened so far has been beyond incredible. I'm not surprised at our chemistry or the fact that Callie loves to talk in bed, but what does get me is how beyond amazing it is to kiss her. Something about her lips on mine feels so incredibly right and not friendly in the fucking slightest.

Holding her close, I kiss her harder. If "friends" hasn't been kissed out of her vocabulary yet, then it's about to be.

With our lips melding together, Callie lets out a little whimper then adjusts her hips. My eager girl.

Sitting back, I admire her for a second and since she likes to talk so much, I'm going to tell her every thought I have while looking at her. "Shit, Blaze." My hand grabs her chin and my thumb brushes over her swollen lips. "These lips.

Kissing you feels like a damn wildfire. So extremely hot, but I'll gladly suffocate in them."

"I thought I told you we don't joke about fire safety." Callie smirks for a moment then pulls my thumb in her mouth to suck on it.

"Oh, baby, I don't ever want to put out your fire. I want to ignite it." Pulling my hand away, I fist my cock and drag my eyes all the way down her body to her perfect cunt. I watch as I take the tip of my cock and slide it up and down from her clit and through her folds, teasing her.

"And this is how I'm going to do just that."

Still sliding my cock up and down, Callie moans as her eyes fall shut.

"Callie, look at us," I demand, and her eyes fly open, but she looks at me first. "Not what I said, baby. Look. At. Us."

I circle my tip around her clit and a little whimper escapes her. She's been way too quiet for my liking—it's almost like she's holding back despite all the confidence she had earlier.

"Tell me, what do you see." Callie groans when I repeat the small circling again. "I want to hear you."

"Fuck, Will. I-I..." Callie's breathing starts to get sporadic. She's close again, I can feel it and I don't think it's from my dick teasing her. No, I think it's the communication.

Callie swallows and lets out a low moan. "I see this guy I really fucking like about to take his incredible cock and put it inside of me"—Callie cuts her eyes up to me now—"and if he doesn't do it soon, I'm going to ignite this fire myself."

I can't fight the tug of my lips. There she is. She might still be holding back a little but I'll fix that. Any doubt anyone ever placed on Callie speaking her mind is about to be erased. In the bed or out of it.

"Should I?" I motion toward her dresser where she mentioned the condoms would be. I know she said she was covered, and I know I'm good too, but I'm not one of those assholes who thinks they're too good for condoms. But if she is okay with bare, I'd love nothing more.

Callie pulls her lips together for a moment while she thinks. I love watching her work through things. I can see her considering all the possible options in her eyes.

Finally letting her lips go she reaches up to pull me to her. "No, I trust you."

I can't help the smile, I fucking trust her too. Lowering on top of her I kiss her again and she hooks her legs around me.

Callie moans my name and her nails dig into my back as I slowly push in her. Her back arches and I move down kissing her neck while palming her breasts.

"Fuck, Callie." She feels so fucking good. I'm riding the edge of losing it already just from entering her. I never really thought about the idea that someone could be made for you, but hell, Callie was fucking made for me. In more ways than one.

Callie's nails claw down my back. "Please move. Fuck, I need you to move."

Following her request, I pick up my speed happily. "Tell me what you need, Blaze."

"Will," she moans. "This. I fucking want this."

My thrusts start to teeter the line of manic because I can't control myself. "I said need, Callie. Tell me what you fucking need."

Sitting back again I pull her ankles up to my shoulders, then lean down slightly, deepening the angle. Callie's back arches and her arms reach for my biceps. "Fuck, Will. I need you. All I've ever needed is you."

Careful to keep my pace I grip her chin and force her to look at me. "You've got me. I'm yours. Now show me how you're mine by coming on my cock. Sear me with your flames, Blaze."

Her eyes roll back and I take the opportunity to pick it up, going harder and faster. Words now seem to be lost to her, but she's not quiet either and with every little moan, whimper, scream out of her I'm getting closer.

"God, yes, Callie, let me hear you."

"I'm. So. Close," she grunts out in between thrusts.

"Give it to me, Callie, I promise I'll be right there with you." Her pussy tightens around me and that nearly does me in, but I can't until she does first. Leaning down I whisper in her ear, "I'll always be right there with you, baby."

And like that, Callie screams out my name and we're both falling. I might not know where the extent of us will go, but so far my only thought has been how will I ever be strong enough to let this go?

Sunlight streams in through the window curtains in Callie's room. The light was enough to wake me up about ten minutes ago, but I couldn't bring myself to get out of this bed. The sunlight now radiates off Callie's red hair giving it an almost golden tint.

Her head rests against my bare chest and her legs are tangled in mine. After round one we made our way to her shower to clean up. And while I was a perfect gentleman in her tiny shower, she threw my sweatshirt on after drying off and the gentleman left my body.

I had her ride me after sitting on my face—with my clothes on her, of course. It was fucking awesome.

We both passed out after that one, but now as she clings to me I want nothing more than to roll her over and wake her up with my head back in between her thighs. But I'm not entirely sure how she's going to feel about us today.

I know we both said we couldn't do a fling, but her job's at stake. And depending on how much weight Olsson holds on this rule, the no-trade clause might not be the only thing I lose.

Although, part of me screams that this girl is worth the fucking risk. It's going to be really hard to not walk up to Olsson today at the training facility and tell him, "I don't care about this stupid rule," but I know this job means a lot to her and I can't put that pressure on her. So, I'm working one day at a time here, might as well make it worth it.

Slowly maneuvering out of her hold, I scoot the pillow closer to rest her head on. She stirs for a moment but as I brush her hair back she sighs and falls back asleep.

Picking up my jeans I make my way out to her kitchen before pulling them on to start a pot of hot water for some tea.

When Callie still hasn't stirred by the time I put the tea bags in I decide to head over to my place to brush my teeth and change. The thought of leaving a note did occur to me, but with no pen or paper in sight, I decide I'll be fast. Even if she gets up, I'll be right back.

Moving as quickly as possible I make it back out of my apartment with the only thought being to get back to Callie.

"Will," Adam hollers from the end of the hall.

Fuck.

Walking toward me I'm at least grateful he called before I turned toward Callie's door. At this point it just looks like I'm going out.

"Hey, how's the head? I thought for sure you'd be out until at least noon." I try to play it cool, but I'm fucking sweating.

"Oh, come on, have a little more faith in me. Nothing some heavy aspirin and water can't fix. I was actually heading down for a light run, wanna join?"

"*Light?*"

"I said have a little faith, not mountains of it. But you're fine, so you should come down with me."

Nope, no way. Not happening.

"Sorry, count me out for today."

Adam pinches his eyebrows as he looks at me. "Are you not wearing any shoes? What are you doing anyway?"

Shit, shit, shit.

"Oh, I was just headed to check my mail." It's the only excuse I can possibly think of, not that it doesn't come off fucking weird that I wouldn't put shoes on to go into the lobby but I'm just praying for this conversation to end.

"Right, so put your running shoes on and you can check that after."

"Dude, come on, I don—"

"Do you have somewhere better to be, Anderson?" Adam clips.

Yeah, back in your sister's bed.

Well, that's definitely one way for me to get punched first thing in the morning. But really, I just want to spend time with Callie and I can't fucking say that.

Great, I've gone from not being able to tell Callie how I feel about her to not being able to tell anyone else.

"Fine, I'll join. But I'm not running anything over three miles."

"Whatever you say."

Slightly cursing this whole situation, I go grab my shoes. Then curse out loud when I realize that my phone's back at Callie's place so not only will she wake up alone, she'll have no explanation for where I went.

Maybe she'll take me leaving my stuff behind as some context clues that I didn't intend on abandoning her this morning, but I still feel like shit. This is not how I wanted today to go. If I can get my miles in fast I might be able to salvage this disaster of a morning and get a couple hours in with her before I have to be at the training facility.

Making it down to the gym in our complex I fly through the stretches and warmups. I just want to get these miles in and get out of here.

"Dude, where's the fire?" Adam asks as I jump on the treadmill.

Upstairs, in my clothes. "I just want to get this run in so I can get back—" I stop myself immediately. Fuck, I just started talking and didn't think about what I was saying.

"Back to?"

Shit, shit, shit.

"Just back to my place. After dealing with you drunk idiots last night, can you blame me for wanting to relax a little?"

I turn up my speed hoping that will be the end of it, but it's Adam, so of course it's not.

"Nah, I don't blame you, but just find it odd how much you're rushing this," Adam says. "I don't know, it just seems like you're trying really hard to get back to something…or should I say, *someone?*"

Oh, fuck, he knows. He has to know. Slowing my speed back down, I at least want to be off this thing if he decks me.

"Listen, it's not—"

"Hey, Callie!" Adam yells, cutting me off.

Following his eyes, I find Callie walking toward us with this deer in headlights look on her face.

I'm having very mixed emotions at this moment because she looks incredible. With skintight black leggings and a matching sports bra, fuck, I'm getting a semi just looking at her. But then there's the glaring issue that we slept together last night, and I essentially ditched her with no explanation. And now she finds me running with her brother.

"Hey," she says, her voice falling just short of a whisper.

I need to talk to her.

Adam goes to her side and hooks his arm around her shoulder. "Did you get any sleep last night? Will here was just about to tell me about the girl he hooked up with last night."

"*What?*" Callie shrieks.

"I was not!" Oh God, shoot me now.

"Then why in the hell are you trying to rush out of here?"

Okay, on one hand this at least tells me he doesn't know about me and Callie. It's fucking awkward, but he doesn't know and now I might be able to clear things up with Callie.

"Because you cornered me in the hallway and forced me to come work out. You're supposed to be hungover."

I try not to put all my attention on Callie's reaction to avoid looking suspicious, but I can't help but hold my breath until I see her shoulders drop and her features relaxing a little bit.

Adam simply waves off my response. "You're being dramatic. I don't care what you said, we're running at least five if you don't have anyone to get back to."

This fucker.

"Okay, well who won't be running any miles is me. I came down for the yoga class, needed to work out some tension." Callie gives me a small smirk. "But I'll leave you two to it."

Her voice sounds lighter now, and while this isn't how I wanted this morning to go, at least she knows that I didn't willingly leave her this morning.

"How long is your class?" I ask in what I hope is in a normal tone and not sounding super desperate.

"I think about an hour." She shrugs.

An hour, okay, I can do five miles in an hour. I think.

I attempt it, at least. I fucking push as hard as I can because the moment, the very second I hit five, I'm done. Callie's class ends five minutes early as I'm just short of five when she gives me and Adam a little wave when she walks by.

Pouring sweat, I'm nearly dying from going full throttle from the very start, but as my distance reads 5.0 miles, I'm done.

I heave heavily, as I slow my speed down. "Alright, I'm done."

"Jesus, man, if you didn't want to run that bad, you could have just said so." There's a dose of sarcasm in his voice that I don't care to entertain.

"Fuck you," I huff and walk out with my hands folded

over my head. I swear if my ears weren't ringing, I'd heard Adam laughing at me.

Chapter 25
Callie

I've never been more thankful for yoga in my life. I normally can't stand it, but when I woke up completely alone this morning, I welcomed the torturous distraction.

I don't exactly know how Adam forced Will into a run, but when Will said that sentence I was relieved. I found the tea he made this morning, but there was no note or text so I wasn't exactly sure if the tea was an act of remorse or gratitude.

I was a little bummed when I got out of class and Will was still on the treadmill. I'm not sure how much of the five miles my brother had left but it looked like they were going pretty hard.

After refilling my bottle, I hop on one of my barstools and gulp some water down. I might not have been doing straight cardio, but I definitely worked up a sweat. Yoga is sneaky like that.

I gamble that I have time to take a shower before they get done. Granted, Will might not have plans to come see me after...

We didn't exactly decide on a game plan last night, but the sex was pretty spectacular. Or, at least I thought it was.

Okay, sitting and dwelling on the status of Will's thoughts about last night is not going to help me. I'm going to shower and when I emerge, I will *not* be that girl who sees Will and asks, "What are we?"

I hop off my stool and head to the shower just as there's a knock on my door. I know it has to be him because Adam would have barged in already.

Butterflies tingle my stomach as I turn my doorknob. *Deep breath, Callie. He's just a guy.*

I open the door and see Will leaning on the wall, still trying to catch his breath. "I'm sorry," he rasps as he walks in.

"Ya going to make it? You're breathing a little heavy. Aren't you an athlete?" I tease with a chuckle bubbling out of me.

A sweaty Will sits down on the stool I just got up from and picks up my drink. "Please tell me this is water."

"It is." Shutting my door, I make my way over to the barstool next to him as he downs the remainder of my drink. "Did Adam not let you bring water?"

Setting it back down he sighs heavily. "Is it too soon in the relationship to say I hate your brother, because I do."

I want to laugh because I know he truly doesn't hate Adam, but one little word really outweighed that whole sentence.

"Relationship?"

Will angles to face me then places one hand around my waist to keep me steady while he pulls my stool closer.

"Callie, I didn't mean to have you wake up alone this morning. I had every intention of keeping you in that bed until the very last possible second, but I ran over to my place to change and on my way back Adam caught me in the hall. And if we're being completely honest here, I think he might know something's going on. He's bound to be hungover, no way he wanted to run five miles this morning."

Biting at my lip, I'm not entirely sure what that could mean for us. The idea that he knows could be a stretch. I've seen my brother push through some pretty bad injuries. "But he didn't seem…"

"Like he wanted to punch me? Nah, so he might not, but that's not my point. My point is, yeah, we can't have a conventional relationship right now, but there's no way you're a fucking fling or one-night stand."

"So, friends with benefits?" Ugh, no, I hate even asking but I need clear answers from him. Screw it, I can't do this confusion anymore. I'll be that girl if I have to.

"Okay, listen to me. If I haven't fucked the word 'friends' out of your mouth already then get your cute ass back in your bed so I can rectify that right now."

I needed "no" to be the answer but that's more than enough to erase my fears of being stuck in a friends-with-benefits situation—and enough to make my panties wet.

I try to look away to calm down a bit because damn that got me. Will pulls my face back by my chin. "I'm serious, Callie. I'll make you say we're friends with my dick in your mouth. Doesn't seem very friendly to me."

"No, not friendly at all," I whisper, and I can feel the blush creeping up my cheeks.

"We can keep this relationship between us until we figure it out, but don't get it twisted, Blaze. We're not fucking friends."

A smile pulls at my lips. *We're not friends.*

Will pulls my face toward him for a small but sensual kiss.

"What's your plan for the rest of the day?" he asks with his face just an inch or two away from mine.

"I've really got to get some editing done at some point, and I was about to take a shower. What time do you have to be at practice?"

Will glances at my clock on the stove and sighs. "I've got about an hour and a half. Not exactly the time I thought I was going to get, but taking a shower with you will serve as your apology."

"*My* apology? What about your apology? I'm the one who woke up and thought I had been abandoned. You know, a text would have sufficed."

Will chuckles. "I have no clue where my phone is. I was too busy thinking about making you tea and having fresh breath for you, but then *your* brother happened."

I roll my eyes and hop off the stool. "Are you going to keep whining about Adam or are you going to enjoy what little time we have left?"

"Oh, I plan on enjoying every second." Will stands up and pulls me to him by my hips. "Just as soon as you lock your door."

Chapter 26
Callie

For a moment, I kind of blacked out the idea of what flying to Aster Creek would be like. A roughly three-hour flight really isn't that long in the grand scheme of things, especially when your brother pays for your first-class ticket. It really should feel like a luxury.

However, being on a flight with your brother on one side and your secret boyfriend who you spent the night before naked with on the other...well, let's just say it complicates the luxury of first class. Hopefully, it's just me who felt weird.

As we wait at baggage claim, I feel pretty proud of myself that I didn't let any of my overthinking come out during the flight. Maybe it's because I got little to no sleep last night, so I'm too tired to ramble.

I try to stifle what has to be my fifth yawn since we started standing around baggage claim when my phone vibrates in my pocket.

WILL

Quit yawning. It keeps reminding me that I'm the reason you're tired and then I get this mental picture of you naked in my bed.

Oh, you poor man. What a horrible picture to have. Maybe I should just always keep my mouth closed, would hate for you to picture me on my knees with my mouth wrapped around your dick.

WILL

What a fucking picture that is. Can I frame it?

Sorry, dream frames only.

WILL

I want a whole fucking gallery then.

A light chuckle escapes me.

"What are you laughing at?" Adam asks with simple curiosity.

"Oh, it was nothing. Just some silly picture," I reply, locking my phone and shoving it in my pocket. I don't exactly pick up the same vibe that Adam suspects anything between Will and me. I mean, he would be pissed, right? Isn't it like some unspoken rule that your sibling's friends are off-limits?

Damn, am I in a forbidden relationship right now?

"Oh, and you didn't think that I would want to laugh at the picture?"

Rolling my eyes away from him, I wave him off. "Believe me, you wouldn't have thought it was funny."

"Yeah, what about me?" Will asks with a smirk. "I like pictures."

This mother— "It's too bad, you'll never get to see." I shrug. "Probably won't ever come across it again."

The smirk on Will's face doesn't falter, he actually laughs a little. When the conveyor belt kicks on, Adam steps up closer to watch for our bags, but Will takes a small step closer to me.

"We'll see about that," he mumbles.

A small blush creeps to my cheeks, and I hum a "Mm-hmm."

After picking up our bags, we make our way out to the front of the airport. Jett texted Adam that he would be waiting out front for us. I had hoped Wyla would come with him, but she said Stevie was grumpy. I still have days to enjoy girl talk.

But the moment I walk out the sliding door I hear my name squealed from around the corner. "Auntie Cals!"

"Ah! My Stevie Bug!" I shout and race to her and Wyla. "You guys tricked me."

Stevie launches toward me with open arms. "It was my idea! Did we surprise you?"

"You did! Best surprise ever."

Wyla comes up to me next, wrapping her arm around my shoulder for a small hug because Stevie's gone full spider monkey and clings to me tight. "She forced me into this scheme. There was no way I wasn't coming."

Jett comes up next, greeting the guys before prying his daughter off me. "Let her breathe, Stevie."

Adam makes his way around to Stevie next and sets down his bag to flip her upside down and she giggles. "Stevie, I missed you. I need a hug."

"Ah-Dum... Put. Me. Down." With her giggling uncontrollably, she barely gets the words out.

Adam flips her all the way around and as soon as her little feet hit the ground and he lets her go, she takes two quick steps to me, wrapping her arms tightly around my waist again.

Adam pretends to put his hand over his heart. "You wound me, Stevie. Why does everyone like my sister more than me?"

"Probably because she's smarter than you," Jett jokes.

"And prettier," Wyla adds.

"Cause she's nicer than you!" Stevie yells the final blow.

Will doesn't pile on and while I know that's for the best, it just reminds me how much this whole sneaking around is going to suck.

Making it back to their house, we start to unload. Before Adam can even offer to stay at a hotel, Jett insists we stay with them. Based on the nonstop word-faucet that their four-year-old is, I'm guessing our stay is more for them than anything.

The moment my feet hit the cement Stevie is pulling me to the door to meet her dog, Poppy, and then dragging me upstairs to her room to see her canopy bed. Not that I mind too much. I love the sassy britches, but I feel bad leaving everyone to carry in my stuff.

She launches off her bed and bounces back to me. "Come on, now let's go look at my swing set."

She yanks my hand trying to breeze past me, but I tug her gently back and kneel next to her. "Stevie Bug, I promise I want to see all of the things, but let me go get my stuff out of the car, okay?"

Her lip hangs so low it hurts my heart. "Okay," she mumbles.

"Hey, we're going to have so much fun over these next few days. I promise."

I squeeze her hand and give her a big smile. I feel a little better when her lip goes back in and she nods eagerly.

"I'm gonna go find Mommy, and then you can meet us at the swing set."

"Sounds great," I say and she bolts down the stairs. "Slow down, Bug."

I chuckle as I watch her stop then reach for the handrail before going the rest of the way down. Shaking my head, I go to follow her down but then someone grabs my hand.

Jumping, I almost yelp but swallow it down when I realize Will's pulling me into a small bedroom.

"Calm down, woman, it's just me."

"Oh, because I'm supposed to know that?"

Will pulls me flush to him the moment I move to hit his shoulder with my free hand, not letting the hit land like I wanted. I try to push away but then he's kissing me and suddenly I don't even remember why I was irritated at him to begin with.

A small hum of approval comes out of me when his tongue glides in my mouth. When he pulls back I want to protest, but he sighs. "As much as I'd like to keep you up here, I know they'll start looking for us."

I nod, stepping back. "I need to go get my stuff anyway."

"I got 'em." Hooking his thumb over his shoulder, Will points to all of my bags on the bed. "Think I'm going to let my girl carry her own bags?"

"Don't make this harder than it already is, Will. I already want to add another mental picture to your gallery."

"Can I make a pose request?"

I chuckle. "We'll see."

"Come on, let's head back down," Will says with light taps to my ass.

"You go ahead. I'll give it a minute then follow."

He shakes his head but smiles before kissing my forehead. I wholeheartedly check him out as he walks out the door. In order to maintain my positivity about this secret relationship I keep focusing on the moments that I get with Will. This past weekend it was easy to do that. Other than the interruption from Adam and practice, we practically spent every second wrapped around each other.

Those moments were fun and easy, but we're officially starting the season and with the schedule we have we'll basically be just coexisting around each other for most of the day. I'm not exactly sure how I'll handle that. I have big emotions and I like to feel them. I'm all for cleat chasers shooting their shots with the single players, but Will's mine...even though I'm not allowed to show it.

Ugh, calling us quits should be the decision. It's the smart one, but it's also the one that makes me feel like I'm going to throw up and have heart palpitations.

Taking a deep breath, I try to keep the thoughts in my brain under control. One day at a time. One hour at a time honestly feels more manageable to me at this second and when I can't do that anymore then I'll walk away.

Finally making my way downstairs, I can hear the negotiations happening from the living room.

"But, Mommy, why can't we go outside?"

"Because, Stevie, it's barely forty degrees. I'm not making Callie stand outside and you just got over a cold. Why don't we play inside?" Wyla's using her soft mom voice and despite truly being a great kid, Stevie's still only four.

When I make it into the living room the tears are flowing and big pleas are being made.

"Please, Mommy. I'll wear a coat, I promise!" Stevie pulls at Wyla's arm and before she can even respond to her daughter, Stevie continues. "Daddy says it's springtime, why is it still cold? I want to go swing!" Stomping her foot for good measure, I can see the tantrum coming.

Scooping Stevie up I plop her down in my lap. "Okay, Bug, let's talk about it for a second."

Her little head turns her teary eyes to me. "Please, can we go outside?"

Ah, hell, how do Jett and Wyla ever say no to this face? I don't want to backtrack on Wyla's reasoning. Wyla's the best mom; I could never undermine her. "Stev—"

"Daddy!" Stevie interrupts as the guys make their way back in. "What season is it?"

Jett takes the seat next to Wyla. "Spring, Little Bee," he says, and I already know what argument has started.

"It is not, it's February. It's winter." Wyla tries to keep that soft mom voice but I can hear the edge starting.

"Nah, it's spring," Adam piles on.

"See, Mommy! It's spring, why can't we go play outside?"

Wyla sighs. "She's going to start pre-k in the fall, you guys have got to tell her the truth."

Jett just laughs and pulls Wyla to him. I've been around them enough to know that he just loves to get a rise out of her. "Sorry, Wy. Spring Training starts next week, so it's spring to me."

"Me too," Adam adds.

"I'm not getting involved," Will says. I try to hide my smile by planting a small kiss on Stevie's head, but I can't help but give him a small wink when he looks my way.

"I give up," Wyla exasperates.

"So, does that mean I can go outside?"

I squeeze Stevie and try to stifle my laugh. Wyla looks like her head might explode, so I bump Stevie on my lap, having her look back at me. "Ya know, I think I noticed a Barbie Dreamhouse in your bedroom. I would really love to play Barbies with you."

"Okay," she grumbles, but her little body bolts off my lap and up the stairs.

"Don't worry, Wyla. I'll explain the whole seasons thing to her through the people she'll actually listen to."

"And who's that?"

"Ken and Barbie, duh."

Chapter 27
Will

Pulling into the college baseball fields bright and early, Callie shivers next to me in the car the moment I open the door. It's really quite ironic that a girl whose whole being is fire is constantly cold.

She climbs out of the car and pulls her jean jacket over her Blues crew neck. Her skintight leggings make it near impossible for me not to check out her ass, which sucks because I know every other fucker on this field is going to want to do the same.

She flashes me a quick smile before turning back around to grab her backpack off the floorboard. Her long red hair is pulled back in a low ponytail that is tucked in from when she put on her jacket.

Not even thinking about it I reach for those fiery waves and pull them out from under her coat. The action is innocent enough until my fist is wrapped around her hair, and I give it a light tug. She goes completely still and I swear she's holding her breath. I don't wait for her to turn around, even though I'd love to see the pink on her cheeks. I walk to the back of the car and grab some of the equipment to take to the fields.

I might not be able to stake my claim on her in front of people, but I can take every opportunity in private to remind her that she's mine.

Throwing the last bag down by home plate, Callie shivers again. "Why did we have to do this so early? Why does it have to be so cold? I thought the south was warm?"

"Cals, we've never lived anywhere but up north. How are you always cold?" Adam huffs. "It's nowhere near what we normally experience."

"I don't like the cold. I like to be warm," she states, clearly unamused.

"I brought a sweatshirt that I don't think I'll need if you want it," I state in the most nonchalant way I can. I knew she'd be cold, so yeah I planned ahead. I might have *coincidentally* brought the one with my number on the back.

Oh, you're cold? Put this on, because I want to send a fucking message.

"It should warm up pretty soon, Cals," Jett promises. Dream crusher.

"We'll see." Callie rocks on her feet and crosses her arms. "I'm going to go get organized in one of the dugouts."

I give her a slight smile as she walks by. I overhear Adam say something to Jett, but I don't really pay that much attention because there's only been one person occupying my thoughts as of late.

"You might want to dim the lights on the heart eyes a bit, Will?" Jett says.

Looking over at him, I realize Adam's halfway to the parking lot now. "Don't know what you're talking about."

"Okay, I'll be blunt about it. I don't know if there's something going on between you and Callie. I don't need to know, but either way, if you're trying to be subtle about liking her, you're not."

"Thanks for the tip, but Callie and I are just friends."

"That 'just' you threw in there really made it sound believable." Jett laughs. "And I'm *just* Wyla's baby daddy. The statement itself is true but the added 'just' is so very false."

"Right, you're also her ticket for the senior discounts, right?"

Any upper hand Jett felt he had was lost in that moment because he knows Wyla begged us to make all the old jokes we could today. She's seven years younger than Jett. They met in their twenties, so it really isn't that bad, but she lives to call him old.

"That woman," he grumbles under his breath, but there's a hint of a smile.

"Hey, Jett, some more of the guys are here," Adam says, walking back up with three other guys. I recognize them all immediately. There's Damon Moreitti, the Chicago Knights shortstop, and Logan Pettersen, an outfielder and one of our old teammates back in Seattle. Both of them are great, never had any problems. The third guy, however, is the Knight's new designated hitter and a complete asshole, Nic Collins.

I may or may not have intentionally hit him with a ball in Chicago last season.

Logan makes his way to Jett, clapping him on the shoulder. "Hey, Ellison, did you lose all your good contacts after retirement because I know these assholes lost their edge the moment they became a part of the Blues."

"Yeah, I was desperate, so I called you too," Jett throws

back, then turns to Nic. "No offense, I don't remember inviting you."

"That's on me," Damon says. "I don't think you guys have formally met Nic. Well, I think Will has... He got called up midseason as our designated hitter."

"Oh, shit. He's the guy you intentionally hit." Adam hits my shoulder and jokes, "Go on, say you're sorry."

Not fucking likely.

"Nah, I deserved it. Plus, it didn't even leave a bruise." Nic shrugs to cover up the obvious lie. I pitch ninety-six miles per hour on an off day. Didn't leave a bruise, my ass.

"Not that it matters anymore," Damon cuts back in. "When Jett mentioned the Blues' team photographer was going to be here, we thought this could be some good PR exposure. That is, if you guys don't mind."

"You'll have to talk to her about it," Adam replies. I know Jett talked to Callie about taking pictures of the fundraiser as a whole, but I'm relieved that Adam isn't straight up volunteering Callie for more work. Adam's also been sizing up Nic like he's trying to place him from somewhere.

"I can do that," Nic says, a little too enthusiastic for my liking.

As if she knew we were talking about her, Callie walks up to us while looking down at her camera. "Hey, Jett, can I get your car keys? I think I will get—Nic?"

Callie looks as white as a ghost.

"Hey, Cupcake, long time no see." And with those words it's like the whole atmosphere changes. You could hear a pin drop on the dirt right now.

Callie's mouth gapes and the only conclusion I can make is that this has to be her ex. The ex who made her swear off baseball players—before me that is.

"Wait, that's why you look familiar," Adam says, breaking the silence. "Your parents are friends with ours."

"Yeah," Nic responds but his eyes don't leave Callie. "Calliope and I might have taken the friends things a little further, though." He tilts his head, addressing Callie now. "You were in your last semester getting your master's in finance when we started dating, but—you always did love photography, didn't you? I just assumed you liked being *in front* of the camera."

What the fuck does that mean?

In a millisecond I see Callie go from shocked to outright pissed. She takes two steps, shoves her camera at Adam and punches Nic right in the face. "Fuck you."

It takes all of us a couple seconds to recover, and before I can even process what just happened Callie's halfway to Jett's car.

"I see you leaving didn't make you any less of a stuck-up bitch," Nic hollers after her.

I'm pretty sure Adam and I both see red at those words. But where Adam's red comes from Nic, my red is blazing away and I need to check on her. Adam grabbing Nic's collar is the last thing I see as I chase after Callie.

"Callie, hold on!" I shout after her, but she doesn't stop. "Callie!"

When she reaches Jett's car she yanks on the door handle trying to rip it open but it's locked. Tears stream down her face. Fuck if someone sees. I turn her to me and cradle her face.

"Callie, it's just me, baby. It's okay." I wipe away her tears, and she sighs.

"I'm sorry, I thought when I saw him at a game or something I would be more prepared. Practice being professional, but I didn't expect—"

"Shh." I pull her in, holding her tight with my hand on the back of her head. "Don't apologize. What did I tell you about apologizing on behalf of men?"

"I was apologizing for hitting him, Will. My action, not his. "She sniffles.

"His actions caused it." I kiss her head.

She snorts a sad laugh. "You don't even know what he did."

"It doesn't matter. He deserved it, end of story."

Her arms squeeze around my waist a little tighter and it seems that her tears have stopped. I should probably let go, but I don't want to.

"Callie," Adam calls.

We get a small arms distance away from each other before he comes barreling around the other cars.

"What the fuck just happened?" he barks.

"Adam. Chill out, man," I throw back at him.

It takes Adam a minute to register my words and for a moment I think he might lash out at me next but then he takes a deep breath. "You're right. Callie, are you okay?"

Callie wipes the tears off her cheeks. "Yeah, I'm fine. But I'm not staying here if he's going to be here. I was going to manage when you played against Chicago and hoped I would be too busy to interact, but not here. I'm also not taking any pictures of him, so don't even ask."

"I wasn't," Adam replies. "Jett's called him a car to take him back to their hotel. Damon is going to stay, if that's okay?"

She nods. "That's fine."

I probably shouldn't be the one to ask this—to Adam it might come off weird, but fuck it. "Callie, what happened?"

She exasperates a breath. "Can we do this later?"

Adam sighs next to me. "I'm sorry, but I'm going to need some sort of answer. I rarely play the brother card, but I am now."

Rolling her eyes, she huffs. "Fine, but can we go somewhere else for a minute?"

Chapter 28
Callie

Well this day has taken a drastic turn and it's not even nine in the morning. I fully anticipated not handling my first interaction with Nic very well when we ultimately crossed paths again but that? I did not expect that.

Punching him was an out of body experience. A very freeing experience. but I surprised everyone—myself included. Now I'm begrudgingly following Adam and Will to one of the college locker rooms to hash out this entire issue.

I guess it's good I'm getting this out now. If dating Will could get me fired, assaulting a player at a game would be ten times worse...even if he deserves it. Maybe the guys can help defend me to Olsson, if it comes to that.

Walking in, Adam huffs when he realizes he can't lock the door from the inside. "You probably have ten minutes before people start showing up. I don't know if any will come in here, but hit us with it, Cals."

I'm a little surprised Adam hasn't questioned Will being

here for this. But I'm going to follow his lead and not question.

"Okay, but I'm asking you to just listen to me first. Start to finish." I raise an eyebrow and wait for them both to nod.

Let's get this off our chest.

"It started at Mom's extravagant Easter Egg party almost two years ago. Mom was on the hunt for a potential husband for me, like she had been since I was seventeen. Over the years I had mastered different ways to shut it down: annoy them with my incessant talking or 'lack of manners' but when one of the dads had too much to drink and got a little too touchy—"

"*One of the dads?!*" Adam yells. Will doesn't look happy, but he already knew about this.

"Why do you think I started kickboxing in college? When I thought my only option was to break his nose, Nic showed up. He pulled me away from it in the diplomatic way Dad would have loved.

"Fast forward a month, we started dating. He was playing for Sutton's minor team so he was only half an hour outside New Haven. I was in my last semester for my master's and things were going great for the most part. Then I graduated, got the job at Dad's financial firm, and Mom and Dad were finally off my back. But things with Nic started moving too fast.

"Nic was getting really pushy about marriage and getting shared bank accounts. Begging me to break into my inheritance even though I told him repeatedly I didn't have access until I turned twenty-five. After a few months I tried to compromise and I moved in with him. But it only got worse. I tried pushing through because it kept Mom and Dad at bay and there was no way I was moving back to that hellhole."

"Callie—" Adam can't help himself at that part.

"Let her finish," Will snaps.

Adam runs his hands over his face. "Sorry. Go on."

"Thank you. So, right before New Years, Nic completely blindsided me by proposing at a family dinner. I said no," I add immediately because I can see the riot going on in Will and Adam's eyes. "That, naturally, did not go over well. There was a lot of yelling, and a lot of name calling on all fronts. Nic's family starts blaming our family for being the reason I said no. That went over like a ton of bricks and all hell broke loose.

"Nic's parents kicked me out of *our* apartment that, apparently, they were paying for. Dad was furious at the scene he thought I made, and I had to sleep in my car for a few nights until everyone calmed down. When I showed up to work the following Monday there was a whole new problem."

"God, it gets worse?" Adam looks up at the ceiling but holds up his hands. "I know, I'll be quiet."

I take a deep breath. This part isn't going to be pretty. "I have always loved photography, and I was really able to explore my skills with it during college when Dad wasn't breathing down my throat twenty-four seven. And when things were good between Nic and I, I might have taken some...inappropriate pictures of myself." I cringe, avoiding eye contact with both of them.

"At the time, it didn't seem like a big deal, but with me trying to give everyone space for the weekend before getting my stuff, Nic decided to print hundreds of copies. He put them everywhere at work. Every department, every lobby, desk, office, bathroom—everywhere had naked pictures of me. And I know what you guys are about to say—that's very illegal. But dear ol' dad informed me that I would officially be homeless and fired if I pressed charges. Apparently I needed to 'save face,' because it was my fault for taking the pictures to begin with.

"For some fucked up reason, I agreed with him. I don't know why, but he's my dad so I just went with it. I, at least, tried getting all of the photos back, but that was absolutely impossible. As you can imagine—based on the touchy douchebags I mentioned earlier—the harassment started. Every woman in the office looked at me like I had a scarlet letter on my chest and every man thought I was a porn star. No one attacked me directly, but the sexual harassment became bad enough I knew physical advancements weren't too far off.

"I tried talking to Dad, ya know, the CEO—*our father*—about it but he just said, 'You get treated how you act.' So, I walked out of the office, broke into Nic's house, took what I couldn't live without, and flew to you."

Finally, I take a deep breath. I thought that it would feel good to get this off my chest, and I guess it does. But it also kind of feels like it's moved from my chest to my stomach. I just told the two most important men in my life my darkest moments. Shit's starting to feel real heavy again.

Pulling my lips together to let them know I'm done talking, both Adam and Will look at me completely shell shocked. I get it, it's a lot to process, so I wait.

"I-I, hmm..." Adam struggles to start. "W-Why didn't you ever tell me? I'm your brother, Callie! Why didn't you tell me?!"

"Hey, calm down," Will tries to say when Adam's voice starts getting louder.

"No, I will not calm down! Callie, you went through all

of that and never said a fucking word! I was a phone call away! Why?!"

"Because you escaped, Adam! You fucking got out. You think I didn't know where your bruises really came from? You think I didn't hear the curses or yelling? I wasn't pulling you back into any of that. Coming to you last year was my last resort. My last Hail Mary. So, no, I didn't fucking tell you."

The room goes dead silent. Adam's whole body, my bear of a brother, deflates in front of me. He turns around and grabs one of the wooden bats and swings it repeatedly against the closest locker.

The first loud bang sends shivers down my spine and Will pulls me tight to his chest, holding me until the bat finally breaks.

"I'll pay the school back for that," he says with no emotion in his voice, then walks out without looking back.

When the door slams shut, another jump runs through me and Will holds me tighter.

"It's okay, he just needs to cool off."

"And you?" I place my chin on his chest to meet his eyes. "Do you need some space?"

"Callie, I'm going to need zero space. Holding you here is the only thing keeping me from going on a murder spree."

I snort a pained laugh. "I'd be your alibi."

Will places his hands on either side of my head. "Listen to me. If your dad ever calls you, hand me the phone. If Nic tries to talk to you at games, you come find me. Hell, call in fucking sick for every Chicago game. Never subject yourself to those assholes again. I don't care if you want to walk away from whatever is happening between us tomorrow, if I ever find out that you brought yourself back into their fucking mess, I will hunt you down and bring you back to me."

"Kidnapping? Rather bold move."

"Don't joke, Callie. I'm serious. I'd throw away my entire career if it meant you not going back to that. Promise me. I need to hear you say that you'll never let them have any hold on you ever again."

My heart aches in my chest and I feel like there's this baseball of emotions stuck in my throat. "You know, I did some online therapy back in Seattle, and for a while I was so angry. I wanted to get back at everyone, I wanted them to feel the pain I felt. But then my therapist told me that sometimes the best revenge is just having a happy life. That took me a while to come to terms with and it's easy for me to forget sometimes, but that's what I want—a happy life."

Will sighs and places a kiss on my forehead. His lips linger and I shut my eyes, breathing in this moment.

"I want that for you too, Blaze."

The day drags by. The training camp ends at noon and Adam refuses to look at me. The car ride back to Jett and Wyla's is painfully silent. Dinner is tense with only the four-year-old talking up a storm because, thankfully, she has no idea how to read the room.

After dinner Jett takes Adam and Will to his gym for a "workout." Everyone knows it's a ploy to give me and Adam a little space from each other. It feels weird fighting with him like this, if we could even call it fighting. Avoidance? Irritation? Disappointment, maybe? I don't know. But every part of me wants to apologize to him. I know I don't need to, and even if I wanted, I can't bring myself to do it. I remember how upset I was when I was old enough to understand where Adam's injuries really came from, but he never told me. I stand by my decision to leave him out of it.

"Here you go." Wyla holds out a glass of wine then places two bottles on the coffee table. "Stevie's finally in bed, and I say you're due another good cry paired nicely with a merlot."

I take a big gulp while staring aimlessly in a daze. "You hate merlot."

"That's true. That's why I made me this." Wyla reaches for another glass that I didn't see from the side table. "Jack and Coke, you know I love a good whiskey."

The laugh that bubbles out surprises me. "You drink that; I'll stick to this." I refill my glass with a gracious pour.

"So, you told them, huh?"

"Yup, it didn't exactly go over well, as you can see."

"Adam just needs to work through it. I've learned some shocking things that my sisters went through, and it rattles you. Learning that the people you thought you knew struggled so heavily and you had no idea—it's hard to move past."

Taking another big sip, I sigh. "I get it, but Wyla, you know why I didn't tell him, right?"

Wyla's the only person who has ever heard the full story. We had a night similar to this one back in Seattle. By bottle two I started crying profusely and let everything out. The next morning when she made me breakfast and forced a gallon of water in me, I made her swear to never tell Adam.

"Yes, of course I do. It's also the reason I've never told Jett either."

"You didn't?"

"Nope. I promised you I wouldn't tell anyone, and you were no longer in that situation, so I didn't feel like it was my place to tell anyone else."

"Aw, Wyla. You're the best." I rest my head on her shoulder. "I think you're the first real girlfriend I've ever had."

"I'm honored. And full disclosure, if you did try to go back to that whole fucked up situation, I was going to rat your butt out in a heartbeat."

A small humph of a laugh finds its way out.

"Let's talk about something that's more important than the assholes in your past. Let's focus on the good and tell me all about you and Will."

My head comes off her shoulder. "There is no me and Will, remember?"

"Mm-hmm, okay, tell that to your lady boner." She laughs and sips her drink.

"Damn it, see this is why it's not going to work. I know I'm going to blab it to someone and we'll be fucked."

"But at least you're getting fucked."

"Wyla!" I smack her shoulder and laugh. "That's true though."

I take another sizable gulp of my wine when we hear the front door open. The guys file in and the tension still feels thick, but at least it's out there.

Will comes in at the front of the group and gives me a soft smile. Man, what I wouldn't give to get any form of affection from him right now.

I'm entirely sure that thought comes across my forehead in neon letters because as he walks by, he squeezes my shoulder. It's small—it's something.

Jett pulls Wyla away next, and Adam plops down in her seat with a sigh.

"Adam, if you take a bat to anything in my house I'll kick your ass," Jett says.

As Will walks up the stairs he adds, "And if I hear you yell, I'll hit *you* with a bat."

Adam mutters curses under his breath and I can't help but chuckle.

"Okay, but if any of you wake Stevie, I'll kill you then bring you back to life so you can put her down to sleep again." Wyla points a look at each of us. Damn, why did her threat feel the most genuine?

When everyone clears out, Adam places his hand on my knee. "I'm sorry, Cals. I wasn't a good brother to you today and honestly, I don't think I ever have been."

"Adam—"

"Just hear me out. I never allowed myself to think about what could have happened to you when I left. I thought keeping that little bit of communication between us was enough. And this whole year I've never asked what happened out of the fear that the guilt would eat me alive and that was so fucking selfish.

"I spoke wrong earlier when I said you should have told me—Callie, I should have asked. I knew what that man was capable of, but I was too scared to ask."

Taking a deep breath, I inhale every word then exhale all the pain out. Reaching for the opened bottle I top off my glass and hand the bottle to Adam. "Here, I don't have another glass but the bottle works just fine."

"Damn right."

Both of us swallow down a good bit and when Adam makes a sour face I chuckle. "God, that's awful."

"Hey, it's alcohol." I shrug and take another sip. "I like it."

Adam shakes his head and puts it back on the coffee table. "Then I'll let you handle that."

Resting his elbows on his knees, Adam runs his hands over his face. "I really am sorry, Callie."

Sitting up I set my glass down as well. "I know and I appreciate the apology. We unfortunately can't change what happened, but I feel good about where it led us."

Adam finally looks up and a small smile tugs at the corner of his mouth. "Yeah, me too."

Chapter 29
Will

Spring Training honestly used to be one of my favorite parts of the whole season. The weather's nice, it's practically nonstop baseball between practice and games, and all around a good way to get pumped and prepared for the season.

However, one major drawback is that Callie's not here. After a few days in Aster Creek, Adam and I got on a plane for Florida and Callie had to go back to Boston for some issue Shannon called her every fucking day about.

Callie tried talking her into letting her work remotely so she could come down with us, but Shannon would not let it go. We barely had any time together during those few days in Aster Creek, and now it's been almost a week since I've seen her.

I know her flight landed earlier along with the rest of the team, and I'm dying to see her. When I click on my phone I've got a thread of texts that I can't help but laugh at.

BLAZE

Just landed. Shannon's already talking about all the stuff I have to do right away, but I heard one of the pitchers was really hot, so I'll probably go check him out first.

Why does this woman hate me? I have to go with her to the hotel first to make sure everyone's checked in. I'm the photographer! What purpose do I have there?

Now I'm being roped into a tour of the stadium with a guide who specializes in the building's history. You better be one of the attractions or else I'm giving it a one-star review.

Tour rating: one star. Rating for tour with Shannon: negative two.

That's the last one I received and the time stamp is from almost an hour ago. Fuck, I want to see her. Sending her a text letting her know I'm done for the day, I toss my phone back in my bag.

"Nice work out there, Anderson," Dex says as he walks into the locker room. "It's good to know my retirement as a player isn't going to hurt the team too bad."

"Who knows, it might even benefit," I joke, failing to remember that Dex is my coach now and not just another player. It's been a weird adjustment. This was his first week actually on the job, and I might not know the full details, but I don't think Dex was as ready to retire as he leads on.

But I think it might be a mutual thought, because Dex laughs. "I wouldn't get too ahead of yourself. You're good, but remember, you're only here because I retired."

"I think it's a little too early to be talking about your glory days, Larsen."

"Dad!" Dex's five-year-old son, Miles, comes charging in and starts talking ninety miles an hour. "Callie says I can help her take pictures if you say it's okay! So, I'm going to tell her you said okay, okay?"

"Whoa, whoa, slow down," Dex hollers and waves for Miles to come back as he tries to race back out of the locker room. Not that I blame the kid. As soon as he mentioned Callie I had to hold myself back from racing out of the room too.

Dex kneels in front of his son and I'm totally not about to eavesdrop on my coach and his five-year-old. That's a lie, I totally am.

"Callie's working, buddy. She doesn't need you being her shadow."

"But she said it was okay. She's waiting for me outside. Said I would be a great helper."

Bingo. Trying not to come off too eager, I grab my bag and give Dex a nod as I pass by.

Dex pauses what he's saying to Miles and hollers at me, "See you, Monday. Take it easy and ice your shoulder."

"I know the drill." I raise my hand high for a wave because there's no way I'm turning around—I see a fire.

"Hey there, Blaze."

Callie's eyes light up and a smirk comes across her face. "Ah, I see my covert operation was successful."

Walking to her I wrap my arm around her waist and pull her around the side of the door and back into a corner. "We've got maybe two minutes before that kid swindles his dad into letting him follow you around. Lucky little fucker."

"Ooo, think you can make those minutes worth it, Anderson?"

Cupping her face, I pull her in for the kiss I've been dying for, but the moment my lips touch hers, her phone rings.

Callie starts to mutter as she pulls out her phone. "I swear if this—ugh!" She takes a deep breath then she throws on the fakest smile I've ever seen. "Hi, Shannon."

I sigh, taking a step back because I know our moment is gone.

"Yes, I'm on my way. Yes, I know how to take pictures with moving objects. Yes, even direct sunlight. I'll be there in two minutes."

Callie clicks off her phone and that smile disappears immediately. "I swear she hates me."

I take the chance of tucking a strand of her hair back behind her ear, mostly because I can't resist. "Please tell me you get out of here soon."

"I wish. Shannon has me doing two brand shoots with some of the other players. They don't start for another twenty minutes, but she wants me to come show her that I can take the actual photo." Callie huffs. "Tell me something, Will. Do I have clown makeup on my face?"

I chuckle. "No, baby. You'd be one sexy clown, though."

"No, don't try to make me less angry, Will. No, I was mad. Feed into my pettiness."

"Callie!" Miles's little voice calls from around the corner.

"Time's up," I whisper and plant a quick kiss on her forehead. She shoves me playfully and mouths *"Bye"* before turning the corner.

I walk out of the stadium and it feels fucking amazing

outside. There's no way it's over seventy-five, and a nice cool breeze comes by every once in a while.

Damn, it'd be nice to have my bike down here. The idea comes to me immediately and it might not be my most thought out idea, but fuck it.

We have tomorrow off before everything gets fucking crazy. I'm calling dibs on you for the day, so be ready at ten. We're going on a date.

I wait for Callie on the side of the road, a block down from our hotel. Being as Shannon has been all over her ass lately, she insisted we meet somewhere away from the hotel.

She tried to tell me to meet her at a street three blocks down but there's no way I was going to let her walk that far. So we compromised. I asked her if I needed a disguise too and Callie sent the middle finger emoji back.

Standing on the side of the road by my brand new red Ninja motorcycle, I hear a whistle. "Hey, biker, can I get a ride?"

Callie strolls down the sidewalk with a smirk. Her red hair is down with her usual waves, a pair of jeans, a white tee, and a brown leather jacket.

"For you, baby, anytime." Taking a step to meet her, I pull her in by her jacket. "This looks damn good on you."

"I thought it might impress you." She comes up on her toes to meet me for a quick kiss. "So, what's our plan? Is the car not here yet?"

"Oh, it's here." I let her go to grab her helmet and put it on her head. "You asked for a ride, and if you're good you'll get a different one later too."

Callie rolls her eyes. "Did you seriously rent a motorcycle for today's date?"

"Oh, no. I bought one." I put on my helmet next and make sure both comms are on. "Now, come on. Let's get going."

"But...where are we going?" Callie hesitates. "What if—"

"Callie, baby, I got you always. But if you're really uncomfortable then I can call us a car."

Her shoulders relax and she takes her small bag off her shoulder. "Can I put this in your backpack?"

I take her bag with a smile that she can't exactly see, but the smirk must show through because she smacks my visor down. "No gloating."

"I didn't say anything!"

"I saw it in your eyes," she snarks.

Shaking my head, I help her on and she holds on tight before I even turn it on. "Callie, you good?"

"Yeah, I'm good." Her voice is calm. "Nervous, but excited. Ready to see what you've got planned, Anderson."

The engine roars to life and I feel her arms tense. I shake my head with a chuckle, and an arm moves from my waist and smacks my helmet.

"You better hold on tight, Blaze."

As I take off her arms squeeze tight for a moment, but as we get out of the city she relaxes. "I still can't believe you bought a whole ass motorcycle for a date."

"Well, I couldn't buy half a bike." I laugh.

"Don't be a smart ass right now, I can't hit you on the top of your head." Her arms squeeze around my torso for a second. "What I meant was, it just seems like a lot of money and hassle. What are you going to do, ride this all the way back to Boston?"

"Well, you see, I recently took on this delivery job because of the cute girl next door, but she was a horrible tipper. So I got this multi-million dollar pitching contract instead. Makes paying for this and paying to get it shipped back to Boston much simpler."

I can practically feel her eyes roll. "I'm hitting you in my head, just so you know."

"I know. I can feel the annoyance radiating off you."

She chuckles softly. "So, are you going to tell me what we're doing?"

"And take all the fun out of it? Absolutely not. Just sit back and enjoy the ride, baby."

"That's not exactly the 'lay back and enjoy it' I was thinking of."

"We've got all day. I want you to enjoy all positions."

Chapter 30
Callie

After driving a half hour toward the coast, Will pulls into a parking lot across the street from a pier that has all these cute booths set up. Lending me a hand as we get off, I let him get my helmet as well.

At this point I'm sure he knows I can do it. I like being independent, but sometimes I like letting him just take care of me. And while I don't know what he has planned exactly, the effort is already romantic as hell.

I've felt a little bummed because part of me really wanted to lock ourselves in one of our hotel rooms for our entire day off, but I know that even with a *Do Not Disturb* sign we'd have zero privacy. If Shannon didn't come knocking, my nosy brother would.

Adam texted me first thing this morning offering to take me to lunch. I didn't exactly know what excuse to give so I went tried and true with girly shit. Loaded him up with shopping, me-time, exploring cutesy tea shops—told him anything that screamed girl time. I practically held my breath as those three dots danced and his "Nah, count me out. Enjoy your day" text came through.

"You ready?" he asks.

"For the date I know nothing about? I guess," I snark.

"Look who's being the smart ass now." Will's hand threads through my hair then down to my neck and pulls me to him.

The kiss doesn't start small. It's desperate, claiming—it's "let me suffocate in your mouth because if this is how I go, then I'll die happy."

For a moment it feels as if it's only Will and I around. This is the kiss I wanted to spend hours on in our hotel room. Keeping this a secret just makes less and less sense with each kiss.

Our moment comes to an abrupt end when a group of what looks like high school kids start hollering and whistling at us.

Will pulls back with a chuckle and I can't help but send the guys the middle finger.

Will takes my hand and places a light kiss to the back of it. "Come on, Blaze, we've got plenty of time for that later."

I lean back slightly with raised eyebrows. "I'm going to hold you to that."

"Oh, believe me, after this date you'll be putty in my hands."

I roll my eyes. "Aren't we confident."

Will wraps his arm around my shoulder to lead me toward the pier. "I'm a pitcher, of course I'm confident."

We walk across the crosswalk but instead of walking further down the pier, Will pulls me to the side toward the strip.

"Don't worry, we'll come back," he says when he notices me looking back at it. "I told you we've got *all* day."

He leans over to kiss my temple while walking me further down. The buildings lining the strip are exactly like the pictures of typical beach-style buildings I've seen. "You know, this is the first time I've ever been to Florida."

"Really?" Will glances my way for a moment.

"Yeah, my family wasn't exactly the beach vacation type. Any vacation type, for that matter. My dad's a complete workaholic and my mom hated the idea of any travel. They love New Haven so much, so traveling just seemed irrelevant." I shrug. "You have family here, right?"

"Yeah, some up closer to the Florida-Georgia line. None I'm close with."

"Oh, yeah? How come?" I ask out loud before even really processing the question. When I really start thinking about what I know about Will, it's not much.

I know the basics, I guess. But I feel like there are tons of things Will knows about me. Heavy stuff, too. Maybe I've just been an oversharer. And if Will's tense shoulders are any indication, I don't think I'm about to get much of an answer right now.

"Just not close," he finally mumbles. We walk a little bit further and I have to bite at my lips the entire time to not ask any more questions.

When we walk up to a small restaurant with these picnic tables out front, I shake off the weirdness with the idea of eating at this cute little spot. But when Will asks for his to-go order, I raise an eyebrow. "Are we not eating here?"

"Hey, there she is. I was half wondering what your next question was going to be and half afraid you were going to bite your lip off."

I narrow my eyes at him with a scowl, but he just smiles and places a kiss to my brow. "Let's get to where we're going, and you can ask me any questions you want, okay?"

"Oh, free reign questioning? Do you even know what you just offered? I get to ask any question? And I have time to think of them?"

"God, you're going to want me to talk for hours aren't you?"

I smile eagerly and nod. "I bet a William Anderson ramble is so hot."

Will rolls his eyes and pulls me closer by my belt loop.

"Here we are!" one of the hostesses says, handing Will a brown bag. "And some of the guys were curious...are you the new pitcher for the Boston Blues?"

I peep around Will and see some of the people at the bar looking at us. Will, however, doesn't hesitate. "Nope, that's not me."

He hooks his arm around my shoulder and leads me away with a kiss to the side of my head.

"Those poor fans must be heartbroken," I joke, but honestly I'm relieved he shut it down quickly. I do hate that he felt like he had to lie though.

"They'll get over it. Today I'm not a pitcher anyway."

I swallow down the lump in my throat. "Oh yeah, what are you?"

"Today, I'm a guy taking his girlfriend out for a date."

Oh. Goodness, am I a puddle? How am I walking? I feel like I just lost every bone in my body.

Blindly following Will further down the street, we come up on a small little tea shop. When Will walks up, I pull back.

"It says they're closed." I point out the sign hanging in

the window. It's weird, their lights are on, but there's not a single customer inside.

"Not for us they're not," Will says cooly then knocks on the door.

"Will! We are not—"

"Mr. Anderson, welcome!" An older woman swings the front door open with a huge smile. She ushers us inside and locks the door behind her.

When I step inside it's covered in pastel greens and pinks. Gold antiques accent the walls and roses are stenciled throughout. Not to mention there are fresh cut roses everywhere. And in the middle, there's a table set up with a lace tablecloth and candles.

"This must be Callie." The woman behind me says, bringing me out of my daze. She holds out her hand for the both of us. "Hi, I'm Rachel, the owner of Rose's Dream Tea. I'm so happy to have fellow tea lovers here. Is this the food I suggested?"

"Yes, ma'am." Will hands her the bag and she smiles.

"Perfect, let me get this set up for you guys. Why don't you have a look around." Rachel scurries around us, and I spin on my heels to face Will.

"What have you done?" I can't help but smile already, this seems so elaborate. How did he manage to do all of this?

"I told you, I'm taking my girlfriend out on a date." He shrugs like it's no big deal but he's got that damn smirk on his face. He knows I'm loving this.

"Will, this seems a bit more detailed than a normal date."

"Does it?" He quirks up an eyebrow. "I mean, buying out a tea shop for the day for my girl seems pretty low bar."

"You bought out the whole place?!" I don't mean to say that so loud, but I'm shocked. I'm fucking flattered.

Will places his hands on my shoulders then runs them up and down my arms. "I thought we covered the whole 'I have money to spend on you' deal. Callie, I know how stressed you are about us keeping this a secret, but today let's just be, okay?"

I nod because it's the only thing I think I can manage. Will cups my face, placing a small kiss to my lips.

"One day at a time."

After a few minutes Rachel brings out several trays full of fruit, cookies, sandwiches, tarts, and small cakes. "Okay, you two. If you're ready, go ahead and take a seat."

Will holds out his hand for me to go first, and when we reach the table he pulls out my chair before sitting across from me. Rachel then places this beautiful drink in front of us.

"Alrighty, this is our mango hibiscus tea. Callie, Will told me that you like to keep your caffeine intake low, so two out of the three teas today will be caffeine free."

"Thank you," I say, then flash a smile to Will and he just winks back.

"There's blended mango at the bottom, and I always recommend mixing up the tea at the beginning, but some of my customers say they simply love the mango first, so as my mom would say, 'whatever floats your boat.'"

I pick my drink up, stirring around the fruit with the straw and Will follows suit. Rachel then brings one of the trays full of fruit and small baked goodies in between us. "And these are the starters. I'm going to start on the next tea and I'll be back shortly."

"Thank you, Rachel," Will says as she walks to the back, then holds his drink out to me. "Cheers."

"Cheers." I clink my glass to his then take my first sip. "Oh my gracious. This is delicious."

"Thank fuck." Will exhales. "Do you know how stressed I was that this was going to go so poorly?"

I can't help the laughter that comes. "Why were you so worried?" I pick up a raspberry from the tray and pop it in my mouth.

"Well, I threw this together in less than twenty-four hours. I barely made it before their closing time yesterday to talk to Rachel about me buying out the place for the day."

"I can't believe you did all this," I whisper.

"Day's not over yet." Will winks as he eats one of the macarons.

I hum low. "Hmm, that's true. I also believe I was told I could ask any question that comes to mind when we got where we're going. Is that still true?"

"Fire away, Blaze. I won't promise a ramble, but I'll answer honestly."

Fidgeting in my chair, I pull it closer to the table. I have one question that I've hung on to for a while. "Okay. Why baseball? Why not keep going with motocross?"

Will puts his drink down and leans back in his chair. "I always enjoyed both. Not to come off like an ass, but I was great at both."

"Humble," I huff jokingly.

He shoots me a smirk, but it quickly disappears. "My dad loved bikes. Motocross was where we bonded. Spent hours on end at dirt tracks—so bad that Mom would have to drag us off when it was too dark."

"That's sweet." I have to take a sip because I'm dying to ask more follow-up questions already, but I know that he's working up to more, I just need to be patient. Granted that's not always been my strong suit—hence drinking my tea to occupy my need to talk.

"Yeah, well, I'm sure you've wondered why I haven't offered to introduce you to him, or mentioned him for that matter. He had always been a drinker. As a kid I didn't really understand what was going on but after a while he got more brazen with it. We went out to dinner after one of my races and he drank a few too many but drove us home anyway. We barely made it out of the parking lot before he ran off into a ditch and into a street pole."

"Oh, God, Will. I'm sorry. I didn't mean—"

"Hey, it's okay. I was fine other than some scratches from the glass. He was the same, but not at all remorseful. He obviously got arrested and Mom picked me up at the hospital. She was furious—rightfully so. She gave him an ultimatum—get sober or leave. He left the next week and never looked back."

My stomach turns in knots, and I feel like my heart dropped out of my chest. "So that's why you never drink."

"Not a drop. I also quit motocross immediately after he left. I wanted to quit baseball too, honestly. I was just angry at everything, but my mom refused to let me stew in it. She forced me to stay in some sort of activity, said she didn't care if it was chess club, but I had to do something. So I stuck with baseball and here we are."

I smile softly. "Can I selfishly say I'm happy your mom did that?"

Will humphs a small laugh. "Yeah, it turned out okay."

"I'm choosing to ignore the small insult for the sake of me still getting to ask questions."

Will takes my hand from across the table. "Keep 'em coming."

"And your family here, is that your dad's family?"

"Yeah, Mom tried to keep them involved in our lives but everything shifted for my mom after that. She loved my dad, probably still does on some level, but there was no coming back from that for her and they couldn't really understand that. The holidays were always her favorite in Rowley anyway, so that's where we stayed.

"Reagan and Lucie had a hard time understanding everything at first. Mom and I really tried to shield them from the whole drama, but eventually it got easier and it's been the four of us ever since. When I went to Seattle, I was far away from them and really they needed me less and less. Now, granted, because of that I did get back into riding. Kind of felt like I was giving my dad too much power in taking away something I enjoyed for so long, so I bought my first bike with my first payout from my contract."

I scrunch my nose thinking of him on his bike. After today's ride, it's growing on me.

"I really must have distanced myself because I never knew about the bike until the night at the bar. Don't get me wrong, I definitely noticed you—"

"Did you have a crush on me, Blaze?" Will interrupts me with a shit-eating grin.

I roll my eyes. "Finding someone attractive and having a full-on crush are two different things. I'd like to think I had the same effect on you."

"Alright, I'll agree to that. Your presence was always noticed, but I never acted on it. So I get what you mean."

A blush comes to my face as I sip my tea. "Back to my original point. I never really paid full attention in Seattle. All I allowed myself to think about was you being a baseball player then shut it down from there. I'm sorry."

"Don't be. Honestly, that was really all I was. After a while I think I was just going through the motions of what was required of me as a player. I didn't have anyone there who I really cared for, and I got lost in that. But then you sat next to me on the plane, and I don't know, you opened your mouth and it felt a little bit like home to me."

Biting at my lip, I don't know if I have any more questions after this. Really I just want to give Will a hug.

Will leans back in his chair and waves for me to continue. "Come on, Callie. Give me another question."

Pushing back my chair, I round the table and lean over to give him a tight hug.

Will chuckles lightly and pulls me into his lap. "Now you've done it. If you think I'm letting you go back over to your own seat, you're fucking wrong."

Sitting up I readjust in his lap to face the table and reach for my drink to bring it over to this side. "One day at a time, right?"

"Right." Will brushes some of my hair behind my ear. "Oh shit, I almost forgot." Will wraps one arm around my waist to hold me to him while he leans over to get his backpack and pulls out a blue Polaroid camera. "I'm going to need my photographer girlfriend to document this killer date."

"Shut up!" I snatch the camera from him, then kiss him on the cheek. "This is perfect."

"That was the goal." He places another kiss on my temple while I fidget with the camera.

Double checking there's film in it, I turn it around. "Smile," I say, then click our picture. Screw being scared of someone finding these, this date deserves to be documented.

Rachel comes back out a few minutes later with an Earl

Grey raspberry tea and the sandwiches Will picked up from the restaurant down the strip. Will stays true to his word and keeps me in his lap the whole time.

I don't think I would have ever made it through any dinner sitting in my boyfriend's lap without feeling uncomfortable, but with Will it was fun. It felt flirty and connecting. We laughed a lot and I took so many damn pictures we go through two packs of film before we've even left the tea shop.

Finally back at the hotel, I think Will might have put me in a "best date ever" trance because I don't even care as we walk toward the hotel together. Screw someone seeing, this man rented out a tea shop for me today. Then practically let me make him my model for the day. I went through almost every pack of film he bought. The amount of Polaroids I tried to carefully place in his backpack was insane.

Will stops at the corner and turns to me. "What's your room number, Callie? I'll do this in whatever way you're most comfortable with, but I'm not quite ready to give up our day off yet."

Me freaking either.

"I mean, there's no harm in walking me to my hotel room. You could just be super protective over your team's photographer. That's very professional."

Will pulls me in closer to him. "But I plan on doing so many unprofessional things to you."

I inhale his scent and sigh drunkenly with a small smile. "Have I ever told you I love the way you smell?"

Yup, I'm pretty sure I'm high off all the freaking romance of today.

"Nope." He laughs. "This would be the first."

"Well, I do. You smell manly but also like coconuts. Just know, whatever soap, deodorant, cologne—I don't care what it is—don't stop using it."

Will smiles that damn smile. "Okay, I promise," he whispers, but then takes a step back. "Now, Callie, can I please escort you to your room safely? The gentleman in me insists."

I can't help my laugh. "Thank you, I would love that."

I follow him through the lobby, shoving my hands in my pockets to resist my need for physical affection. I let out a small sigh when we get in the elevator alone and it makes it all the way up to my floor without any stops.

I swipe my keycard at my door. "It seems I've made it safely."

"Then is my job done?" Will smirks.

"For the gentleman in you, it is." I pull Will in my room by his coat and with the click of my door, it's on.

Chapter 31
Callie

Ripping away our clothes, my lips only leave Will's for the seconds it takes for us to pull our shirts over our heads. Savoring this moment is a predicament. I want this man right now—so greedily that it's near painful. But at the same time, I want to revel in this because I have no idea when this will happen again.

When every stitch of our clothing hits the floor, Will backs me up to the bed. His hands tease my body as they travel down from my face, grazing my hard nipples, then squeezing my ass.

"Talk to me, Callie. Tell me what you need," he whispers in between kisses.

What I need? Fuck, that's a great question. I need so many things. I need more of him. I need this rule to go away. I need more than just today with Will.

Will's hand comes to the back of my head, gripping my hair tight as he pulls it back. "The only time I want you speechless, Callie, is when my dick's in your mouth. But even then I still want to hear you choking on it."

Oh, hell. "I want that," I pant. "Will, I want to let you take control tonight."

The corner of Will's lips turn up in a sexy smirk. "As long as I can still hear you, baby."

Will doesn't wait for my answer before tossing me back on the side of the bed. I squeal at the unexpectedness of it. As I look back Will's already started to come around to the other side.

"Come on," he says as he stands directly behind me. "Hang your head off the edge and open those pretty lips for me."

"With pleasure," I purr.

Once I'm where he requests, my body feels like it's vibrating with anticipation. Will looks down at me while fisting his dick then spits on his dick.

"Fuck, that's so hot." I watch as he works his hand up and down his shaft.

Will's eyes trail down my body, then come back up with this glint in his eyes. "If you need me to stop or pull back, you tap my leg twice, understand?"

All I can manage is a nod because he steps closer, teasing my mouth with his tip. I try to pull him in, but he pulls back. "Words, Callie."

"I understand." I smirk, then he steps closer and takes control of my mouth.

My arms wrap around his thighs, and he slows for a moment, but I'm not fucking tapping. I let out a moan and tug at his legs to let him know that I want him to keep going. Yeah, sometimes I like to play with control, but not tonight. And the part I love the most is that explaining that to Will doesn't seem necessary. I think if I asked to be dominant next time, he wouldn't bat an eye.

"You look good like this, baby." Will's hands trace down from my throat to palm my breasts. "Fuck, this is going up in my mental gallery."

My noises barely qualify as moans anymore, but with him still thrusting into my mouth and playing with my tits, I'm so turned on there's no way I could be silent.

My arms hold on tightly as I start to gag a little. Will doesn't stop entirely but he slows down enough for me to calm down and breathe through my nose.

"Good girl. You take me so well, Callie." Will moves one hand and it clasps around my throat. "I fucking missed this mouth. All week I've thought of it. About kissing those pink lips." *Thrust.* "About filling it with my cock." *Thrust.* "About every noise, word, and ramble that comes out of it." *Thrust. Thrust. Thrust.*

My legs rub together because after that, fuck, I'm soaked down there and I need some friction.

"I see what you're doing, baby." Will's hand tightens around my throat. "Don't worry, I'm going to spend the whole night worshiping that pussy of yours. But for right now, I'm going to come down your throat, and I want to feel you swallow it."

Small whimpering noises are the only response I can give, but I'm screaming *yes sir* in my head. Will picks up his pace and I can feel how close he is. Letting go of his legs I let him take full control as my hands play with my tits.

"Fuck, Callie," Will grunts then comes down my throat.

Being the good girl I am, I swallow just like he told me too. As he pulls out slowly I lick his tip one more time.

Will leans down placing a sensual kiss to my mouth then down to my chest. "Touch yourself again," he commands.

When he stands back up I already have my hands

working over my tits and he shakes his head. "Lower," he growls.

I let my hands travel down my body slowly. I'm eager for a release, but I keep a slow pace as I hold Will's eyes as he watches me intently. By the time he makes his way back around to the other side of the bed, my fingers run over my clit.

"Will," I moan because I want him to know that even if it's my hand, it's him that has this effect on me.

"Fuck, another picture I want seared into my brain." Will's hands grip my ankles as he pulls me further down the bed so my head is no longer hanging off. "So, damn perfect."

Will's fingers slowly make their way up my legs and suddenly the idea comes to me. I blurt out, "Why don't you take an actual picture?"

Will's hands make it to my knees and he goes still. "Callie, I don't—"

"With the Polaroid." Stopping, I sit up to meet Will's face. "We have a pack left. They're more private this way. We don't have to, I just—I know it seems like a horrible idea. Maybe I should know better but this feels different. I trust you."

Cupping my face, Will kisses me deeply. "If this is what you want. But if you so much as regret it for a single second we burn them in the bathroom sink after this."

"Can I take some pictures of you too?" I whisper.

Will lets out this low sensual hum as he leans me back down flat on the bed. With hands on either side of my head, he hovers over me. "How about pictures of us?"

This man. "Oh, I can picture us perfectly, Will."

Chapter 32
Will

Moving back off the bed, I leave a trail of kisses as I go get the camera. Knowing what happened I would have never anticipated this. But she's right, this is a completely different situation. In our past we've both felt alone, and that ends now.

I hand her the camera, and she smiles softly. "Are you sure you're good with this?"

Grabbing her ankles again, I pull her further down the bed and she giggles lightly. "Now I'm not the photographer here, but I think the first picture should be of me on my knees for you."

I push her knees apart as I get down on mine. "And don't forget—I'm not a model either, so tell me what to do."

I don't wait for her to agree because I know my girl will do exactly that. And I love that it won't stop at just the pictures.

With my mouth on her pussy, she sits up on one hand to adjust her angle and lets out the most intoxicating moan. "Yes, Will, just like that."

Using my hands, I lift up her ass so I can eat my girl

properly. After circling her clit slowly a few times, my tongue trails down to her center, then slightly further to feel her out.

Her hips jerk and she lies back on the mattress. "Fuck, no one's ever done that before."

Gliding back up, I flick her clit one more time. "Want me to do it again?"

Callie sits back up with a sexy smirk. "I want you to keep doing everything you're doing."

With that I have my mouth back on her, but I know her—she's not done talking yet.

She lets out a small moan and pulls the camera up. "I still have a picture to take. Eyes on me, Will." When my eyes meet hers, she smiles and says, "Good boy."

Fucking hell. I thought I could convince her to stay with me by pulling out all my tricks and ruining it for any other man, but this—she's ruined me.

Holding her ass up with one hand, the other teases her everywhere while my tongue circles her clit. When her body arches back, she drops the camera.

"Pick it back up, Callie," I tell her as I push a finger in her center. "Take another."

When she doesn't do it right away I pump my finger in her twice before replacing it with my tongue, then going down slightly further again.

"Will, I'm going to—" she pants.

"I know." I flick my tongue on her ass again. "Take a picture and come." Moving back up to her clit, I circle it while fingering her tight pussy. And just as her walls squeeze the hell out of my finger, her legs wrap around my shoulders, there's a click of the camera, and she comes.

Just as I had her do, I lick up every drop of her orgasm.

Her legs shake around me and each pant of my name feels like a damn prayer that I never want to end.

When her body slows and her legs go lax, I ease my way up onto the bed to hover over her. Looking into her glossy, green eyes I suck the taste of her off my finger.

"That's...so...hot." Callie's breath sounds strained.

"You okay, baby?"

"Yeah," she huffs. "I think I'm just still waiting for my soul to return to my body."

I chuckle. "You really know how to inflate a man's ego, Blaze." Leaning down, I place a small kiss on her lips then pull back for a second to let her breathe before going back in.

"Just kiss me, damn it." Callie wraps her arms around my neck and spreads her legs for me to settle between her thighs.

Happy to fulfill her request I cup her face and kiss her slowly but with every bit of passion in me. Callie's nails scratch up and down my back, sometimes lightly and sometimes, when our tongues glide against each other, her nails dig in harder.

"Will," Callie mumbles. "I don't want this to end."

I'm not entirely sure if she means this night or us, but either way I agree. Rolling us over so she can straddle me, I look up at her and brush her hair behind her ears. "Callie, baby, I'm yours."

I pull her back down for another sensuous kiss, but don't hold it long because I know she's about to get in her head about this.

Raising her up by her shoulder, I grind my hips into her with the command, "Go on, put it in. It's my turn for some pictures."

The fire in her eyes ignites as she raises up on her knees

and lines herself up. Locking her eyes with mine, she smirks when I pick up the camera.

"Sit on my cock, baby."

Callie lowers down slowly, watching me intently, waiting to see when I'm going to take the picture. But as sexy as she is the whole way down, nothing beats the arch in her back and the look of pure bliss on her face when she takes all of me in. That's my picture.

Callie moans as she moves her hips. "I bet that was a good one."

"There's not a doubt in my mind." My hands travel up her thighs as she rides. "Fuck. Nothing beats the live show."

"Wanna know a secret?" Callie whispers.

"Tell me, baby, but don't you dare stop." My hands grip onto her hips and lift her up slightly before bringing her back down.

Callie's head rolls back with a moan. "I like being on top. It makes me feel powerful." Callie places her hands on my chest then takes over with her own rhythm.

My hands fall off her hips. "Fuck yes."

Her fingers dig into my chest and she leans down. "I know I said I wanted you to take control, but I think I want a little."

"Baby, I lost control the moment you moved in next door."

Callie arches back, clawing her nails down my torso. "Why don't you take another picture."

My fucking pleasure.

I grab the camera and look up at my gorgeous girl. She's close already, I can feel it. "I'll take the picture as soon as you come, Callie."

A wicked smile comes to her face and her hands go up to

her hair. Fuck, I thought she looked good bouncing on my dick before, but now she's putting on a damn show. She's going to kill me. Callie Reyer will be the fucking death of me, and I'm not even remotely scared of her blaze.

When her pace picks up, I raise up the camera with one hand, then tease her tits with the other.

Callie's head falls back with my name on her lips and the moment I feel her climax take over I take the picture, then flip us over. Her nails dig into my back as I tear her apart. And with her name now my prayer, I pour into her.

Now I know precisely what she meant earlier—my soul has completely left my body, but the only difference is, I don't expect mine to come back. I'm pretty sure I'm lying on my soul now.

I start to push up on my hands, but Callie wraps her arms back around me. "Hold on. One more picture, please?"

"Anything you want." I kiss her temple. She reaches for the Polaroid and holds it around my back.

Sliding to the side slightly I grip her chin. "Take it now," I tell her then kiss my soul.

Practically dead to the world after the night Callie and I had, I'm dying to hit snooze just one more time on the alarm.

But when I hit the small alarm next to me the pounding continues. Fuck, is someone knocking? The clock reads just a little after seven, so it's not like I'm late for pictures today.

Aimlessly I walk up to the door, throw on my pants, and rip it open to find Beck on the other side. "Fuck, man, what's with the loud knocking?"

And the moment the words leave my mouth, and I see the look on Beck's face, I know I've fucked up.

"Well, considering this is Callie's room, the real question is, what are you doing here?" Beck tries to hold in a laugh. "I was coming over here to ask her if she's seen you. Guess I got my answer."

Beck's laugh starts getting louder.

"Beck, shut the fuck up."

But he doesn't, his laugh continues on.

"Will!" Callie whisper-shouts behind me. I turn around to find her wrapped up in a sheet and panic in her eyes. "What the hell is going on? What are you doing?"

Grabbing Beck by his shirt I yank him inside to get him out of that damn hallway before he gets the attention of anyone else.

"Good grief," Callie mumbles under her breath.

"Hey, Callie Bear, I like your sheet." Beck's grin is a mile-wide and as much as I'd like to punch it clean off, this mess is my fault.

"Hey, watch it, man," I snap, then step around him into the bathroom to grab Callie's robe. Draping it around her shoulders, I help her get covered while she looks up at me with sad eyes.

I have to fix this.

The bright side is this could at least give us an answer as to how serious this rule is.

"Okay, I get how this looks."

"Oh, I know exactly how it looks. The claw marks on your back and chest don't really leave much room for interpretation." Beck turns to Callie again and looks her up and down with a smirk. "It feels like Callie Cat is more fitting now. I might change—"

"Beck! Shut the fuck up. Stop looking at my girl like that and fucking listen!"

"*Your girl?*"

Callie runs her hands over her face and mutters, "We're screwed."

"No, we're not." I take her hand and pull her closer before turning back to Beck. "Look, we've been secretly seeing each other for a few weeks, but we've been dancing around this attraction since the trade. So we're not just fucking around. This is serious, Beck."

Beck shrugs and crosses his arms. "If this is serious, then why are you keeping it a secret? Just because of Adam—wait, nooo. You two aren't allowed to date."

And just like that the bubble of hope I had pops.

"So, that's an actual rule?" Callie asks just barely above a whisper. Damn it.

"Yeah." Beck nods. "We had a couple of players over my years here who wouldn't leave the staff alone. It got really messy—from both sides, really. Almost all of the players were traded and some were sent back to assignment. There were two girls who were let go but others just left. After all that shit, the rule was strictly enforced. Olsson might be the new GM but he was still a coach through all that mess. It wouldn't surprise me if this was still his rule."

"Fuck." I pinch the bridge of my nose. What the fuck are we going to do?

A punch comes to my other shoulder and Beck looks angrily at me. "Why the fuck did you answer the door anyway?"

"The fuck was that for? I didn't do it on purpose. I was working off little to no sleep."

"Will!" Callie slaps at my other arm and while she looks upset still, her cheeks are rosy.

God, I'm on fire this morning. Not only have I put her in this situation, now I'm afraid she feels like she's going to have to make a decision. Fuck knows I can't.

"Callie, I'm sorry, I—"

"Now, hold on." Beck interrupts. "First, might I say I'm rather impressed. All night stamina." Beck lightly claps.

"For fuck's sake," Callie mutters.

"Second, you assholes are not about to break up in front of me. I'm a fucking romantic!"

I raise an eyebrow. "You? Really?"

Beck shrugs. "For other people. I'm happy where I'm at, but damn it, now that I know about this...I fucking ship it."

What the actual fuck is happening right now?

Beck looks at Callie and takes a step toward her. "I mean, don't get me wrong, I'm a little heartbroken I wasn't even considered, Callie Bear. I mean, just think about—"

"Okay." I step in between them. "That's enough. Was the whole 'my girlfriend' part not clear?"

Callie chuckles and wraps her arms around my waist. "Relax. Beck, you look like you could be my brother, it was never on the table for me."

Putting my arm around her, I kiss her head with a laugh while Beck digests that rejection.

"Okay, I'm just going to push through that." Beck shakes his head. "My original point is that all of the other instances were issues because it always led to huge drama. If you can show that it won't be a problem for you two, then maybe, he'll let it go."

"But we still run the risk of both of us losing our jobs, right?" Callie whispers.

"Yeah, if you want to look at it that way." Beck shrugs. "Or you could look at it as a way to make it work."

Callie looks up at me with the question I know she's afraid to ask.

"We'll make it work." I kiss her forehead.

"Hey! Did you guys get a Polaroid camera?" Beck asks, pointing at the nightstand where not only the camera is, but the *pictures* are too.

"Okay, time to go." Pulling him by his shirt again, I yank him to the door.

"Seriously? Dirty Polaroids?" Beck has this coat-hanger smile on his face. "Fuck, you guys, mad respect."

And with that I push him out into the hallway and swing the door shut.

Turning back, Callie's already got her arms crossed. She's got to be pissed—I'm pissed at me. "Alright, let me have it."

But she doesn't yell or get upset, she laughs. Her arms come uncrossed and she laughs. "I would have bet so much money that I was going to get us busted first."

I pull her chuckling butt to me by the belt on her robe. "You're not mad?"

"I was a little bit when I woke up to Beck's laugh. But it was good to at least get an idea of what we're working with, and it was just Beck. I don't think he'll tell anyone." She giggles some more, but then wraps her arms around my shoulders. "Really, you just answered my door? I was lying right next to you. If I fucked your brains out last night Anderson, it's okay, you can admit it."

"Woman." I pick her up and toss her back on the bed. Crawling on top of her, she wraps her legs around my waist.

"You didn't even hear the knocking. I fucked the consciousness out of you."

Callie hums with a smirk on her pretty lips. "Are the pictures as hot as I remember?"

I reach over to the nightstand and hand the stack to her. "Why don't you look through them?" I slide down her body and pull the knot of her robe loose. "And please describe them to me in heavy detail."

"Hmm, and where are you going?" Callie's voice might sound coy but the little minx moves her legs, spreading them for me already.

"I'm going to have my breakfast." I kiss down to her hip before both of our alarms go off. Both of us groan and curse at the same time.

"I'm going to kill Beck. Fucker waisted valuable time this morning," I mutter after we both turn off our alarms.

Callie laughs before rolling off the bed. "You answered the door, Will! The one time I have a locked door and you answer it!"

"We might not have a ton of time, but I'll still bend your smart mouth over."

Callie leans over and places the dirty Polaroids on my chest. "You love my smart mouth. Now I have to get ready to go take pictures of you all day, but, unfortunately, they won't be as hot as these."

Chapter 33
Callie

"So how was your day off?" Adam asks the moment I slide into the back of the car he had waiting for us.

"It was..." *Mind blowing. Life altering.* "Great. It was nice to have a day off before games start."

It took quite the amount of self-restraint to not pull Will back into my hotel room the moment his foot stepped out of the door. The interruption this morning might not have been a part of our plan, but there is now a bright side—we have a little hope.

At first, when I heard Beck at the door, I assumed the worst and expected Will would want us to call it quits. But when he agreed that we'd make it work, I was beyond relieved. All the unknowns are still really daunting when I think about them too much, but Will and I can keep it professional. We can stay out of drama. We have to.

After buckling and getting settled I realize that Adam's in his uniform. "Hey, I haven't gotten to see the uniforms in person yet! These are nice!"

I looked at a million pictures with Shannon, and I hate to

say it, but she picked out a good jersey. It's white with royal blue pinstripes. "Blues" is written across the front, and on their hats have the bird logo on the side.

Adam looks down at the jersey. "Yeah, I figured I'd just put it on now. I brought some clothes for a workout after, if I have time. So, you may have to get a ride back with one of the other players if that's okay?"

"Oh yeah." *Cool, calm, and collected, Callie.* "I don't mind."

"I would ask Will, but when I asked if he needed a ride this morning, he said he was taking his bike. The guy bought a brand new motorcycle, out of nowhere."

It's a little odd to me that Adam's so shocked by this. I mean, yeah, I guess it was a little extravagant, but they are million dollar athletes.

"He's an adult, Adam. I think he knows how to handle his finances."

"I know he does. What I'm saying is it's just out of character for him. I mean, he bought that one when he first signed with the Mavs, but he's never mentioned buying another. He's going to have to get it transferred back to Boston. Just seems like such a hassle."

"It's his life." I shrug, trying to be nonchalant about it.

I can see why Adam thinks it's odd behavior for Will. I thought that at the beginning of our date as well. But the more I thought about it, the more it made sense. He told me in Seattle he was basically just surviving, but since this trade, I think he's actually living...and I'm a part of that. That thought sends butterflies fluttering in my stomach and I can't help but think about what it could be like for us if this does actually work out like we hope.

Once Adam and I get to the stadium where we'll be

taking our headshots and team pictures at, I barely make it in the front door before my phone rings. I don't even have to look to see who it is. It's the same person who's already called me four times since my alarm went off.

"Ugh, go ahead without me, Adam. I have to take this." Adam nods and when he walks off I plaster on a fake-ass smile because it forces my voice to not come off so snarky. "Hi, Shannon."

"Callie, are you at the stadium yet?" Shannon snaps with her usual accusatory tone.

"I'm walking in now." I check my watch. I'm here ten minutes earlier than the time written on my schedule.

"Oh," Shannon mumbles. "Well, I'm running behind. Just stall the shoot until I get there."

My fake smile tactic is really struggling right now. For years I've used it to hide my true emotions, but Shannon's testing my patience.

"Why do I need to stall the shoot?" I know for a fact that her name is not on my list of headshots I need today, nor do I need her hovering. At this point I'm not even sure what she does during the day other than try to micromanage me.

"I think I should be there. I have the list of pictures we need."

My eye has to be twitching right now.

I hear the front door open behind me and Olsson strolls in with a smile.

"As do I," I reply with the least amount of sarcasm I can manage. "But I'm here now, I'll let Olsson know you'll be here when you can."

It might be a little rude, but I hang up before she can retort. All she was going to do was argue with me. And despite what she thinks, she's not my boss.

"Good morning, Callie. You ready for today?"

"Good morning," I chime back to my actual boss. "I am. I have the full lineup printed out, so we should be able to knock pictures out pretty quickly."

"Sounds great. I don't know how we lucked out, but we're the only team at this stadium today. A lot of teams decided to do this yesterday, I guess. But after headshots, I was thinking of engaging in some friendly competition with the players and having a scrimmage. Think you can stay and get some pictures of that too?"

Can I? I've mostly been taking pictures of them at the training facility or staged branding photos. I have been dying to get some game-time pictures, and I know an opportunity when I see one.

"Can I be slightly reckless and be out on the field?"

Olsson raises an eyebrow at my request. I'm sure he's picturing every liability now. My camera getting hit. Me getting hit. Medical bills and scrambling for a new photographer.

"Here me out. Every game from here on out I'll have to be in my own little space, or somewhere out in the crowd. But since this isn't an actual game, I could move around and get some different angles."

Olsson sighs and pinches the bridge of his nose while he thinks. "Okay, you're right. Just, please, don't hurt yourself."

I just smile back to that because I make no promises. "Oh, and Shannon said she should be here soon," I add.

"Here? She's not supposed to be here today. She said she was working from the hotel."

She what? Oh, that bitch. Then what was she calling me for?

Okay, deep breath. We're drama free, right?

"Oh, I don't know. Maybe she just wanted to get some fresh air or something."

"Well, if she's getting out I've got some errands she could run. I'll give her a call and you can start with the players first."

"Will do."

I walk out to the field where some of the guys are crowded around. I scan for Will, but I don't see him yet. I try not to let worry take over my brain, but it's hard. Seeing him brings me a little bit of peace when things feel like they could get overwhelming.

He's probably in the locker room changing. Man, I really want to see him in his new uniform. It's been entirely too long since I've seen him in baseball pants. Goodness, probably since they won the World Series back in Seattle. But now, I don't have to feel guilty about appreciating his ass in God's gift to women—baseball pants. I just have to be secretive about it.

"Hey, Callie Bear," Beck says as he comes up behind me and hangs his arm around my shoulder. "How was your morning?"

I roll my eyes. I do trust Beck to keep our secret, but I knew the moment he said he was a romantic that he was about to be up in our business any chance he could get.

"It was fine, how was your morning?"

"Only fine? Anderson not fulfilling you already?" Beck whispers, then slows us down to a stop before we make it over to the group on the field. Taking his arm off my shoulder he turns to me. "Listen, I'm really sorry about this morning. I didn't mean to—"

I chuckle. "Beck, you're fine. It wasn't your fault."

"I know, it was your idiot boyfriend's. But still, I saw the worry in your eyes, Cals. I promise your secret is safe with me."

"Thank you, I appreciate that."

"But, I do have to say one thing. I gotta put it out there."

I can tell by the mischievous smirk on Beck's face that this is not at all about to be serious.

"If this does blow up in y'all's face, I'm lobbying for you to keep your job. Will can manage just fine, and I know he'll agree with me." Beck puts his hands on my shoulders. "So, no matter what happens, I got your back, okay?"

Well, I was wrong. "Damn it, Beck, don't make me cry on a baseball field right now."

Beck starts to laugh, but it's cut off.

"Daines, hands off," Will barks as he walks up beside us. "You're going to make this fucking hard on me, aren't you?"

"Oh yeah." Beck winks at me then removes his hands before turning to Will. "That's a non-negotiable, but you can relax since apparently Callie has doomed me in the brother-zone. Friendzone is clearly escapable, but a sibling label? I'll never recover from that."

I snort a laugh. "I said you look like my brother, not that you are my brother."

"Eh, I'll take the role anyway." Beck shrugs before walking off to the group ahead, leaving Will and I alone for a moment.

"Am I crying? Will you make fun of me if I start?"

"Damn fucker. Just tell me my chances of keeping you if he dyes his hair."

I roll my eyes. He thinks after last night some sweet words and box dye would sway me? Magic eight ball says "not likely."

"I'm not going anywhere, Will." I give him a small smile

before walking away to get started, but I don't make it very far before I'm interrupted again.

"Callie!" Miles shouts as he races toward me on the field. "Can I help you take pictures again today?"

I chuckle as he bounces up and down in front of me with such vigor. Dex comes up behind him and places his hands softly on his shoulders.

"Before she even answers, what are we not going to do if she says no?"

Miles looks up at his dad with such confusion on his little face. "She's not going to say no."

Suddenly, I see the same look I've seen on Wyla's face a million times—the *I won't be a smart ass back to my child* look, and it's usually accompanied with a deep breath.

When Dex exhales, I cut in. "He's really fine, I promise."

"See!" Miles yells.

Poor Dex's shoulders slump. "Callie, I'm serious, you don't have to—"

"I know I don't. And if it helps..." I reach into my bag and pull out my shot list. "I put him to work. Don't I, Miles? We're hard workers, aren't we?"

"Yeah!" Miles cheers as he takes the paper from my hands.

I chuckle. Miles is great, and this is really what I like when it comes to kids—fun for a few hours then I get to send them back to their parents. Growing up, I had always thought I wanted them, but now my cool aunt status feels like the right fit for me right now.

Dex still hovers hesitantly, but I don't take it personal. I'm not fully versed on the extent of what happened, but according to Shannon, Miles's mom got a job at a major law firm, then left Dex and decided she only wanted to see Miles one weekend out of the month. My heart hurts for the kid but from what I've seen, Dex gives him his all. I know he's been worried about how everyone would respond to having a five-year-old so present during the season, but so far, everyone has loved having Miles around.

I squat down in front of Miles and point at the list of players and their numbers. "Okay, bud. We've got a lot of pictures to take, and I need your help getting everyone in order. Think you can help me keep 'em in line?"

Miles nods eagerly. "You got it!"

I take a quick glance down the list and note that I won't need Dex for several shots. "But first, tell your dad it's not even close to his turn so he can go work without worrying right now."

"Hit the road, Dad," Miles snaps, and then snickers. "I've got work to do!"

And, boy, did he take his job seriously. I was allotted three hours to get every player, every coach, and team pictures done. But with my little drill sergeant of an assistant, we got it done in two.

Apparently, the key to keeping grown men in order is to have a five-year-old yell at them. Miles also wasn't afraid to throw some threats around. I heard him tell many players that he would have me draw mustaches and black out some of their teeth in their photos if they didn't listen.

With the team all set up for the final picture I look down at Miles. He's looking at the guys so proud. "Psst, hey, Miles."

He jerks his head up to me. "Yeah?"

"Do you want to take one with everybody?"

"Can I really?" Miles squeals.

With a chuckle I turn back to the players. "Okay, two

more. Ready?" I click the last one I need and now for the one I want. "Okay, Miles, go where you want to stand."

As he makes his way up with a little strut in his step, all of the guys start cheering his name. With a massive smile on his face, Miles runs next to his dad, and Dex pulls him onto his shoulders.

"Alright, Miles, you ready?" I yell, and when he gives me a thumbs up, I take the last picture. "Okay, Mr. Olsson, I'm all good here."

I know I need to get resituated for the scrimmage, so I head back to my bag so I can start reorganizing my things and changing my lenses. But before I can put anything away, Dex comes over with giggling Miles still on his shoulders. "Hey, Callie. I hate to ask, but could I possibly get one more picture?"

"Ah, of course!"

I move Dex over to the side so the stadium is in the background as opposed to all the players. "Ready, one, two, three."

It was around two that Miles threw his hands up with peace signs and the biggest smile I've ever seen. Goodness, melt my heart into a million pieces.

I pull the picture back up and step up to show Dex. "I must say, the best picture of the day."

Dex smiles at the photo then turns his head up to his son. "What do you think?"

"The best picture ever!" Miles cheers. "Callie always takes the best pictures."

"Miles, you flatter me," I joke as Dex places him back on the ground. I kneel next to him. "Thank you for helping me today. And listen, you did a really great job, but I'm about to take some pictures on the field and I need you to do me the biggest favor ever."

Miles bounces up and down at the excitement, and I hate to burst his bubble, but I know I can't risk him getting hurt.

"I'm going to need you to stay in the dugout with your dad, okay?"

"Oh," Miles pouts. His lip hangs so low I fear he may trip on it.

"Hey, I promise there will be so many more times that you can help me, but this time I think your dad might actually need your help. Think you can keep the players in the dugout in order?"

Miles nods his head quickly. "I can do it."

"That's my boy." I hold out my hand for a high five and he smacks it as hard as he can manage then bolts down the field.

I chuckle as I stand back up. "I'll send that picture to you first thing, Dex."

"Thank you, Callie. I'm not exactly sure what I'm going to do when he starts kindergarten this fall, but for now, you've been a huge help."

"Eh, I do what I can," I say with a smile. It feels good being appreciated here and the weird thing is, I didn't feel overwhelmed or anxious at all today. I was in charge the whole morning, and yeah, some encouraging looks from Will were nice boosts, but I felt confident in my abilities today.

"Callie!" Olsson calls from where he's standing in front of the team, waving me over.

Damn it, I should have knocked on wood.

When I walk up, Olsson turns back to the team. "While I want this to be an actual scrimmage, I'm going to have

Callie out on the field getting some action shots." Olsson takes a huge sigh. "If anyone hurts my photographer, I will send your asses so far back into the minors, you'll be a rookie all over again. Understood?"

Why is everyone on this team trying to get me to cry happy tears?

Chapter 34
Will

Scrimmages are usually fun for me. There's friendly competition, no major stakes, and we just get to play. But this whole game I've been a nervous wreck.

Why the fuck Olsson told Callie she could be out here taking pictures is beyond me, but having her out here is about to give me a freaking aneurysm. I've never really been an anxious person and in reality, if this was anyone else, I wouldn't bat an eye. But it's my girl and if any of these fuckers do something stupid and get her hurt I'll lose my shit.

Adam is on the opposite team and he's up to bat. Callie comes to stand behind me.

"Blaze, you're going to give me a heart attack. What are you doing?"

"I want to get some good pictures of your butt in these pants," she whispers.

I flash her a quick *not funny* look. I can manage when she stays off to the sides, but directly behind me—

Callie sighs. "I have an idea and it will look really cool.

So if you'd please let my brother hit one of your pitches, I'd greatly appreciate it."

"Callie—"

"Pitch the damn ball, Anderson," Adam yells.

Well, I was going to do what Callie asked but one strike will be okay. Glancing back at my girl, I nod then throw my knuckleball.

I hear the clicks on her camera then the beautiful sound of the ball hitting my catcher's glove.

"Will!" Callie whisper-shouts behind me. "I said I need him to hit it."

"Callie, I'm going to need those pictures to hold over his head forever," I say as I get the ball back then turn to her. "I'll ask nicely if I have to."

Callie raises her camera to her face to cover her oncoming blush. "Get me my photo, Will, and we'll see."

So, I do. Callie beams the whole scrimmage. Every time she looks at the photo she successfully gets, she smiles. And if there's time, she'll show the player the picture she got. There's not an ounce of jealousy that runs through me either when the guys then make a fuss over what she showed them. Back in Seattle she never even spoke to the team, but here, she is the team. It makes me happy to know she feels safe here.

There was only one close call toward the end of the scrimmage at first base when a rookie let a ball get past him. Beck was trying hard to annoy me by standing so close to Callie, so luckily he was there and caught it before it hit her.

Back in the locker room I change out of my uniform and back into my riding leathers. Adam mentioned wanting to go on another run, but I told him to count me out. When I pull out my phone to text Callie, messages from my sisters await.

When Will met Callie.

LUCIE

How's Florida? More importantly, how are things with Callie in Florida?

REAGAN

At this point if you haven't told her how you feel I don't know if you deserve her.

You're right, I probably don't.

LUCIE

Well yeah, but what does that mean? Like you don't deserve her because you've done nothing, or you don't deserve her because you have done something?

REAGAN

Luce, I think you're too invested in this.

LUCIE

I'm a first grade teacher. I've seen my students be more upfront about their emotions than our twenty-eight-year-old brother.

Will has left the group chat.

"Hey, Will!" Miles yells at me from down the hall.

"Hey, bud. What's up?" I ask as he races to me.

"I'm looking for Callie. Have you seen her?"

Me and you both.

I kneel in front of him. "Well, you've found the perfect person to help you look. Let me help, I'm sure we'll find her."

Walking back to the front, I shoot Callie a quick text

asking where she is, but I don't want to spoil the fun for Miles. I'm pretty sure he's now turned this into a scavenger hunt, and Callie's the treasure.

"Maybe she's in here," Miles says as he tries to open a locked janitor's closet. I chuckle as he shrugs when the door won't open and we're off to the next door. "Did you know that I'm going to marry Callie one day?"

"Oh, really?" Damn, little man's coming after my girl. "Isn't she a little old for you, bud?"

Miles rolls his eyes. "That's what my dad said, but that's silly because I'll grow up one day and then I'll marry Callie."

"What if she married someone else by then?" The question kind of tumbles out of me before realizing it might crush this kid's dream.

At the beginning of all of this between us, I told Callie I wasn't sure where things would go, and I guess part of that is still true. I don't know what will happen, neither of us do, but it's getting harder and harder to picture my life without her in it.

Miles hums while he thinks about my question. "I don't think she will because she always says that I'm the best helper. That means she likes me too."

"That makes sense." I laugh. Even though Miles is staking his claim on my girl, I'm not about to ruin his first crush by telling him I might marry her first.

"Hey, you two. Were you looking for me?" Callie says, walking up to us.

Miles practically jumps toward her. "Yes! I wanted to talk to you before you left."

Callie flashes me a smile before going back to Miles. "Well, you found me. What do you want to talk about?"

Miles starts with the first thought that pops in his head.

I'd cut in with what he told me earlier but that might mess up his game. Don't want the guy to seem too eager and fuck up his chances.

For now.

I stand by watching them intently. I love how into the conversation she is. It doesn't matter that he's five, Callie's giving him just as much attention as everyone else. And she looks so happy to be talking to him. I hadn't ever really thought about kids before. But here I am, picturing all sorts of ways my life could turn out.

Kids with Callie. No kids with Callie. Making a home in Boston. Moving to another state. The traveling. The experiences. All of the options.

After a few minutes Dex yells to Miles that it's time to go back to the hotel. He protests for a second, but Callie kneels and gives him a goodbye hug and the kid's back on cloud nine again.

As he races down the hall, I hold out my hand to help Callie stand up. Looking around I see we're alone in the hallway.

"Hey, I have a question for ya."

Callie narrows her eyebrows with a quirked smile. "Okay?"

Now that I'm actually asking the question, I realize how fucking heavy it is. Swallowing down my doubt I push through. "Kids"—I clear my throat—"do you want them?"

Callie's face falls a bit as she tugs at the sleeves of her sweatshirt. "Oh, I, um...I do love kids, but I don't know. Lately I've liked the idea of not having them." Callie shakes her head, clearly rattled by my question. "I guess that sounds a little contradicting. I mean—"

"Hey, Callie." I cut her off and take her hand. "Whatever

you want, is what you want. There's no pressure, it was just a thought that came to my head. But if it helps, I think I'd be a killer uncle."

Callie smiles, and I pull her in with a quick kiss on her forehead. I don't care about my stakes anymore. Whatever I have to do to keep her and have her stay at this job she loves, I'm going to do it.

Chapter 35
Callie

I had always known Adam's game schedule was demanding, but nothing could have prepared me for it being my schedule also. When I lived with him in Seattle, I only went to the home games, and never Spring Training.

We've had games every day for a month—some with double headers. Then, right after that we all hopped on our chartered plane and flew to Texas for a week to play the Drakes.

We finally got back to Boston late last night and it's so good to be back at my apartment. I'm not sure what's better: being in my own bed with all my stuff, or the fact that, the moment Adam closed his door, Will abandoned his place to come get naked in mine.

"Callie, we need to get up." Will speaks softly next to me as he lightly runs his fingers up and down my back.

I'm not sure what time it is, but when Will tried to get up earlier, I pulled him back down to sleep with me longer.

"No," I grumble with my eyes still closed. "I want to sleep in so late that it's embarrassing to talk about."

Will chuckles. "What if I told you I had Alex deliver some tea to my place and they are sitting in front of my door right now getting cold?"

That gets me to open my eyes as I look up at him. "Which one did you get me?"

"Well, you'll never know unless you let me get up."

"Ugh, fine." Rolling off the bed, I throw on a pair of leggings to go with Will's shirt that I slept in. "I suppose I can get up and let my boyfriend make me breakfast shirtless while I sip my tea."

"Whoa, now, that's not what I said." Will pulls up his gray sweats and he's like a damn wet dream.

I walk over to him and pop a kiss to his cheek then run my hand down his chest and abs. "It's what I heard."

Walking into my kitchen, I smile because it feels so good to finally be home. We have home games for a whole week and I'm so happy I could cry. Keeping up this secret relationship hasn't exactly been the easiest. It's been impossible to find alone time to be together, except for when we sneak over to each other's hotel room for the night. I do love sleeping next to him, but I want to be able to go on dates more. Show affection in public. You know, be that obnoxious couple people make fun of.

I know I told myself I would walk away when it felt too hard or interfered with my job, but I think it's reversed on me. As much as I do love this job and want to keep it—I want to keep Will more.

We've been nothing but professional this past month, and Olsson has given us both high praises individually. Maybe it's time we test Beck's theory.

Walking past my island, I turn to Will. "Why don't I grab the tea and you start breakfast. There should be some groceries in the fridge. Adam had me place an order with his guy to get some food delivered yesterday before we got back."

"Was he able to get your stuff delivered because you never lock your door?"

"Okay, one, I resent that. And two, Adam has a spare key for emergencies so that's how."

"Mm-hmm." Will gives my ass a little smack.

I roll my eyes as I make my way to my door. "Hey, what do you know, it's locked. See I remember—"

"I locked it last night, Blaze. Nice try."

Damn it. I think he's right. I don't exactly remember what happened after I opened my door and immediately thought about being in my own bed.

I give Will a pointed look before I open my door and, much to my surprise, find Lucie and Reagan standing in the hall.

"Hi, Callie!" Lucie cheers.

Reagan holds out the tray of tea and I take it, unsure how to respond. "This was in front of Will's door, but we've been knocking for a bit and then it dawned on us that he might finally be hooking up with the neighbor he's been obsessed with for months."

"I...um..."

"For fuck's sake," Will mutters, coming up behind me. "What are you guys doing here?"

"Please don't even start, Will. We saw this coming from a mile away," Reagan snarks.

"We had a group chat pressuring him to actually do something about it." Lucie smiles.

"A group chat I left repeatedly," Will huffs.

Reagan rolls her eyes and leans on my door frame.

"Which did not help your case by the way. Denial is usually stage one."

I chuckle under my breath and Will nudges me. "Watch it."

I step back into him with a smile on my face. I don't hate at all that his sisters are here. I liked them before any of this even got started. I'm not going to miss my shot at friendship.

"Will was just about to make me some breakfast, do you want to come in?"

Reagan and Lucie don't waste a second before coming in and taking a seat on the island barstools.

Will leans down, wrapping his arms around my waist, and whispers in my ear, "Hey, I need my shirt back."

"Hmm, so would it be rude for me to kick them out now?" I laugh before pushing off his chest. "I'll be right back."

After changing into one of my oversized cream sweaters, I walk back into the kitchen and toss Will his shirt.

"We didn't mean to barge in on your romantic morning, but it seems *someone* has been leaving important details out of the group chat." Reagan gives a pointed look to Will.

"I left that group, remember?" Will replies after pulling his shirt on.

Lucie rolls her eyes. "I remember. A group chat with a name I very creatively named, that you didn't appreciate at all. But since you're together now, I guess I should change it." Lucie whips out her phone and taps on her screen. "Callie, give me your number. I'll add you and maybe that will make Will stop leaving."

Will closes the fridge with a sarcastic laugh. "Not likely."

"Hey, do you not want to talk to me?"

Will sets down the milk and eggs on the counter then

lifts my chin. "You, always. Them, sometimes. That's what direct messages are for."

Will winks before letting go of my face and grabbing a mixing bowl from the cabinet. "And before we get too far off topic, what are you two doing here anyway?"

Reagan scoffs dramatically. "Can we not come visit our dear brother who we haven't seen in over a month? I mean, the audacity to not want—"

"Reagan," Will snaps.

"Okay, fine. We wanted to have a girl's day and while we were going to stop by your place to say hi, we wanted to see if Callie wanted to come with us."

"Me?" My voice sounds oddly high, but hell, who cares?

"You." Lucie beams. "Full disclosure if our brother hadn't told you how he felt yet, we were going to use this as a secret ploy to get you two together."

"What the hell, guys?" Will stops what he's doing and huffs. "What were you planning exactly?"

"Nothing weird!" Reagan exclaims. "Lucie's making it sounds more like this extravagant plan. We were just going to take her out, talk you up, and you know, essentially lie to her about how great you are."

I can't help my laugh as Will gives his sisters the most dumbfounded look. "I don't know how to respond to that. You get the first burned pancake."

"I don't want the burned one. What I said was nice!"

Will starts to mix the batter and shakes his head. "Half of it was nice, which is why you can get the first one, but then you added the lying part, therefore you get the burned one."

I chuckle. "Why does the first one have to be burned?"

"He always burns the first one," Reagan and Lucie say at the exact same time.

"Ah, jinx!" Lucie cheers.

Will simply rolls his eyes, then gives me a small kiss before turning to the stove to burn his first pancake.

"Even though our plan is no longer needed as you two are clearly together..." Lucie beams. "We'd still love for you to come with us."

Be cool, Callie.

"Yeah, I'd love to."

With that my phone dings on the counter with a message.

When Will Finally Dates Callie.

LUCIE

I think I'll update this name often! This is Lucie by the way.

Once we finish our pancakes, I quickly change and freshen up my hair and makeup for us to go out. As I spritz on a little bit of perfume there's a knock on my bathroom door. Will leans against the frame in such an effortlessly sexy way.

"Hey, you about ready to go? Adam just messaged asking if I wanted to go work out, so I thought I might go ahead and let you have your day."

"Yeah, I'm ready," I say, putting down my bottle. Then the guilt hits me as I realize what I've done. I probably should have asked Will if this was okay, now that I think about it. This is our first day off in a while, he might have wanted to spend it together. I've been dying for quality time, and yet I just threw it out the window.

"It's probably a little too late to be asking this, but is it okay if I go with your sisters today?"

Will raises an eyebrow with a frown. "Yeah, of course. Why? Do you not want to go? I can talk to—"

"No, no, I want to go. We just haven't had a day off in a while. I just kind of robbed us of spending it together."

Will chuckles softly then pulls me to him by my belt loop. "Callie, I would have loved to have spent today with you, but"—Will reaches into his sweats pocket then holds up one of his cards from his wallet—"if you don't take my card and spend a shit ton of money on yourself today, then we're going to have a problem."

Oh, man, if that's not one of the sexiest things to say to a girl then I don't know what is.

I take the card with a soft smile. "Thank you, I promise I won't go too crazy."

"Oh, you won't be able to because that's the card that my delivery boy check comes to."

"I make one joke!" I laugh, and Will pulls me into his arms kissing my neck playfully, only making me giggle more. "Okay, okay, that's enough."

Will stops the kisses but doesn't let me go from his hold. "Have fun today, and don't let my sisters talk you into leaving me."

"Will, you just handed me your card and said go spend a lot of money...I don't think there's anything they could say to make me do that."

Will's eyes go wide with an amused smile. "Oh, golddigger? I didn't expect—"

Grabbing his face, I shut up his little joke with my lips on his. Will's hands thread through my hair as he turns me against the door frame, deepening our kiss.

"Hey, just so you guys don't forget, Lucie and I are still here!" Reagan yells.

Will stops our kiss but doesn't let go of me yet. He turns his head back toward the living room, so he's not yelling in my face. "Let me get this straight. You show up uninvited, complain about my breakfast, then plan to take my girlfriend away for the day, and now this? Beggars can't be choosers."

"They are when they're sisters!" Lucie yells back.

One realization I've had today is that I've been robbed. Robbed of having a sister. Do I love Adam? Yes, absolutely. And yeah, I'm glad I don't have another sibling for my parents to abuse, but I wish I had a sister.

Reagan and Lucie are by far the most polar opposite people I have ever met, but I think that's what makes their dynamic so great. It's also been nice to be out with girls that I feel like I can let go with. The only girl I've ever had that with is Wyla, and I was worried I might not ever have it again.

For our last stop of the day we go to the nail salon Lucie loves for some mani-pedis.

"I went ahead and made you an appointment, Callie, because I kind of assumed we were going to kidnap you either way," Lucie says as we sit in the big chairs. "Hope this is okay."

"Are you kidding? This is perfect. Don't get me wrong, I love my job, but I've been drowning in testosterone. I need this."

I rest my head back on my chair, shutting my eyes briefly before I hear, "Callie?"

Looking up, I find my fellow weirdly-named girl. "Ah, Jensen! Hi," I cheer.

"Oh, hey Callie!" Jensen waves, walking over to us.

When we met at the restaurant she was wearing a long-sleeved button-up, but as she takes her jacket off I see both her arms are full of tattoos.

Jensen smiles and takes the open seat next to me. "One thing I refuse to give up is a mani-pedi. Self-care, and all that."

"Heck yeah, I like you," Lucie says leaning over to wave at Jensen. "Hi, I'm Lucie and this is my sister Reagan."

Reagan leans over next and adds, "We're Callie's boyfriend's sisters."

"Oh?" Jensen looks at me with her eyebrows pulled together with a silent question.

"New guy." I laugh. "Not the rando from the bar! Jensen, are you kidding? That man was a nightmare."

Jensen relaxes in her chair. 'Thank God, I was afraid I wasn't going to be able to be your friend if you went back to that loser after I helped you escape him."

"I'm sorry, escaped?" Reagan asks. "We're so going to need this story! Is this the date you went on before Will?"

"He told you I went on a date?"

Lucie nods. "Yeah, he left the group chat after I told him that Harry and Sally dated people before they got together."

Jensen chuckles next to us. "Oh, like from the romcom?"

"Yes, I love a good romcom!" Lucie beams. "But you know Will never told us what happened that night."

Reagan leans back up in her chair. "Callie, we're going to

need the full rundown here. Leave out any mentions of bedroom times with our brother but otherwise spare no detail."

Jensen leans up next but grabs the attention of one of the workers. "Hi, we're going to need some wine over here."

"Oh, yes we are." I laugh. "I'm glad we're going to be here for a minute because I promise you, I couldn't tell a short story short if I ever tried, so keep up. I'm going to ramble."

Recapping everything that happened from the post-birthday miscommunication, to the not-a-date date, to the speech—which Lucie was really proud of Will for—to not being able to actually date, to now. I leave out the bedroom details and the downfall with my ex, but otherwise they are all caught up. It only took the whole damn appointment for me to get through it.

"Okay, hold up." Reagan waves her now freshly manicured hand around across from me at the drying table. "So, you're telling me that we've been hanging out all day and you didn't tell us that you're not actually allowed to date our brother?"

I wince a bit at her tone. "I'm sorry, I was just really enjoying some girl time, and with you guys I don't have to keep it a secret, so it was nice to just not have to think about it."

"No, that's totally fair," Reagan says. "I'm just shocked. Listen, if you need someone to tell your boss that's a stupid rule, then hi, use me!"

"Me too," Lucie adds.

"Count me for the trio," Jensen says as she blows on her nails.

"Believe me, I've thought about it myself. And Will

offered the same thing. I find it really sweet that you all had the same reaction."

Lucie snorts a laugh. "Well, that's not really that shocking considering he's totally in love with you."

Butterflies flutter in my stomach immediately. I want nothing more than to have her expand on that thought, but my phone starts to ring with the man in question's name on my screen.

"Hey," I answer, putting him on speaker so I can keep my nails under the light. "Everyone can hear you so keep that in mind."

"Okay, Callie. Thanks for the heads up." Will laughs. "So, fair warning for you, you're about to get a text from Adam. A couple of the guys are wanting to go to the bar tonight, same one we went to the first night after we got here. It'll be pretty chill if you guys want to come. If not that's fine, but my sisters are invited as long as they keep their fucking mouths shut."

"Hey, we've been team Callie and Will from the start. We're not going to be the fuck-ups," Reagan snarks.

"And isn't he the one who got y'all busted with the team-mate?" Jensen backs up Reagan.

"Okay, I'm not sure who that was, or how they know about that," he says pointedly, "but that was a genuine mistake. Anyway, I've got to go to Beck's. A couple of the guys are meeting over there to play PlayStation first, but I'll see you tonight?"

Glancing at the girls, Reagan and Lucie nod first, but then I look at Jensen and she points back at herself. "Wait, me too?"

Reagan nudges her with her elbow. "Yes, you too, dummy."

"Yeah, we'll be there. Talk to you later."

"Okay, see you soon."

The call clicks off, and my phone immediately buzzes with a text that I'm sure just came from my brother.

Lucie pulls out her nails and carefully checks them to make sure they are completely dry. "Do we have time to go back by your place, Callie? I'd love to change into that pink dress I bought today. Since, ya know, hot baseball players will be there."

Clicking on Adam's message I read it through. "Oh yeah, he said they'd head there around seven, so we have plenty of time. Oh, and Jensen if you don't want to come you don't have to. I just—"

"Eh, it could be fun." Jensen clicks her nails on the table. "I'm all dry. If you don't mind, can you send me the name of the bar and I'll meet you there?"

"Yeah, no problem." I shoot the text to her real quick then remind her. "Wear something sexy. There will be hot baseball players—just one of them is secretly taken."

Chapter 36
Will

Going out wasn't exactly at the top of my list of things to do tonight, but when the guys said it would be lowkey and Callie agreed to come along, I figured it couldn't be that bad. That was until Callie strolled into the bar wearing a sexy black, long sleeve dress that fit her too damn well, and boots that go all the way to her thighs.

I've been able to keep my composure in public for months. I've wanted to lose my cool on some of the guys who hit on her before, but I trust her and I'm always close by in case the assholes don't get the hint.

But this is pure fucking torture. I'm going to lose my mind. I can't touch her. I can't make every fucker in here so insanely jealous by having her on my arm. I clench my fist to keep the tension at bay.

"Hey, guys," Callie greets the table. "I brought Reagan and Lucie, who are Will's sisters. And this is Jensen, she's a new friend of mine who works at the wine bar around the corner."

I'm not sure who everyone is looking at—and if it's one of

my sisters, I don't want to fucking know—but I swear the whole group does a collective gulp.

When none of us say anything, Callie tilts her head. "Guys?"

"Right." Adam shakes out of his trance first. *Again, I don't want to know who.* "I'm Callie's brother, Adam. Jensen, this is Will. Then we got Beck and Tripp. We should have enough seats, but I'd recommend going up to the bar first if you want a drink."

Callie looks back to my sisters and Jensen. "Okay, we'll be back."

When they get far enough away Beck clears his throat. "Um, as someone who is not related to any of them, I feel it's safest for me to say, *holy fuck.*"

"I second that statement. I mean, did you see—" Tripp starts, but I cut him off.

"I'm going to go ahead and stop you. If it's about either of our sisters, keep it to your fucking self." The statement comes off as concern for Adam, but that's just my cover. I will not do well if he starts talking about my Callie.

"Yeah, I think it's best we all just move on from that moment completely," Adam adds.

Not able to help myself I look toward the bar seeing Callie in the little dress again. *Fuck me.* Her eyes find me and she winks before turning her attention back to the bar.

"Agreed," I grunt, coming back to reality. "Let's talk about literally anything else."

Our table goes silent again with this awkward tension filling the air.

"So..." Beck starts, but nothing follows it, so he just starts picking at the label on his beer.

The silence continues and it's borderline uncomfortable.

Tripp takes a drink of his beer then sighs. "Can we just talk about—"

In unison, Adam, Beck, and I all cut him off with a resounding, "No."

We remain in our awkward silence for what feels like several minutes until the girls finally come back. Callie takes the seat in between me and Adam. My sisters take the end seats and Jensen across from Callie in the middle of Beck and Tripp.

"So, Beck, are we rematching on pool tonight?" Callie asks.

Beck finishes off his beer with a sigh. "Oh, hell yeah. Let's make it interesting, though."

"Oh?" Callie shuffles in her chair and crosses her legs.

I know it's risky, but her leg is pretty hidden under the table, and I'll seek out any contact I can get. Leaning up, I rest my hand on her knee and a slight smile comes to her face.

"How do you feel about teams, Callie Bear?" Beck sits back in his chair. "Are you as strong when you're not playing one-on-one?"

Callie rolls her eyes. "I'm pretty strong, I don't mind carrying the weight. I'll still kick your ass."

I squeeze her leg because if anyone is going to be her partner it's me. And somehow, I'm sure Beck has a plan to make that happen. As flirty as Beck is with Callie, he's had our backs since he found out.

"Alright." Beck claps. "Who's in? We could go full tourney style."

"I'm in," I say.

"Me too," my sisters say at the same time. I shoot them

both thankful looks, I didn't even have to ask they just followed my lead.

And with Jensen joining next, it's not exactly surprising that Adam and Tripp follow.

Beck shoots a quick look around the table and pauses on Callie for a second. "Okay, ladies, since you are always right...look to your right, and you've got your teammate."

Callie turns her head to her right and looks right at me with a smile. "How are your pool skills, partner?"

Beck's the wingman of the century.

Abandoning our table, we all head over to the pool tables. Callie and I play against Reagan and Tripp first, while Beck and Jensen play Adam and Lucie at the table next to us.

While I'm not terrible at pool, Callie's amazing at it, so we beat Reagan and Tripp pretty quickly. Granted, it also had to do with the fact that Reagan and Tripp were quite possibly the worst pairing out of our whole group. The two are practically the same person. However, I've noticed Reagan missing some pretty easy shots.

Beck and Jensen take the win on their table and when Beck suggests that the losers can play each other, my sisters shrug.

"Or we could just go back to the table and drink?" Reagan says.

Lucie hooks her arm around Reagan. "Oh, I would love a giant pizza. Adam, Tripp, you guys coming?"

Tripp has this dumbass look on his face and I can already tell it's going to be some playboy pick up line. "With you, angel? Absolutely."

I don't even bother saying anything because Reagan

laughs. "Yeah, listen, call me when you have a vagina, and we'll talk."

Adam claps Tripp's shoulder as he registers my sister's implication. "He acts like he has one sometimes. Does that count?"

All in complete unison the girls say, "No."

When the other's walk off, Beck laughs. "I thought I was the only member of Team Will and Callie, but it seems you guys might have a fan club."

My phone vibrates in my pocket and Callie reaches for her as well, so I already know what group message it's from.

When Will Finally Dates Callie.

REAGAN

Not to be dramatic but the sacrifice we just made needs to be noted.

LUCIE

Our old table was taken so we grabbed a new one as far away as possible. You guys are completely out of eyesight.

Callie shoves her phone back in her small bag and laughs as I immediately pull her to me. Her back rests against my chest and I kiss the back of her head. "You ready to win, Blaze?"

"They don't stand a chance." Callie looks back at me with a smile and I place a quick kiss to her lips.

"Okay, guys, don't go too crazy. Social media is still a thing." Beck laughs then turns to Jensen. "Jenni-cakes, rack 'em up!"

I have sisters, so I've seen a million eye rolls. I've never seen someone's eyes roll as hard as Jensen's do toward Beck just now.

"Did you see that?" Callie snorts a small laugh.

I pull her tighter to me. "Stay close, the temperature in here just got a lot colder."

At the start of the game, Callie has a great break and gets us a good lead, but after a while Beck catches them back up. I stand off to the side as it's Callie's turn at the eight-ball, and Beck practically hovers over her.

"You're much better than that dick I helped her escape from," Jensen says as she comes up next to me. "But your friend is annoying as shit."

I laugh. "Hey, I got to give him credit. He's covered for us quite a bit. Don't write him off so quickly."

Jensen hums. "Have you tried slipping him a Xanax? Does it calm him down any?"

"Damn it, Callie!" Beck shouts and throws his hands up as Callie sinks the eight-ball and wins us the game.

I go to take a step toward her but before I can make it Adam comes back over.

"My sister kick your ass again, Daines?"

"I swear she cheats." Beck shakes his head.

Callie shoots a quick smile my way before turning back to her brother with a shrug. "Will and I just make a good team."

After a few more rounds of drinks and some pizza we call it a night. Lucie and Reagan aren't super drunk, but I don't feel comfortable having them drive. So I tell them to crash at my apartment. Fuck knows I won't be there.

Given that I was technically the designated driver again, I drove all of the guys here. Adam, thankfully, stopped drinking after two beers hours ago, so he drives Jensen home and my sisters and Callie back to our complex. I have the displeasure of delaying my night with Callie to drop Tripp and Beck off.

The speed limit might have been pushed a bit on my way back to my place. Walking down the hall I take a glance back just to be sure and immediately pass my apartment door. I know my sisters will make themselves at home, and after looking at Callie all night, my mind is on a one-way track. I'm getting really tired of pretending that I don't worship every move she makes. If we can't convince Olsson our relationship won't be a problem soon, I might lose my damn mind. A whole new take on this "we won't be a problem" idea.

Reaching for her doorknob, I'm not at all surprised that it's unlocked. What I am surprised by is opening the door to find Callie no longer in her black dress.

Closing and locking the door behind me I'm damn near tempted to fall on my knees. Callie sits leaned back in one of her dining table chairs, her red hair pulled up in a ponytail and, from what I can tell, only wearing my jersey.

"Fuck, woman, you are out to kill tonight."

Callie pushes up off the chair and pulls out a pair of handcuffs. "You know when I got these from Wyla as a gag gift, I almost tossed them out. But I just couldn't bring myself to do it."

She strolls to me so slowly. Such a tease.

"Oh yeah, what did you have in mind?" When she

reaches me, I pull her closer by her hips. My hands go down to the seams then travel back up under the jersey just waiting to be stopped by the fabric of her underwear...but that doesn't happen.

"Mmm, please tell me you weren't like this all night. That little black dress was torture enough."

"Wouldn't you like to know?" Callie pushes me back with a smirk. "Take off your shirt."

I let go of her and pull my shirt over my head. Looking back at her she smiles. "Now hands behind your back, Anderson."

Oh, shit. Me? When I move my hands back her eyes light up. She loves this. Fuck, that makes all of this even hotter.

"All night, I've been dying to touch you, and now this?" I keep my voice playful so she knows I'm definitely into this, but I do hate the fact that I can't touch her.

With my hands locked back, she comes to my front and starts to unbutton my jeans and pulls them down. "That dress was hot, wasn't it?" Callie lowers down on her knees while I kick the rest of my clothes to the side.

"You looked so good in that dress baby, but now? Fuck, my jersey? You better be glad you cuffed me, or I'd bend your ass over and absolutely tear into you."

Callie's hands slide up my thighs but instead of touching my dick they slide right up to my abs as she stands back up. "Why don't you take a seat."

Callie steps to the side and watches as I lean back in her chair, letting my linked hands rest behind the seat. She takes a step toward me, but I know her, she likes to be told what to do.

"Nuh uh, Blaze. Crawl."

The fire ignites in her eyes, and she drops down to her hands and knees. "I like this. I like the push and pull we have."

Callie crawls agonizingly slow to me. I know she's doing it on purpose and every minute since I came through her door, I've thought I can't possibly get any harder but, fuck, it's got to be stone by now.

"Which one do you want right now? Do you want me to push by telling you to get your cute ass over here and suck me? Or do you want me to pull and beg because I need that mouth of yours?"

Callie hums happily at the thought of both. I know she wants both—this push and pull has become very clear to me over these past few months, even outside of the bedroom.

Callie wants control but she also wants to be wanted and let go when she feels comfortable. She wants to be desired and loved but also come off as strong and independent. I don't like to think about her past, but I can confidently say that no one else understands this about her.

When she reaches me, she sits back on her knees with her hands in her lap. She looks so sweet and innocent—ya know, if you take away the fact that she just handcuffed me and is mere inches away from my dick.

"Go on, Callie. Why don't you make me beg for you?"

A wicked smile tugs at her lips. "Okay, let's see how long you last."

I would have a flirty comeback, I really would, but Callie leans up and spits on my dick. When her mouth takes me in, I'm pretty sure my brain malfunctions because every word in my vocabulary immediately disappears.

"Fuck, woman," I hiss when Callie starts using her hand in tandem with her mouth. Looking down at her, I see my name lining her back as she sucks the life out of me. "You look so fucking sexy right now."

Callie moans and flashes those piercing green eyes up at me.

"I like my name on your back, baby. It looks like it belongs there."

Callie pops off and lets her hand take over. "Maybe it does," she purrs. "Isn't this the jersey you're supposed to wear tomorrow?"

"It is." God, how am I going to ever be able to wear this jersey without getting a fucking hard on?

Callie hums happily as her hand continues to work me over. "Well, I'm about to use your jersey to make myself come and you better not come with me."

"You're going to wh—"

I get cut off when her mouth goes back to my dick and when I look down, she's pulled the corner of my jersey in between her legs.

"God—fuck." My hands instinctively want to go to her hair, but I'm quickly reminded by the metal digging into my skin that I can't. Callie continues to take me as far as she can while she works her clit over with my jersey. Her moans turn into quick whimpers and her speed in both places picks up.

"Damn it, Callie. Take these fucking cuffs off."

But she doesn't, she only moans louder. I don't have to be touching her to know she's close. Hell, I'm close. Thrusting my hips in the small way I can at this angle, Callie starts to choke for a moment. Instead of stopping completely I just slow my thrusts down until she regains her breath.

"So fucking hot, Blaze. You don't want me to come down your throat? How am I supposed to do that when you're about to make yourself come with my dick in your mouth?"

Callie looks up at me again, smiling with her eyes because her mouth is fucking busy. "Callie, undo these cuffs because I am going to fuck you senseless."

Callie pops off again. "No," she whispers. "I'm not going to uncuff you." Callie stands then straddles me in the chair. "Not until I come."

My head falls back as Callie starts to bounce up and down. Her hand goes back to her clit and her back arches with my name on her lips. Her pussy is already squeezing the hell out of me. Not being able to touch her right now is fucking torture.

"Damn it, Callie, I can't move my hands." I'm trying to move the best I can, but I can't reach her. I just want to feel her. "Please get down here and kiss me."

Callie smiles as she lays her chest against mine. She doesn't kiss me yet, but she's close enough for me to claim her mouth myself. Kissing her deep and slowly, I can feel her hand moving faster and when I slide my tongue in her mouth she starts to pulse around me.

Her moan comes so loud that I try to swallow it up with my lips. Her whole body trembles as I take over thrusting into her until her body practically melts against mine.

Still keeping slow and shallow thrusts, I kiss the top of her head. "Callie. Un-fucking-cuff me."

Callie picks her head up and with a satiated smile she slides off me and grabs the key off her small dining table. She unlocks one of my hands and I turn, pulling her back to my front. I want her straddling me again, but this time turned the other way.

Her head falls back with a moan as I slide into her. "Now, this one," I say, holding up the other cuff and start slow but steady thrusts.

"I was working on that, you impatient man," Callie huffs breathlessly as she fiddles with the other lock.

"That's right, I am impatient." I start to thrust into her harder. When my other hand is free, she drops the cuff and nearly falls forward at my momentum. I catch her by her arms pulling her back.

"Fucking impatient because I've had to pretend for a month that there's nothing between us." I pull her against my chest and stand us up. I turn so she can put her hands on the chair. "I'm impatient because you were the most beautiful girl in that bar tonight and I couldn't make every fucker in that place hate me because you were on my arm."

"Will," Callie pants and her walls clench me like a vise. "Fuck, keep going."

"Oh, there's no stopping this and that includes us, Callie." Keeping my bruising pace, Callie arches her head back and I reach up to wrap that pretty ponytail of hers around my fist. "You're mine, Callie, and I'm getting really impatient about not being able to show everyone that."

"Yes, Will. Fuck. I'm going to come again." Callie reaches one hand back up to her center.

She moans at her touch, so I let go of her hair and pull her hand back to replace it with mine. "You had your turn. I want this one coming from my touch alone."

Callie lets out a small whimper as my fingers circle her clit. "Will, please," she begs.

"Oh, Blaze, I like hearing you beg. But I love it when you take, so please come for me."

And just like that Callie takes her orgasm and mine right alongside her.

When both of us feel like we can move again, I pull out

of her and turn her around to sit back in the chair. "Wait here. I'll be right back."

She nods with a sleepy but satisfied smile, then I head into the kitchen to get a warm wet rag to clean her up. Her body jumps a little when the rag touches her center, and she lets out a laugh. "Sorry, still sensitive."

I set the rag down on the floor then scoop her up in my arms. "I think I told you a while ago not to apologize for men's actions."

"Hmm, I suppose you're right." Callie rests her head on my shoulder. "And I'm not sorry about that at all."

I laugh as I lay her back down on her bed. "Yeah, me either." I place a kiss on her temple and climb in next to her.

Callie turns to cuddle up next to me. "Will," she mumbles. "Thank you. I've never had this. Before you, my ideas were always shut down and that's me talking about normal stuff outside of the bedroom. I thought it would have gotten better when I got into Yale, that maybe they just needed that superficial proof that I was competent. But I've never had someone that doesn't look at me like I've lost my head when I talk or suggest something until you. You make me feel safe to be myself no matter the context."

My entire being hates that her independence and outspokenness were viewed so negatively—to me they're everything.

"That's their loss. To them you're Calliope, but to me you're my Callie. I love when you let me take care of you. If there ever comes a day when you don't speak your mind or tell me you want something, I'm going to handcuff you and give you so many orgasms you'll be blurting out every thought in your head just to make me stop. But then that won't work because I love to hear your voice."

Callie snorts a small laugh but doesn't say anything.

"Oh, are we looking for that punishment now?" I tickle her side, and her laugh comes out loud and beautiful.

"No, please stop." She giggles and tries to push away from me.

I chuckle at her fighting me, but when she gets even an inch away, I stop and pull her back to my side. My hand runs up and down her back as she tries to even her breath, and I'm reminded that she's still wearing my jersey. "When did you steal this?"

Callie's arms tighten around me as she snuggles deeper. "I might have stolen it after saying bye to your sisters. It was in the bag by the door! It was too tempting."

"It looks good on you, Callie. I don't know how I'm going to put it on tomorrow and not get immediately hard at the reminder of you in it."

Callie shrugs and I can hear the smile in her tone. "Maybe you're just really excited about baseball?"

"I'm really excited about something." I kiss the top of her head.

"Hey, Will," she whispers. "I'm impatient too. Let's tell everyone this week."

Chapter 37
Callie

"So, you're sure about this?" Will asks as he pours me a cup of the lemon ginger tea that *he made* for us first thing this morning.

My heart swells in my chest as he hands me my mug before he grabs another for himself. His sisters stopped by before their drive back to Rowley. Before they could even step in the door, Will informed them he wasn't sharing me this morning.

"Yeah, I'm sure," I say, taking a small sip. My eyes shut briefly as I feel the burn all the way down. "Mmm, I know you're just a delivery boy, but I think you need a promotion. This has got to be one of the best cups of tea I've ever had."

Will chuckles. "I think you just like to inflate my ego."

"I like to inflate something." I dance my eyebrows at my innuendo, and he just laughs.

Will takes a small sip of his tea before setting the mug down and making his way around my island to the back of my stool to wrap his arms around me.

I lean back and let my head rest on his shoulder. "I don't

want to keep this a secret anymore and I'm okay with the consequences, but I can't make that same decision for you. I know the no-trade is important to you for your family and losing that is the best-case scenario, Will. You could get traded to another team or even sent back to assignment if Olsson wants."

Will sighs and kisses my temple. "Callie, at the start I told you I didn't know where this could go, but not anymore. I can picture it. I can picture us in every scenario you could possibly think of."

Will takes my mug out of my hand and spins me around so I face him. He cups my face so gently. "There's nothing more important to me than having you in my life. We'll get through this week of games and on our day off we'll both go in and talk to Olsson. We'll make it work no matter what."

My heart swells in my chest. "Okay."

The smile on Will's face and the relief in his eyes at my admission threatens to bring tears to my eyes. I meant what I said last night—I've never had anyone like Will. I know Adam loves me and he's done a lot for me, but Will's made me his priority, even when we were "just friends."

I go to pull him closer as he leans in and kisses me slowly, passionately.

It's a kiss that I never want to end, but unfortunately for us we both have to be at the stadium in a couple hours.

"Hey, I have to take a shower. Wanna join me?"

"What kind of question is that?" Will kisses my forehead. "I'll get it started. Drink some more of your tea."

I smile as I watch him make his way back to my bathroom. When I turn back around, I reach for my mug as soon as my phone starts to vibrate on the counter. When I register that the name on my screen reads Mom, I freeze. I know

Adam told me to block both of them and after my run in with Nic, I did find the strength to block our dad.

Picking up my phone my first instinct is to ignore it, but as I hear the water turn on, I remember that Will's here. I remember the love Will shows me. I have no need for their affection or approval, and if I'm going to cut them off, I'm going to let them know why.

"Hello?" I answer.

"Calliope, finally." My mother sighs. We're off to a great start. "Your father tried calling you, but it went to voicemail. It's really quite irresponsible of you to not answer your father. I tried for years to teach you manners, but I thought human decency was a given."

I pinch the bridge of my nose, regretting this immediately. "Mom, I don't want to talk to dad. I only answered so I could explain that."

"Explain? Really, Calliope, you exhaust me. You always wanted to talk as a kid, I just—can't. Here's your father."

"No, Mom, I don't—"

"Calliope," my dad cuts me off with his usual self-righteous tone. Even my name sounds like an insult coming from him. "I tried calling you, but I take it your brother had you block my calls as well."

I sigh. "Can you blame me?"

But that wasn't the right thing to say because yes, he can most definitely blame me.

"How I got the two most ungrateful kids, I'll never understand. You treat me as if I'm—"

"Dad," I try to cut in, but I'm not the only one who can exhaust my mother with their excessive talking. He plows through with insults and disappointments, and the next thing I know my hand is being pulled back from my ear.

I jump at the surprise and yank my arm back, but Will's already figured out who I'm talking to.

"Let me have the phone, Callie," Will demands. The soft demeanor he had just a few moments ago is gone. Right now, he looks down right pissed.

I put my phone on mute while my dad's tantrum continues. "No, Will. I need to handle this."

Will cups my face again and the moment he looks in my eyes his features soften. "Callie, baby, we talked about this. The push and pull is something I love but just let me handle this."

The look of pure love and concern in his eyes almost has me folding but this is something I have to do.

"No, Will. I need this."

Will's eyes shut for a moment as he takes a deep breath, the harshness I saw a moment ago comes back as he looks at my phone. "Speaker phone. Non-negotiable."

I nod, clicking it on as my dad is starting to realize he's being ignored.

"Calliope, are you even listening? Of course you're not. You couldn't—"

"Dad," I snap, cutting him off. "You must have had Mom call for a reason, so what is it?"

The line goes silent for a second and I swear I can hear the thuds of his shoes landing on his desk. That was my dad's favorite move when he felt he was about to make the final blow. I can picture him clear as day in my head—laid back in his obnoxious leather chair and his feet crossed on his grand mahogany desk.

"I've talked with your grandfather, and in light of your recent actions we have decided to pull your inheritance and officially write you out of the family will. Adam has been written out already, I see no future for him, but this is your final chance. Come back home and we can just write this whole year off as you 'finding yourself.'"

And at that I burst out laughing. It might be an odd response, but that? That's what he thinks his checkmate is?

"Calliope!" my father shouts, and I imagine sits straight up now. "Stop laughing this instance. I'm not kidding. You will be stripped of your family name."

Another laugh bubbles out of me. "I'm sorry, I just— phew, you thought that was going to win me over? Make me come back home like a scared little girl?"

The line goes silent for a moment and I almost want to start counting to five to see if the explosion happens, but I don't wait.

"I'm not coming back. You can take my name, my inheritance—write me out of your will, that's fine." I turn to face Will with a smile on my face. "I've got my own, I'm not worried."

"Cal—" my father starts but I hang up before I can hear that awful name again.

Will laughs, picking me up from my stool and walking me back to the running shower. "Damn, it sure is a good thing I got a promotion today. I would have never been able to provide for you as a delivery boy."

"I make one joke!"

For the rest of the morning, I'm on a high. Will and I have a plan. I've put my past and my family completely behind me. I feel good.

Almost too good…that should have been my first warning sign. The moment I walk through the entrance at the stadium, Shannon's there. I asked Olsson on the flight back home if I could come in half an hour earlier to the stadium so I could get pictures of the guys walking in. It appears that plan got back to Shannon.

"Callie, we're on a very serious schedule today. I need you to be close throughout the day because it's all hands on deck for Opening Day."

My high immediately gets knocked down a few pegs. "Okay, Shannon. I'm scheduled to do walk-in pictures for the next hour and a half. I have a pretty full day as well. I don't mind helping you when I have free time, but I'm going to stick to my schedule that Olsson and I agreed on before every game."

"Callie, your schedule isn't really that set in stone. You can get your silly little pictures anytime." Shannon turns on her heels not even waiting for my response. She just expects me to follow her.

Deep breath, Callie. No drama, right? But damn it, I have to do my job too.

"Shannon," I call before she gets too far. She clicks her heels as she turns back to me. "Hi. So, listen, I don't want this to come off rude because I love this job, and because of that I'm going to do it right. Now I can still be a team player and help you when I have breaks, but right now I'm going to go set up to get pictures of the guys coming in and then I will check in."

Shannon stares at me with this deadpan look on her face. "Fine. If that's what you need to do, then so be it."

She clicks on her heels again and my high takes a nose-dive. I can't dwell because I've wanted to get these pictures all month. I know Shannon will force her two cents in on mine and Will's relationship, and at this point I've lost all hope on her showing any support. I'm just hoping the work I've done so far can speak for itself.

After dropping off some of my stuff in my small office, I go to get set up out front to get the pictures I've been wanting for a while now. I shouldn't let Shannon get to me. I've had a pretty empowering morning. I've officially closed the door on *Calliope* and now I feel like I can be Callie. Well, almost. I just have to get through this week because I honestly don't feel much like me without Will.

Unsurprisingly, Adam is the first player to show up. When he spots me sitting on the concrete taking pictures he laughs. "What are you doing? It's like forty degrees out here."

"Shh, I'm not here. I want pictures of you guys in your element for Opening Day." I click a few more pictures and Adam shakes his head.

"Hey, you're the one who got me this job. I'll endure the cold for the shot." I laugh.

Adam stops next to me and pats my head lightly. "I'm really proud of you, Cals. I'm happy you're happy here."

"Thank you." Peering up, I can feel myself getting misty already. "For everything."

Adam shrugs. "Eh, it wasn't just me."

I raise an eyebrow at him. "Who—"

"Your next player's here, Cals," Adam cuts me off. "Get back to work."

I turn to see Mateo walking in, so I pick my camera back up. I can't help but turn back to my brother for one more question. "Who are—" is all I can get out before Adam walks into the stadium.

Damn it. I sigh and try to shake off the funk of this weird day. I get my shots of Mateo and laugh when he strikes a pose. A lot of them strike poses honestly. I'm pretty sure every man on this team is just one big goofball.

Nearing the end of arrival time, I have three players left and lucky me, my personal favorite walks up next.

I pick up my camera as I see Will walking up. I take a quick glance around to make sure no one's in ear shot before doing a cat-call whistle. "Damn! Excuse me, sir, what are you doing after the game tonight?"

I snap my pictures just as Will starts to laugh. Ugh, I'm going to get these framed.

"You, Blaze." When Will reaches me, he hands me the to-go cup in his hand. "Here, to warm you up."

"Ah, you angel man, you." I take the cup and want to cry happy tears as it warms my frozen fingers. "What's this one?"

"Black tea with tangerine, I think. It was the special at Spilled Tea today," Will says. "Have you gotten everyone yet?"

"Nope, Tripp and Beck are my lone stragglers." Reaching for my phone to check the time, I unfortunately find a text from Shannon telling me that the moment I'm finished I'm needed for pictures at the concession stands. "I'm pretty sure Shannon's going to kill me today."

"What's she doing now?" Will asks as I pull out my schedule to make sure I'm not forgetting something.

"She says I'm supposed to come take pictures of the concession stands or something, but I'm supposed to have fifteen minutes in between this and warm-ups to set up my camera for wide shots." I groan and toss my phone back in my bag. "This is because I told her this morning that I needed to focus on doing my job first then I would help her after. She's probably about to run my ass all day for useless shit, like concession photos. What the hell does that mean? They aren't even open right now, Will."

Will starts with a chuckle but when I give him the side eye he shuts right up. "I'm sorry, you're right, not funny. Want me to scare her with an accidentally close pitch at warm-ups?"

I let that image play out in my head for a moment and now it's my turn to laugh. "As tempting as that sounds, I think that might push our 'we won't let our relationship affect our work' argument. I can snap her silly little pictures if it means we can make this work."

Will smiles down at me. "Yeah, yeah, but if my hand slips, just know it was intentional."

"Will!" I smack his leg. "Go inside."

"Yeah, I got to go warm up my arm." Will starts to stretch as he walks toward the entrance. "Would hate for a pitch to go a little sideways."

Chapter 38
Will

Man, Callie wasn't kidding when she said Shannon was out for blood. My girl ran all over the place during warm-ups. It was a damn miracle I didn't say anything...or throw anything.

I tried hanging back on the field for a little while longer, to catch a moment to check in on Callie, but Shannon wasn't about to let that happen. Before I could even step in her direction, Shannon stepped in and sent her somewhere else.

Heading back to the locker room, we have time to kill before the game actually starts so I might venture back out to see if I can find her again. Reaching for my phone I text her asking for her schedule, so my completely harmless walk later just happens to be where she's at.

"Hey, Anderson. Good luck today," a man says in front of me.

It doesn't take long for me to register why the voice sounds so familiar. Looking up slowly, I take a calming breath. "Nic, what are you doing here? Aren't you supposed to be in Chicago right now? Oh, don't tell me, did they send you back down? It happens, you just have to keep practicing."

An unsettling smirk comes to his face. "Oh, you haven't heard the good news. I got traded to the New York Crimsons." Nic takes a step closer and shoves his hands in his pockets. "And wanna know the best part? I got an early flight, so it looks like I'm playing today."

The fucker has such a smug look on his face that I'm dying to clean it right off with a nice left hook, but this is exactly what me and Callie talked about. I won't risk her.

"Yeah, well, good for you," I say plainly and try to step around him toward the locker room.

Nic matches my step. "Ya know, I was hoping I could talk to Calliope. Any chance you might know where she is?"

"Stay the fuck away from Callie." The words come out instinctively. I should have known this prick would want to bring her into this. Cutting my eyes to him, I say, "Was her right hook not subtle enough for you? Leave her the fuck alone."

Nic huffs a laugh. "Calliope is quite addicting, isn't she? I don't know if you've seen her in her true element, she's insane with numbers. Although, no one in her family ever really did give her any credit—which I'm sure is the reason for her outbursts. But I suppose she's not shown you that side of her." He shrugs. "Or maybe she has...I thought it was so interesting the way you chased after her a couple months ago. She likes the chase, trust me."

My blood is absolutely boiling. "I don't know what you're talking about," I grit out.

"Sure you don't." Nic leans forward and says quietly, "Just between us, she's great in bed. A little mouthy, but hey, she makes up for it—"

I don't think at that moment. I grab Nic's throat and slam him against the nearest wall. "Shut your fucking mouth. You useless piece—"

Before I can even start my threat, Beck's pulling me back. "Whoa, what the fuck is going on out here?"

Nic falls forward with a strangled breath. "You think she's worth it, but she's fucking not."

I'm going to kill him. I'm absolutely going to murder him here in the stadium.

But this time when I go after him it's not just Beck holding me back. Tripp must have come out with him and I've just been in too much of a blind rage to notice.

"Get out of my fucking way," I yell when Tripp steps in front of me.

"Will, calm down." Tripp pushes me further back and keeps his focus on me, while Beck tells Nic to fuck off.

But then in that moment everything shifts when I see fire. Callie strolls down the hallway toward us with no warning of what she's about to walk into.

"Calliope, it seems you've already done a number on one of your brother's teammates and your co-worker... I just thought if you were going to keep being a slut, you'd try to maintain some sort of respect for the workplace." Nic spews his words so easily.

And in that moment, my blind rage immediately spreads to Beck and Tripp.

"The fuck did you just say?" Beck spits out.

Tripp takes a step away from me, toward Nic. "I must be hearing things because I know you didn't call Callie a slut in front of her team. Who the fuck are you, anyway?"

"He's fucking dead," is all I get to add before Callie steps in the middle.

"Okay, everyone shut up right fucking now." Callie holds her hands out and all I want to do is pull her toward me, but she's pissed. "Nic, I don't know what you're doing here and before you even start to tell me—I don't care. That shiner I gave you was the final reaction you'll get out of me, so move on. I truly care more about the gum on the bottom of my shoe than you."

Nic straightens his spine at the look on her face. "You made a mistake when you left, Calliope."

Callie huffs a laugh. "Oh, yeah? Do me a favor and hold your breath while you wait for me to realize that."

Nic rolls his shoulders back with an arrogant laugh. "Whatever you say, *Calliope*."

I absolutely hate the way he says her name. As if it's a way to put her down.

Callie watches until he walks out of sight, but I don't want that fucker getting another millisecond of her attention.

"Callie," I say softly, and reach for her hand. The moment my skin touches hers she jumps back.

"Will, what was that? We just talked about this! We talked about how to make this work and now you're making death threats in the hall. What if Shannon saw you? She's been all over my ass today and you knew that."

"Baby—" I try to stop her, but she's not done.

"And you." She turns to Beck. "This whole 'keep it professional' thing was your idea. What the hell were you doing?"

"Oh, because I was just going to let him say that to you?" Beck holds up his hands but he's not going to be able to stop Callie either.

"I don't want to hear it," Callie snaps. "He's not worth it. I don't care what he calls me, what he says, or the air he breathes. Now I have to go deal with Shannon's insistent, pointless photos in addition to my list of pictures needed today. So, I need you guys to let this go. I will not let that asshole impact my life any more than he already has."

Before any of us can respond to her Shannon yells from down the hall, "Callie! Any day now."

Callie takes a deep breath then looks at me one more time. Her green eyes are eerily bright and glossy, and I know she's fighting the urge to cry, but not because she's hurt—she's stressed.

"I'm sorry, baby," I say quietly. "It's going to be okay, I promise."

Beck shakes her shoulder slightly. "We got you, Callie."

Callie nods with an exasperated breath. "Okay. I've got to go," she whispers then heads down the hall.

When she gets far enough away, Tripp clears his throat. "So, I'm gonna go out on a limb here and say that Will and Callie are together."

"Yup," Beck and I reply at the same time.

Tripp tosses his hands up. "Oh, so the new guy gets to break the rules but when I flirted with her in the beginning I was told to back off. When did this even happen? She went on a date not too long ago, was that the guy?"

For fuck's sake.

"No, that's her asshole of an ex." I sigh. I hate that I let Nic get the better of me, but he got off way too easy to begin with. I would never tell Callie's story to anyone, but I'm also not the only one who knows it.

"Listen, Adam can't know about me and Callie. Not yet, at least. But we do need to tell him about Nic. The prick did some pretty serious stuff and I don't imagine he'll have a better response than I did."

"Alright." Tripp nods. "I think we should talk to the team anyway about this guy. I'm sure you're not surprised by this, but even if none of us are actually gunning for your girl, she's one of us now. If he starts spouting off like that, the whole team will riot."

Fuck, he's right.

Beck places his hand on my shoulder. "We've got to tell the guys something. We can leave the relationship out of it easy enough, but I don't want that prick touching a base tonight. Either you strike him out or we make sure he never makes it to first."

Tripp laughs. "Hope that arm of yours is warmed up because if you strike him out the entire game, you, my friend, will be my new hero."

Hm, it won't exactly be as satisfying as punching him in the face, but it'll do.

"Alright, I think I can do that."

Telling everyone goes about as well as I expect it too. There are many questions and a lot of anger. I don't speak about a single thing Nic did to her in the past, just going off what he said in the hall is enough to piss everyone off. My girl's loved, so it's not exactly shocking.

Adam was naturally the most upset. It takes a lot of convincing to get him on board with our plan as opposed to "putting him six feet under the base." Frankly, I was on his side, but we were clearly outnumbered.

The locker room's atmosphere has completely shifted. I don't think I've ever seen my team more determined to play a game. Even back in Seattle when we were about to play the World Series there was still a bit of excitement in the air. Even I was fine, though granted in Seattle I didn't care like I do now.

A World Series trophy is great, but my relationship with Callie? It's everything.

Chapter 39
Callie

I am an emotional trainwreck right now. I've wanted to lock myself in one of the janitors' closets and just have the most therapeutic cry ever. Despite the disownment from my father this morning and the name calling from Nic, the person I'm most upset with is myself.

I shouldn't have lashed out at Will like that. He was standing up for me when I wasn't there to stand up for myself. But when I walked in on that it was like my worst nightmare, except it didn't have anything to do with the things Nic said or did to me, it was the idea of Nic ruining my revenge of a happy life.

The moment I hung up with my dad this morning, I felt this weight lifted off. I was finally going to be able to put everything behind me. But then here comes Nic trying to fuck it up again.

It hasn't helped that the entire work day Shannon has had me running the stadium. It was so bad that when Miles hunted me down to ask to help me, I had to break the poor kid's heart and tell him no. I'll never forgive her for that one.

I thought my declaration of doing my job would suffice, but it only egged her on. She's memorized my schedule now and if I had a moment to breathe today, she was there with something for me to do.

All day I've thought I could escape her and the tension she brings at the start of the game, but now I'm switching to a whole new stressor. Earlier the guys were ready to go at it in the hall—now they have bats and a crowd.

Taking my position in my designated photo hole next to the dugout, I try to steal a glance at Will, but he never looks my way. Fuck, I can't have a full breakdown here. I just have to get through this game, and we can talk it out.

I can do hard things...I have done hard things.

By the bottom of the fourth inning the Blues are absolutely killing the Crimsons—five to nothing. The guys are playing better than I've seen all month. Will's pitching better than I've ever seen him. Period.

So far he's struck out Nic every single inning. It's been both extremely satisfying and beyond nerve wracking because Will has yet to look at me.

Abandoning my little hole, I decide to take some pictures behind home plate. The angle isn't as great as opposed to being directly on the field, but it still does the job. Plus, with Will still not even sending a glance in my direction, I'm starting to get in my head.

Moving as quickly as I can to the new spot, I miss one player making it to first. I do, however, make it just in time for Nic to be up to bat again and while I could pick up his anger from my old spot, from here it's palpable.

With Will's first strike, I can't help the tug at my lips. I won't apologize, it feels so good to see. With Will's second strike, I swear Nic says something, but with this rowdy crowd there's no way I can hear anything. Nic spares a glance back down to my brother which gives me a little pause, but it's fine, right?

With Will's final strike, the umpire calls Nic out for the fifth time tonight and it feels so freaking good to hear. But then my heart stops because Nic slings his bat back at the fence then charges the mound straight at Will.

"Oh, fuck," I mutter to myself. As soon as Nic makes it to the pitcher's mound, Will lets him get one hit in before losing it.

After that it's an all-out fight. Will's laying into Nic. Beck's fighting off the guy who made it to first. And it just escalates from there. Adam pulls Will off Nic, but not to stop him, to take over. Then every fucking player is out of their respective dugouts.

I'm pretty sure the shock and fear hold me in place as I watch the mess unfold. The crowd roars around me, eating up the drama, but my heart is in my stomach.

Finally, between the coaches' and the umpires' intervention, the fighting stops. Nic, Adam, and Will get ejected. Olsson starts yelling. Whether it's to Adam and Will or the umps, I don't know. I don't care. The moment Will walks off that field I move—no, I run to find him.

Pushing through the crowd, I race down the hall and bust through the locker room doors.

"Will?" I yell, looking around so frantically I almost yell for him again before he comes out of the bathroom holding a rag to a cut on his eye.

"Callie, I'm so sor—"

He doesn't get to finish that apology because I launch myself at him in relief. Wrapping my arms around his waist, it takes him a second to fully embrace my hug. With the rag removed from his head, I look up to inspect the gash above his eyebrow.

My hands go to his face. "Shit, Will. Are you okay?"

Will chuckles as he pulls my hands down. "I'm fine, Callie. It's worse than it looks. Nic, on the other hand—"

"I don't care about him," I snap, cutting him off. "Will, I only care about you. I'm sorry this is such a mess. I shouldn't have gotten mad at you earlier, I'm sorry, I ju—"

"Hey, hey," Will says softly. "I don't usually stop your rambles, Blaze, but this time I have to. Never say you're sorry about anything that remotely involves that guy. I swear, Callie..." Will sighs as he trails off.

He's holding the rag to his brow, so I gently reach up and take over for him. "Let me see."

Reluctantly, Will lets me have the rag and sits down on the bench close by so I can get a better look. With the bleeding now mostly finished, it really isn't that bad.

"I suppose you'll live." I chuckle lightly.

"I know I will." A smile tugs at the corner of Will's lips as he pulls me in for a small kiss. "Now, you should probably get back out there. I've made enough trouble for us today."

"Oh, that's an understatement."

My eyes shut the moment I register whose voice that is. Turning around, I find an outraged Olsson and my brother who's staring at me and Will like we were the ones that punched him.

Will shoots up. "I can explain. We're not—"

"Don't start, Anderson!" Olsson snaps. I've never seen him look so pissed. We're fucking screwed. "I don't want to hear a single fucking word from you. All of you, for that matter."

Sighing, Olsson runs his hands over his face. "Adam,

Will, you guys are obviously ejected. I'll have to wait to hear about the penalty the league decides on for you two, but for now, go home. You too, Callie. You're suspended for tomorrow's game as well. We'll discuss this relationship after I clean up this fucking mess."

My heart sinks and I can practically feel the anger radiating off Will. Before he even opens his mouth to argue, I place my hand on his back lightly.

"I understand." I nod to my boss because, fuck, I should have known.

"Sir, she—" Adam tries but Olsson holds up his hand.

"Not a word." He grits out. "Now I have to go deal with the fact that you two assholes broke a player's nose and possibly his jaw. So, for all that's fucking holy, not another word."

When none of us say anything, Olsson hits us with another sigh before he turns and slings open the locker room door on his way out.

Shit. I'm going to lose my job.

Chapter 40
Will

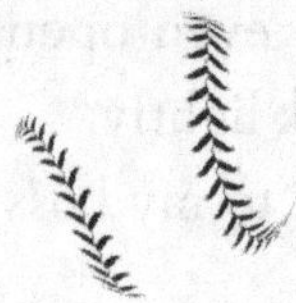

Fuck. The moment the door to the locker room slams shut, Callie deflates beside me.

"Callie," I breathe out. "It's going to be okay."

"I—Um." Callie takes an exasperated breath. "I'm going to go get my stuff and we can go." I can practically hear her fighting the tears through the cracks in her voice.

I glance at Adam. He doesn't exactly seem happy, but he hasn't lashed out at me yet, so I dare a step to my girl and try to pull her closer to calm her down. "Baby, it's—"

Callie steps forward. "Sorry, I just...I want to get my stuff and I want to get out of here."

"Go," Adam tells her. "We'll wait for you here. Just get what you can, but Will and I aren't allowed back on the field. If you forget anything, Beck will get it."

Callie nods but hesitates for a moment to look back at me. I know what she's thinking. "Go, we'll be fine."

I already took one punch today; I can take another.

Callie bites on her lip like she always does when she wants to say something. I hold her glossy-eyed stare until she finally turns and heads out of the locker room.

A solid ten seconds go by, and Adam doesn't say anything. He doesn't move to hit me—he just stares.

"Look, Callie's—"

"I know," Adam cuts me off.

A little taken aback, I huff. "You didn't let me finish."

Adam chuckles lightly. "True, but you were essentially about to tell me that Callie's more than a secret hook-up to you, which I already knew. You planned her birthday party. You made her tea...Will, I don't even go to that place and I knew they were closed on Christmas."

Yeah, that one was a stretch.

"Wait, so you knew this whole time?"

"Oh yeah, the whole time." Adam laughs. "Did you seriously think I wanted to run five fucking miles hungover? I stopped by your place earlier searching for some Advil but you weren't there. I shrugged it off at first but when I came back with, ya know, shoes, I was going to go out to the store but caught you in the hall. I put two and two together and couldn't pass up the opportunity."

"You fucking—you egged it on!" I know he should be the one hitting me, but I really want to hit him instead.

"Oh yeah, that was fucking priceless. Your face—I thought you were going to have a heart attack."

"And you don't care?"

Adam shrugs. "Do I love the idea? No. But your saving grace was that it was obvious you cared about her. If I thought you were just fooling around, I might have hit you, but you bought a motorcycle in Florida to take her on a date."

Fuck, is Adam all-knowing or something? "How did you know about that?"

Adam gives me a pointed look. "You bought one bike in Seattle. You lived there for five years. I thought it was odd when you said you bought one on a whim, but it didn't exactly click until I remembered the text Callie sent back after I asked her to go to lunch. It was an extremely over-explained message about all the girlie shit she was going to do that day."

I laugh at that. "Yeah, her 'annoy them with talking' tactic isn't subtle once you get to know her."

"No, it's really not. I kept waiting for one of you to tell me, but I figured there was a reason you hadn't, so I thought I'd just wait it out."

Sighing, I sit back down on the bench. "Yeah, this wasn't exactly the way we had in mind."

"I'd say not." Adam takes the spot next to me. "For what it's worth, I'm happy you two are happy, but I have to ask—what happens now?"

Isn't that the fucking question of the hour. Olsson was pissed, that part's obvious, but he didn't outright fire Callie either. "The main thing we have to wait on is Olsson. Our plan was to show how our relationship wouldn't impact work...but today kind of fucked that plan over."

Adam laughs. "Do you think you broke Nic's nose or jaw?"

"Oh, I got both for sure." It took all of my will to let Nic take that first punch. I let him be the first aggressor, but after his hit landed, every hit of mine carried the thought of what he did to Callie.

I shake my head. "I love your sister. So, yeah, this might not have been the way we thought it would go, but she's all I really care about."

"I know." Adam claps my shoulder. "But I'm not the person you need to say that to."

Oh, I have every intention of telling Callie how I feel about her. I kicked my sisters out of Callie's place this morning because I actually needed them to help me with what Lucie calls my "grand gesture."

"Hey." I shoot off the bench. "Can you bring Callie home?"

"Yeah, I can." Adam gives me a puzzled look. "But I think it would be better for you to."

"I know, but just trust me. I have a plan."

Chapter 41
Callie

My ride home with Adam has been silent. I can't say I hate it. I'm not exactly in the mood to talk, but the fact that I left Will alone with Adam and came back only to find my brother waiting...

It wasn't what I had hoped to see, but I'm trying not to jump to any major conclusions. When I asked where Will went, Adam just shrugged and said he needed to go. What the hell did that mean?

Finally, riding up the elevator to our floor, I muster the courage to ask some questions. "So, did you tell Will to leave?"

Adam turns to me with a sigh. "No, I didn't."

Okay, that doesn't help me much. I swallow before asking, "Are you mad at me?"

"Fuck no." Adam laughs. "Cals, I haven't said anything because I thought you needed some time to process. I've known about you and Will before you guys even knew. I might not have been the best brother, but I'm not blind."

Part of me wants to feel relieved that he genuinely seems

fine with it, but also slightly annoyed because Will was right about Adam knowing from the beginning.

"So, you're okay with this? I might lose my job, Adam. I know you pushed for me to get it, but even if they don't fire me...if Olsson says I have to break up with Will to keep it, then I'm quitting. I love the job and I'm grateful for it, but it's not worth losing him."

With that declaration out in the open the elevator dings at our floor. Stepping out I look down my hallway then back to Adam. "I know you said you were proud of me and if this changes things, I'm sorry, but—"

"Callie." Adam puts his hands on my shoulders. "It's okay. Fuck the job. I want you to be happy. You *deserve* to be happy."

Pulling my brother into my version of a bear hug, I fight back the tears. "*We* both deserve to be happy, Adam."

Adam huffs a small laugh. "We will be. You just go get your happiness first for me, okay?"

Stepping back, I wipe the tear that escaped. "I don't even know where Will went."

"I don't think he's gone far." Adam squeezes my shoulder. "I'll talk to you tomorrow?"

I give Adam a small nod before turning to walk to my place. I hesitate in front of Will's door for a moment but then I hear banging coming from my apartment. When the noise stops, I wait outside my own door until I hear it again.

"What the—" I mutter as I swing my door open and find Will walking to me with a hammer in his hand and a spare nail in his mouth. Damn, if today hadn't been an absolute clusterfuck of a day I might have jumped him from this look alone.

"Hey Blaze," Will mumbles before taking the nail out of his mouth and stepping toward me. "Close your eyes."

My eyes close immediately upon his request but he didn't say anything about being quiet. "What, why?"

I hear him lay down the hammer and nails, and when his hand takes mine, I jump for a second. "Callie, baby, relax, I—"

"No, I will not relax when you leave me after a very emotional day," I huff, still keeping my eyes closed. I probably shouldn't be so irritated, but he left without a word.

"You're right, I'm sorry." Will's hand cups my cheek with a soft caress. "Can I show you something?"

I nod and he links his fingers through mine. "I would ask how you got in here, but I already know the answer."

Will chuckles softly as he pulls me to what I'm pretty sure is my living room. "Yeah, thanks to that, it made my grand gesture a little easier to pull off."

What? "Grand—"

"Open your eyes, Callie."

At first I'm a little scared too, but when Will squeezes my hand I open them to find my wall full of pictures of us. Some look like blown up versions of our Polaroids from our date and some are ones of Will that I've taken over the last month.

"I—Will...how...what..." I fumble words as I take them all in.

"I started going through our Polaroids during Spring Training. I knew I wanted to do something special with them, so I sent a couple off to get scanned and resized. The pictures of me are obviously one's you took, but I feel it's important to note that they are all ones of me looking at you."

Walking up to the wall I look over every picture he hung

up. The ones of us together and the ones where he's smiling at me.

Will wraps his arms around me and I rest my head back on his chest. "I knew I wanted these hung up the day that we told Olsson about us. I must've had some sixth sense or something because when I kicked my sisters out this morning it was to get these."

A happy tear slides down my face as I look at the photos in front of me. "I love them. Thank you," I whisper.

Will spins me around and cups my face. "Callie, I know this wasn't our plan, and I know today was stressful, but selfishly, I don't care. I don't feel bad about hitting your asshole ex. I don't care about the fines or the penalties for me because *you* are the only thing that I care about.

"I love you, Callie. So, if Olsson gives us an ultimatum just know that you're the one I'm picking."

"I love you too, Will. So much." My lip trembles for a moment but then Will captures my mouth with his in an all-consuming kiss.

His hands thread through my hair as he pulls my face closer to deepen our kiss. God, I don't think I'll ever get over how he kisses. Every time it feels like some form of revival.

"I love you, Blaze." Will repeats his declaration and even though I'm supposed to be the flame, I want to melt.

"I love you too," I whisper back. "Wait, where are these frames going?" I ask, pointing at the stack leaned up against my couch.

"Oh, those are going up in my place." Will steps back to the stack and takes the small one that was turned around backward. "But this one goes in your bedroom."

Turning the frame around it's our tamest Polaroid that

we took that night where Will's gripping my chin and kissing me.

A blush creeps up my cheeks. "Hmm, this might be one of the best pictures I've ever taken."

Will leans down, picking up a new unopened pack of Polaroids. "Want to see if we can top it?"

Waking up the next morning I had hoped it would be to Will lying next to me. Instead my bed is empty and I can hear several voices in my kitchen and loud clunks of pans.

Rolling out of my bed, I throw on Will's sweatshirt and a pair of sweatpants before stumbling out to find not one, not two, but three baseball players in my kitchen. None of who are my boyfriend, mind you.

Beck's standing over the stove with the unmistakable sound of bacon popping in his pan. My brother is stirring something in one of my mixing bowls, and Tripp is using a juicer I can only imagine he brought with him for homemade orange juice.

"What the hell is going on?"

All of the guys' heads whip to me with an overzealous cheer of my name. My face must show every bit of confusion I feel because Adam walks over to me with a chuckle. "Will called us, thought you might need a distraction."

My heart skips a beat. "A distraction from what? Where is he?"

Adam sighs. "He went to talk to Olsson."

Chapter 42
Will

Beck has named the group chat *Operation: Contain the Blaze*.

BECK

She's up and she's pissed.

TRIPP

I now understand why three of us were needed to keep her here. I think she's about to claw Adam's face off.

ADAM

They're lying. My sister is a delight…but also, on an unrelated note, no take backs.

I can see them now, all of them trying to tell Callie to sit her cute ass down and just let me take care of this. Tripp's right—there was no way just one of them was going to work. Beck would cave the moment Callie flashed him a pout. Tripp would be lost with any sort of argument that Callie threw his way. And Adam? She would have just steam rolled right through him.

As much as I hated leaving her this morning, I want this behind us. The stress of this conversation would be eating Callie alive and while I know she's not happy that I've left her out of it, she knows my intentions.

I knock on Olsson's office door and take a deep breath before he calls me in.

"Anderson." He nods to the seat across from his desk. "I got the word from the league just a moment ago. You and Adam are each getting hit with a hefty fine and one game suspension."

"Just one?" I was sure it was going to be more.

Olsson leans back in his chair. "I didn't ask questions, but I assume it's because you weren't technically the one to throw the first punch. But I'd say the ones you did throw came from a personal place."

Olsson raises his eyebrows, and I know what he's getting at.

"They might have, but not for the reason you might be thinking." Sitting up straighter in my chair, here goes a Callie ramble. "It wasn't over some petty bullshit. Nic deserved every one of those punches, but if you ask me for the details on it I won't give them to you. What I will tell you is that Callie and I are in a serious relationship and have been since February. Although, I really feel like I could argue earlier because when I fell for her I had no idea about this rule.

"Our intentions were to prove that we could work together and not let it impact the job, and you have to admit that—yesterday aside—we've done that. Callie loves this job and if we're being honest, I think this is the first time I've actually loved playing in years. But if you tell us that we can't be together while being a part of this team, then trade me, send me back to assignment—hell, I'll retire if I have to. But please, let Callie keep this job."

Olsson keeps a blank expression for a moment as he takes in what I said. I couldn't tell you how much time passes because it felt like an eternity to me, but eventually Olsson sighs. "Callie's not going to get fired."

Immediately I feel bricks falling off my shoulders.

"I didn't love that she left her post to go check on some idiot who got ejected. Her suspension for today's game stands because of it, but I suppose her concern makes a little more sense now." Olsson leans forward on his desk. "Listen, I've dealt with a lot of bullshit over the years, but this has got to be one of the first times that a player has requested a meeting to discuss said bullshit. But if it's serious, Anderson, just fill out the fucking form with Shannon."

"Form? What form?" I swear if all of this could have been avoided by a fucking form...

Olsson sighs. "Yes, it's not directly encouraged for you guys to date, and I get this isn't exactly your typical corporate job, but there's still an HR department. Just request the form with Shannon, and fill it out."

"And that's it? We're fine to date? That's not what Shannon told Callie."

Olsson raises his eyebrow. "Well, I suppose in all fairness the last GM would have fired Callie on the spot after that fight, and you would already be on a plane to a different team by now, so maybe that wasn't ill-advised on Shannon's part. I hold a lot of weight on the image of this team—and in truth, I won't tolerate another fight on the field again over a personal matter. The purpose of this dating policy is to limit the liability. People in the past couldn't separate the two. But if you both can keep it professional, then we won't have a problem." Olsson stands from his desk. "And while we're at it, if you keep pitching like you did yesterday—we'll rewrite your contract now."

"I can make that work." Standing up, I hold out my hand for a shake and Olsson returns it.

"I have full faith you can. But unfortunately, you won't be doing it today." Olsson checks his watch as he walks to his office door. "Swing by Shannon's desk. I had her request the form as soon as I got your call for a meeting. Otherwise, I'll see you tomorrow, Anderson."

I nod and follow him out just as Shannon walks in taking a seat at her desk.

Fucking Shannon. I'm going to enjoy this.

I take the seat in front of her desk with a smile. "Hey, I need to fill out the form stating I'm in a relationship with Callie. You know, the gorgeous redhead you constantly run around?"

I make it out the elevator door and I can already hear the chaos coming from Callie's apartment. God, people on this floor probably hate us.

I walk in the door, but they are all too wrapped up in their conversation at the dining room table to notice me yet, so I just watch.

Callie throws her hands in the air. "I'm just saying if a mythical creature did exist it would be a mermaid. The ocean is huge—they could easily hide from us."

Tripp shakes his head. "No, no way. It's got to be Bigfoot. National Parks? I mean, have you even watched the TV show?"

"You're all insane," Beck yells. "It's one hundred percent witches. You want to tell me that there aren't legit witches in this world? I've had some pretty questionable ex's I think I could reference."

Adam just pinches the bridge of his nose as he tries to hold in a laugh.

"Who the fuck started this conversation?" I ask, but I already know the answer.

The argument stops immediately as they all turn to look at me.

"I'll give you one guess," Adam jokes as I walk up to where Callie's sitting.

Callie pulls her lips into a thin line as she holds back asking me the million and one questions running through her head. Scooping her up off her chair I take her seat and hold her in my lap with a sigh.

"So?" Callie whispers.

"Oh, well, it's obviously mermaids," I say with a shrug, and I can see that fire ignite in her eyes.

"Will!" Callie smacks my chest. "That's not what I meant."

I can't help but laugh. "We're good, Blaze. You get to keep your job, I don't lose my no-trade clause, and we're in the clear to be together."

"What? Really?" Callie's face lights up. "But I thought—"

"Shannon and *someone* else"—I turn to Beck—"might not have given us the full information. We just have to fill out a form saying we're in a relationship."

Callie whips her head to Beck, and he's already got his hands up in surrender. "How was I supposed to know that? I was working off past experiences, Callie Bear, I swear."

Callie narrows her eyes at him for a moment but finally lets him off the hook with a smile. "I believe you, but only because you were quite the wingman at times."

I chuckle. "Adam and I each got a fine and a one game suspension for the fight, and your suspension for today still stands for leaving during the game. But otherwise, Olsson was fine. I did get the pleasure of talking to Shannon while getting everything sorted."

Callie's eyes roll back into her head. "What'd she have to say about it?"

"Nothing." I shrug. "I didn't really give her much room to with all the talking I did about how incredible you are and how I love protecting you from petty micromanagers. Then rolled my shoulder a few times and warned her my pitches might be a little off after yesterday."

Callie snorts a laugh. "You did not."

"Okay, I didn't go that far, but I did remind her that you are damn good at your job." I tuck a strand of her hair behind her ear. "Callie, I invited these assholes over here to keep you company while I argued for your job, you think I have—"

"Our jobs," Callie cuts in. "You went in and argued for our jobs."

I smile as I look into her beautiful green eyes. "No, baby, just your job."

Adam scoots his chair back. "You know...I think we'll let you guys have your morning. As cool as I am with this, I've got my limits."

Tripp reaches for another piece of bacon in the middle of the table. "Can we stay?"

"No," everyone replies.

With the guys all saying bye to Callie, I wait for the click of the door before picking her back up and carrying her over to her couch. When I sit this time, I have her straddle me.

"Will, why were you just going for my job? I told you—"

"And I told you that you're the one I'm picking. I know if that was our actual situation, and you went with me, you'd try to quit. I couldn't let you do that, Callie."

Callie looks down, trying to avoid my gaze. "I just don't—"

I lift her face back up by her chin. "Hey, the best revenge is a happy life, right? So let's have one. There are still blank spots in my gallery Callie. I need to take a million more pictures with you to fill it."

That soft smile comes to her face. "It's a good thing I'm still a photographer then."

Chapter 43
Callie

"Callie, I have a question," Miles says next to me in the photograph outpost.

I snap a few pictures as Beck hits a double before turning to Miles. "What's up, bud?" I ask even though I'm pretty sure I already know his question. It's been the same one he's asked me every week since he found out Will and I are dating. It's been nearly two months and he's still not over it.

"Have you and Will broken up yet?" He asks the question so cautiously. Ugh my heart. This kid is so sweet.

"No, Miles, Will is still my boyfriend." I laugh. "We've been over this, bud. I'm just too old for you."

Miles crosses his arms with a humph. "This isn't fair. I told him I was going to marry you first."

Oh, bless his heart. "Hey, you're still my best helper. That's something, right?"

"Yeah, I guess so." Miles scrunches his nose then smiles. "I'll steal you from Will one day."

"Ah, Miles!" I laugh loudly. Will stops short on his walk to the field.

"Hey, Miles, quit making my girl laugh! That's my job."

"Not for forever!" Miles yells back, and now I'm laughing harder.

Will just shakes his head as he walks out on the field, and I try to regain my composure.

"That was a good one, bud."

Miles bounces in the chair next to me. "It's all a part of my plan."

After the game, I return my Casanova back to his dad as he walks out of the locker room.

"Thanks again for helping, Callie." Dex sighs. "I swear I'm going to find someone to help. I've just been trying figure out schooling and with travel—"

"Dex, it's fine." I cut him off. "As I've told you before, I don't mind helping. You'll find someone soon, but until then, we're good. So stop worrying about it on my end."

"Okay." Dex nods, but I can see the stress all over his face. "Will said he'll be out soon. We'll see you guys tomorrow."

I give Miles a quick hug. "Yup, bright and early."

We played at home all this week, but tomorrow we fly down to Georgia for a week's worth of games. Wyla and Jett said they would come to at least one, so I'm pretty excited about that, but then we fly out to San Francisco next.

Shannon makes her way down the hallway, and while we aren't exactly best friends, thanks to Will's chat with her, we're at least on common ground. "Oh, Callie! The *Boston Times* is working on a blog post for how great of a season we are having so far and requested a couple pictures that you've taken. They have specific ones in mind."

This has definitely been one of my favorite parts about

this job. Other photographers come to the games for pictures, but no one quite captures the Blues like I do.

"That's not a problem. If you can email me the list, I will get started on that the moment our plane takes off."

Shannon's smile twitches for just a moment. I know she's actively trying not to tell me to do them tonight. One thing that I've worked hard on since Will and I made it official with the team is work boundaries. "Okay, thank you."

"You're welcome." I beam as I step around her and walk to the person I've been waiting on.

Will smiles the moment he sees me heading his way and even though my brother is talking to him about something, he steps toward me and kisses my forehead. "Hey, Blaze."

Adam sighs next to me. "Well, I guess I'm done talking."

My brother might sound and look irritated, but I know he's not. He's been helping me move into Will's place all week. And even as he just makes that comment, he's reaching for my camera bag because he takes it after every home game so I can ride on Will's motorcycle back to our place. "I'll keep your stuff locked up in my trunk, Cals, since we are all riding together to the airport tomorrow."

"Thank you, my sweet brother," I tease as I slide my riding jacket on. "Have I told you how much I love and appreciate you?"

"Yeah, yeah." Adam chuckles before turning on his heels. "I'll see you guys in the morning. Get my sister home safely, Anderson."

"Always," Will replies and tugs me closer by the belt loop on my jeans. "You ready to go?"

"Yup." I flip my braid out of my jacket. "I've been thinking about hanging those pictures laying on our living room floor this entire game. I want to get them hung up before we leave for two weeks."

Will sighs. "Baby, those pictures and our apartment aren't going anywhere. You need sleep."

"I know," I draw out. "But we're about to be gone for two weeks and when we get back, we get to come home to *our* place for the first time. I just want it to be perfect."

Will shakes his head but there's this smile on his face that tells me he likes the idea too. Linking his hand with mine we head out to the red Ninja he bought in Florida and Will starts to put my helmet on my head.

"Alright," Will says softly. "If you want the pictures done, I'll do them as soon as we get home. Just tell me where you want them."

"No, Will, you just played a long game. I can hang some frames."

Will narrows his eyes at me. "I'll hang the pictures. We've talked about this, Callie. I get to take care of you now."

Will fixes my strap on my helmet and I chuckle. "Will, you know I can do the helmet myself, right?"

Will stills. He knows I know how to do it, but I also know that he likes doing it. He lets out a sigh. "Damn it, woman. Don't take this away from me. If you want to hang the pictures, then okay, I'll watch because I know you're capable. But I do your helmet. Always."

My smile is stupid big but Will can only tell through my eyes. "I love you. If you want to hang up the pictures you can...but can you do it shirtless?"

Will smirks. "That's funny, I was going to make the same request of you."

Back home, Will follows through by taking his shirt off to

hang the last of our pictures. He told me he wanted a gallery, and what kind of photographer would I be if I didn't jump on that?

Granted, it's called for some major rearranging since we're living together now. Originally, we talked about moving into my place as it felt more like our comfort spot, but ultimately his place is bigger, and we definitely needed the extra wall space.

"Okay, last one," Will mumbles with the last nail in his mouth. Why is that just so hot? It's so simple, yet manly. "Callie, can you hand me that last frame?"

Grabbing the picture, I walk over and lift the frame up to him. After seeing my stool-chair combo Will immediately bought a step ladder, which I thought was a pointless buy, but now as I'm eye level with Will's dick I have a brilliant idea. Safe idea? That's debatable.

As Will starts to hammer the anchor into the wall I slide his grey sweats down.

The hammering immediately stops and Will mumbles, "Callie, what are you doing?"

I run my hands over his quickly hardening length before pulling his briefs down next. "You know I don't have any way to pay you for your services today," I say, mimicking a bad porno.

"Cal—Fuck." Will curses as I start sucking on his cock. "I don't know what I did in a past life to deserve you, but shit, you're incredible."

Letting my hand take over for a moment, I pop off and bat my eyelashes up at Will. "Please, finish hanging my pictures, Mr. Handyman, and then I'll finish you."

I don't give Will any time to respond and take him back in my mouth. I feel his eyes watching me though, so I put on a good show—taking him all the way back until I start to choke a little.

"Fuck me," Will breathes. "If I wasn't a saint, then I must have been fucking Superman."

Popping off one more time, I say, "What girl doesn't want to fuck Superman?"

Chapter 44
Will

Opening Day at Blues Stadium – One Year Later

After six years in the major leagues and two World Series wins in my career, I feel I can confidently say this is the most nervous I have ever been for a game.

I wipe my hands off on my uniform for what feels like the hundredth time. I can't ask Callie to marry me with sweaty hands.

"What are you going to do if she says no?" Adam asks, coming up next to me in the locker room.

This fucker. "I know you're fucking with me, but today's not the day."

Adam laughs at my misery—he has been all month. I knew I was going to ask Callie to marry me on the next Opening Day for a while now. So, before we left for Spring Training, I found a ring designer and knocked on Adam's door to tell him I was going to ask Callie to marry me.

I know my Callie, and she would cringe eternally at the idea of me asking for a blessing, but it's the gentleman in me who couldn't say nothing. So I might not have asked, but I damn sure let her brother know how much I love her.

There's just one other person I have to prepare for this proposal and even though he's had a year to get use to the idea of me and Callie, Miles might not take this so well. And right on time, my phone vibrates with the new group chat Lucie started without Callie in it.

When Will asks Callie to marry him.

REAGAN

On a scale of 1 to 10 how nervous are you?

Don't start.

REAGAN

So ten?

LUCIE

Rea, leave him alone. Of course he's a ten.

Not helping.

REAGAN

Mom's already crying and it hasn't even happened yet.

LUCIE

You better have hid her from Callie or she'll ruin the surprise! She tried handing Callie a wedding catalog at the nail salon this week. I nearly killed her.

"I got to go meet Lucie with Miles," I say to Adam and toss my phone back in my bag.

"Oh yeah, how's that going by the way?" Adam asks with a knowing smile. Man, he's really pushing it today.

"I don't ask questions," I quip, turning to walk toward the door.

Adam humphs. "Yeah, I didn't either."

Damn shit stirrer.

"Will," Lucie calls as I step out into the hallway. Her and Miles are decked out in all Blues gear for Opening Day and I'm going not to dwell on the fact that I already know it's not our last name on her jersey.

"Hey, Miles, looking good, bud." I kneel in front of him so I can look him in the eye. "I've got something to run by you."

Callie

I can't even begin to express how happy I am that it's Opening Day. Away games just don't feel as lively. Not to mention home games mean actually being *home*.

I love mine and Will's place so much. To other people it's probably pretty obnoxious the amount of pictures we have on our walls, but I smile every time I walk in our unlocked door. Will does too and that's all that matters to me.

I walk down the stairs to my little photo outpost as Adam runs up behind me. "Hey, Cals."

"One sec," I reply as I set my stuff down to the side and turn on the little portable heater I begged Olsson for. Turning back to my brother, I rub my hands together to warm them. "What's up?"

"So, the guest who was going to do the ceremonial first pitch can't come at the last minute. I volunteered you for the honor." Adam gives me a goofy smile as he sees the look of horror on my face.

"You did not." I blink at him. I've thrown balls with the guys enough to know I can do a decent job—enough to not embarrass myself, at least. But he's not serious, he can't be. "Adam, it's Opening Day. This place is not only packed, it's sold out! It's a fucking televised game!"

Adam laughs. "I know."

"Callie!" Olsson shouts from the field. "You're up."

Looking out at my boss, I freeze. They can't be serious right now.

Adam takes my hand as he slowly starts to pull me back out of my safe zone and, to solidify my anxieties, the announcer comes over the microphone. "Tonight's ceremonial first pitch will be thrown by the Blue's incredibly talented photographer, Callie Reyer!"

"Adam," I mumble. "I'm going to kill you."

Adam squeezes my hand as we reach the pitcher's mound. "Oh, come on, it will be good. I promise."

Adam takes a step back to grab a ball, while I take an unfortunate look at the completely packed stadium. I'm overwhelmed at the amount of people. How Will does this every game is beyond me.

Where is he anyway?

"Here you are, lil' sis," Adam says, pulling me away from the crowd and handing me a ball to throw. "You ready?"

"Am I not throwing it to you?"

Adam simply smiles and takes a step back.

"Hey, Blaze," Will calls as he walks up to home plate. "Show me how it's done."

Shaking my head, I bite my lip for a moment to hold back my comment. I must have been too distracted by the crowd to notice but every player on the Blues is out of the dugout now. Half of the guys are usually getting into game-time mode during this part. And now I have to throw a pitch to my starting pitcher boyfriend. Fuck, guys, the pressure.

I glance back to Adam and he gives me a small nod for me to go ahead and throw it. Taking one more deep breath, I push all the outside stuff away and focus on Will. No one else is here right now. I'm just throwing a ball to the love of my life.

Rearing back, I send the ball straight into Will's glove. Is it as fast or as beautiful as his? No. Not even close. But it's decent, he taught me well.

Will stands up with a smile on his handsome face and starts to walk toward me. Unable to help myself, I meet him halfway. I know we're working, but I feel I deserve at least a quick "good job" kiss. I can keep it PG.

"Nice job, baby. You trying to put me out of a job?" Will half yells as the crowd continues to cheer.

I think the announcer is saying something but as I reach Will, I've completely tuned them all out.

"We both know you have skills to fall back on." I hint at our never-ending tea shop joke.

Will smirks and tosses me the ball back. "You get to keep the ball. And don't worry, I signed it for you."

"You did not." I let out a small chuckle as I look down at the ball, turning it to look for Will's scribbled signature. Every word, syllable, and breath is knocked out of me when I read the words *Will you marry me, Blaze?*

The crowd's noise becomes unignorable, and I look up to find Will down on one knee with a ring box open in his hand.

"We might have to get a bigger place, but what do you say, Callie? Want to put our wedding pictures up on the wall?"

Tears well in my eyes and I don't hesitate. "Yes!" I drop to my knees and wrap my arms around his shoulders.

Tears stream down my face as I hold on to him tighter. "Yes," I repeat barely above a whisper. It's the only word I can manage—a ramble has been knocked out of me.

Will wraps his arms around my waist as he stands us both back up. "Then let's make it official."

Pulling my left arm down Will places a gorgeous engagement ring on my finger. It's got a solid gold band with two pear-shaped stones mirroring each other, and are at least three carats each. One a diamond and one a beautiful orange sapphire.

The moment the ring is completely on, I cup Will's face and pull him in for that "good job" kiss. The man deserves it.

The crowd roars again and the moment I pull back to tell Will how much I love him we're swarmed by the team.

There's endless rounds of congratulations and hugs. Even Miles comes out with Will's sisters and mom to tell me how he's happy that I'm happy. Adam might deny it till the day he dies, but I saw the hint of water pooling in his eyes as he wrapped me up in a hug.

Beck slings his arm around my shoulder. "We've got a kick ass after party too. I sweet talked Jenni-cakes into doing some small tattoos. I told her I wanted 'Will + Callie' in a heart on my arm."

Will lightly shoves Beck back so he can pull me to him. "Maybe when you see it in permanent ink you'll remember to keep your hands off my fiancée."

I place a small kiss on Will's cheek. "Oh, trust me, we're not the names he really wants tattooed on his skin."

Olsson congratulates us next. "I like this scene much more than last Opening Day," he jokes. "I'm happy for you two, but I believe there's a different form for spouses to sign. Think you can manage that?"

I snort out a laugh. "You'll never let us live that down, will ya?"

"Nope." Olsson claps his hands and yells to the team, "Now, let's win this fucking game!"

As we make our way back over to the dugouts, Will takes me over to my spot first. "So, how's that happy life working out?"

I smile. "It's still developing, but I can picture it perfectly."

Epilogue
Will

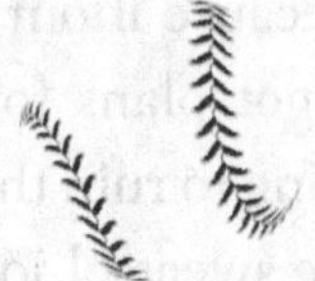

Ten Years Later

"Callie, baby, I'm home," I say as I walk through the unlocked door of our penthouse. Not long after we got married, it became abundantly clear we needed more room for all of our pictures.

It might seem silly to get a bigger place to hang stuff on the walls but fuck that, I told Callie I wanted a gallery, so here we are.

"Bedroom," Callie yells as I take my snow boots off in the entryway. I should peel off the rest of my snow-clad clothes, but my wife wanted the special at Spilled Tea this morning and who am I to deny her?

That and the fact that we're investors in Spilled Tea's franchise. I might have taken Callie's delivery boy jokes too far.

When I walk in our room, Callie's pulled on some leggings and one of my sweatshirts as she sits on our small couch in front of the window that overlooks the city.

"Man, it's really coming down," she says. "I'm sorry I made you go out in this."

I hand her the spiced apple tea. "It's your birthday month, Blaze, I didn't even question it."

Callie gives me her soft smile and takes sips of her tea while she waits for me to pull off my now wet clothes. It really was coming down. I just hope we get some sort of reprieve in a few days because if our flight gets delayed, I'm going to be pissed. I've got plans for Callie's birthday and damn it the snow isn't going to ruin them.

After pulling on some sweats, I join my beautiful wife on our small sofa and pull her to me. "In light of the snow, do you want me to tell you your birthday surprise or should I hold out until I know it won't get pushed back?"

Callie shifts so she's now straddling me. "Oh, tell me now, Mr. Anderson."

I smirk at the fake sternness on her face. "I don't know. It's pretty big. You might not even want to go because I fear it could lead to us having to buy the whole building for the pictures you're going to take."

Callie wraps her arms around my neck. "Well, it's a good thing we're partial owners in a couple tea shops. We can put some pictures in them for decor."

I chuckle. "I knew I married a smart woman."

"What can I say, I'm a problem solver!" Callie beams. "Now tell me—what are we doing?"

Reaching up I tuck a strand of her fiery red hair behind her ear. "How does a whole month touring Europe sound?"

Callie straightens her back and her eyes light up. "No way. Really? Don't lie to me, Will."

"Baby, why would I lie about your birthday present? You know I've deemed it the most important holiday."

I place a small kiss on her lips.

A small smile appears on her face. "I love you," she whispers.

"I love you too, Blaze." I cup her face. "Now where'd you put the Polaroid camera?"

Dick-tionary

Listen, I'm not here to judge, so whether you're here to find those spicy chapters *wink wink* or skip over them, I'm so happy you are about to spend time with Callie and Will!

Explicit content is mentioned through out the book. Pitcher Us is intended for a mature audience only. Chapters of high sexual content are listed below.

Chapter 23 (whole)

Chapter 24 (ends at scene break)

Chapter 31 (whole)

Chapter 32 (ends at scene break)

Chapter 36 (starts at scene break)

Also by Mollie Goins

I hope you enjoyed Pitcher Us! I truly fell in love with this team, and I cannot wait to dive into them again.

Up next will be Dex and Lucie's story in *Coach Me*.

Curious about Wyla and Jett's story? You can find it here in the Aster Creek series! The series can be read as interconnected standalones (chronic out of order readers, you're welcome). However, in order reading will provide the full experience.

Feel It All - Winry and Graham's story

Bring It All - Waverley and Owen's story

Despite It All - Wyla and Jett's story

Acknowledgments

Wow. This book really got my blood, sweat, and tears. But also a ton of love and so many pieces of my heart. First, I want to thank Callie for being the FMC I didn't expect, but wholeheartedly love, and for the story itself showing me how much I've grown.

Thank you to my dear husband, Krischan. Your continuous love and support for me is unmatched. My real book husband, thanks for all the research help! *Wink wink*

Okay, soul sister time. Thank you to Dany for being my complete opposite half. Literally. We could not be more opposite, but we complete each other just the same. Here's to all of our inside jokes that we will forever sneak into our books and the countless adventures ahead.

To Courtney. My girl. No one quite has my back like you do. Thank you for being my encourager and never batting an eye when I send you a voice memo that's +6 minutes long. You are a kickass mom, and one of the strongest women I know.

To Isabella. You have literally been here since book one and I will never let you leave me. My favorite Alpha reader. The person who tells it to me straight, but always believes in me. You are an incredible person, and I'm truly so grateful to have you in my corner.

To Brittany. Please never change. I'm so happy to have

you as a reader. Thank you for loving my work, while still pushing me to be better.

To MK. Thank you for loving my books and screaming about them to readers. I'll forever cherish my doodled books. They are the author dream I never knew I needed. Thank you for supporting me through out this process. Ready to do it all over again? Lol.

To Kristen. Thank you for your constant love and creative brain. You just might be the middle glue between me and Dany. Oh and thank you to both you and Dany for still loving me despite my dislike for musicals.

To my beta readers, MK, Danie, Jes, B, Maddy, Tori, Abby, Isabella, Courtney, Brittany, and Kristen. Thank you for being a part of this journey. Thank you for loving Pitcher Us, while still helping me make it a better book. OH and the most important beta reader: my mom! Thank you for being the comic relief in my docs. Your every growing support and willingness to skim the spicy chapters do not go unappreciated.

To the Bubbly Bookshelf. THANK YOU for making merch for this book. My mind seriously can't wrap around the fact that you all loved this book enough to give it a collection. My author heart is so full every time I look at your incredible creations. To readers please check out @the.bubbly.bookshelf on IG for the collection!

To Lauren! Thank you so much for being this incredible human with a brain that thinks out of the box! You helped me kickass on this deadline and I'm eternally grateful for you and all the many FaceTimes you talked me off the ledge of my author mental breakdown.

A HUGE thank you to everyone who worked with me through out this publication.

Cover design: Kimberly Sable - KBG Designs
Dev & Copy edits: Lauren Sakowski - Author's Best Friend
Proofedits: Caroline Palmier: Love & Edits
Marketing/PA/Team: MK Patterson, Courtney Jeffcoat, and Kristen Owens
Literary Agent: Amanda Wooden

Wow, I had a lot of people to thank this time around. It feels weird but also so right. This community has filled my cup so much that it's overflowing. That being said—THANK YOU to you readers. Thank you for reading my books and recommending them to others. You all are the reason I'm able to do what I love, and I hope we get to continue this journey for a very long time.

No words could truly express my love and gratitude. As contradicting as that sounds for an author, it's true. I'm sending you all a virtual hug. Thank you for being readers.

About the Author

Mollie Goins is a contemporary romance author, with books in the sub genre of small town and sports. With swoon worthy men and strong women, each book delivers on all the sweet, spicy, and emotional moments that you can escape in.

Residing in a small town in Tennessee with her high school sweetheart, Mollie is also a mother to two adorable but wild kids who always keep her on her toes.

Mollie is a chronic out of order reader, so while her books are in a series, each book can be read as a standalone. However, Mollie also loves a good Easter egg, so be looking for callbacks from book to book.

For more information visit molliegoins.com